MURDER IN REVELATION

ANNE CLEELAND

ARTEMIS
PRESS

THE DOYLE & ACTON MURDER SERIES

For the surgeons who work with Samaritan's Purse on the Children's Heart Project; and for all others like them.

CHAPTER 1

One down; three to go.

"𝓘 may not survive this," the witness said to Detective Sergeant Kathleen Doyle, in her soft voice. "But I have decided that it does not matter. There is too much evil, in this fallen world."

The woman, a doctor from Nigeria, was a member of *The Curing League,* and the first one that Doyle could find who'd been willing to admit that she'd been robbed—robbed in broad daylight, whilst walking toward the tube stop after her shift at the London free clinic. The assailant had taken her handbag and had left a black eye, barely discernable against the woman's dark skin.

Doyle had been tipped-off by one of her friends that some of the volunteer doctors who worked in the inner-city projects were getting themselves robbed, even though no reports of these robberies had been filed. It was a worrying trend, and therefore she'd been assigned the task of finding a victim, so as to gather enough information to decide if an investigation should be opened—every protection should be afforded to those who gave their time and talents so unselfishly.

Because the victims were doctors, it could be presumed that they were being robbed for cash, or perhaps in the hope of finding drugs—faint as that hope may be, with narcotics so heavily regulated. Rather surprisingly, however, none of the medical volunteers had admitted to being a victim, and Doyle was beginning to wonder if Timothy McGonigal had it wrong —that he must have misunderstood something that he'd overheard. But then Dr. Okafor had come onto her shift, had taken a long, measuring look at Doyle, and then had asked to speak privately, in one of the offices.

This seemed to be a breakthrough, and—upon noting the woman's black eye—Doyle's detective-sense went on high alert, only to be disappointed when her witness didn't seem as interested in giving the police a useful description as she was in making dire apocalyptic predictions.

"Why wouldn't you survive this, ma'am?" Doyle asked, truly puzzled. It was a strange thing to say—especially for a doctor—and Doyle wondered if she was the type of witness who seized the opportunity to make-up tales out of whole cloth—some witnesses did, either to make themselves seem more important, or because they'd a mental infirmity that left them to live in a fantasy-filled world. And there were always those witnesses who lied because they very much enjoyed the idea of hoodwinking the coppers, but this woman seemed an unlikely candidate for the latter category–what with the volunteering, and all.

"It was a *gargadi*," the woman explained, and paused, so as to come up with an appropriate translation. "A warning not to speak of these things."

"And what things are those, ma'am?" Doyle prompted, trying to keep hold of her patience.

"Terrible things." The woman's dark eyes met Doyle's for a moment. *"Blessed are the dead, who die in the Lord."*

"Amen," said Doyle, who was starting to have the sinking feeling that the good doctor was wasting her time. "Now, if you would—"

Her companion leaned forward, and confided, "I will tell you these things, because you will stop them—you will stop the evil ones. You helped Nanda; you helped her son escape them."

"Oh—did you know Nanda?" This would not be a surprise, actually; Nanda was an African nurse who'd worked at another charity clinic where Doyle had done a volunteer stint. Unfortunately, Nanda had subsequently lost her bearings and become violent, and so she'd been packed-up and sent to her home country to live with relatives, along with her small son.

The woman nodded solemnly. "Yes. You saved them. You saved the others—everyone knows of this."

"Oh," Doyle demurred, a bit flustered. "It was nothin', truly; I'm just doin' my duty, ma'am." Doyle had been awarded two commendations for bravery from the Met, although on both occasions she felt she'd only done what anyone else would do under the circumstances. And so, will-she or nil-she, she was now considered something of a local hero, which was—truth to tell—more an annoyance than anything else.

"My pastor, he speaks of you on the radio," the witness continued in her earnest voice. "You saved his ministry."

Trying to follow, Doyle ventured, "Are you speakin' of the Wexton Prison ministry?" The former Detective Chief Superintendent of Scotland Yard had been sent to prison, only to form a popular evangelical ministry, which was now broadcast on a weekly basis. It appeared this woman was a member of the ministry, then, which might explain her doom-saying; some evangelicals tended to be fatalistic, and dwell on the apocalyptic teachings.

The woman nodded, and then turned her head to gaze out the window with an air of calm conviction—she wore a colorful head scarf, a bit incongruous in the confines of the rather shabby office. "I had a little boy, once," she said. "I go to be with him."

There was a small, silent pause whist Doyle tried to decide what to say. "Please, ma'am; why d'you think you're in danger?" It was a strange situation; Doyle had the sense that the woman truly believed she was slated to die, but it seemed an odd conviction to have, under the circumstances. "Did your attacker threaten to come back?"

"Oh, yes," she nodded, bringing her attention back to Doyle. "He knows I know."

"Knows—" Doyle prompted, leaning forward so as to invite enlightenment.

"That the evil ones are eating the souls of the children."

Doyle digested this for a moment, doing her best to keep her polite-police-officer expression in place, in the face of this alarming accusation. She ventured, "Are you sayin' that the doctors at your clinic are involved in sex-traffickin'?" Unfortunately, this was not as far-fetched as it might seem;

the Met had already exposed a sex-trafficking ring that preyed on poor immigrants.

But Dr. Okafor shook her head. "No—no; instead, they are soul-eaters." As though she was explaining the concept to someone none too bright, she continued, "They take away the souls of the children, and leave them with the wasting disease."

Her brow knit, Doyle considered this. "And so—do the children die?"

"Sometimes," the woman replied sadly. "Sometimes they are only very sick."

Doyle regarded her in silence for a few moments. The perplexing thing was that the woman truly believed what she was saying. Doyle—Irish by birth—was a bit fey, having the innate ability to sense the emotions of the people in her immediate area, and as a result, she could usually tell when someone was lying. Strange as it seemed, a medical doctor in modern-day London truly believed that her compatriots were eating the souls of children, in their spare time.

"That does sound evil," Doyle offered. "I have to say I'd never heard of such a thing."

"In my home country, everyone knows of them. *Maita*," the woman explained. "You must stop them; *the righteous must do right, and the holy still be holy.*"

Taking up her tablet, Doyle assured the woman, "I will certainly do my best, ma'am. Could you give me some particulars? Names and dates?" Doyle wondered if perhaps there was a kernel of truth to this tale, and that the doctor— clearly frightened by the wrongdoers, who'd already given her a six-pack of beat-up—was transferring the blame to the appropriate cultural bogeyman. After all, she'd often heard

Nanda explain medical protocols in terms of tribal remedies, more easily understood and trusted by African immigrants. It was one of the main reasons immigrant doctors were desperately needed in these free clinics; their patients felt an affinity, and thus were willing to take a chance on the treatment prescribed.

The woman shook her head. "I do not know their names, but it is always the last patient, before closing. They wish as few to know of it as possible."

Doyle nodded. "Right, then. I won't say anythin' today, but I'll take a peek at the CCTV film and the patient records, and I'll try to keep your role in this as quiet as I'm able."

Doctor Okafor smiled, rather sadly, and reached to grasp Doyle's arm. "Thank you, Officer Doyle."

It seemed clear that she thought this a faint hope, and on impulse, Doyle covered the woman's hand with her own. "Thank you for comin' forward."

"Yes," the woman agreed. "*In all things, give thanks.*"

That's what my mum used to say, Doyle thought, as she rose to leave; and usually she said it just as the boom was about to be lowered down on our heads.

Doyle then put on her best nothing-to-see-here expression and ambled out to the front desk, to speak with the charge nurse–a harassed young man who didn't much like the coppers coming on-site and interrupting his important work. He'd already claimed not to have heard anything about the alleged doctor-assaults, and he'd been telling the truth, which led Doyle to question the whole premise of the investigation; surely, if there were roaming soul-eaters about, the charge nurse would have an inkling of this, or would have been enlisted by the aforesaid soul-eaters, or something. On the other hand, he definitely wasn't happy that Scotland Yard was here, knockin' about, and—now that she'd Dr. Okafor's story–such as it was—it might be a good idea to plumb him a bit more.

She paused at the counter, and made a show of reviewing her notes. In a slightly bored tone, she told the man, "Poor Dr. Okafor says she was assaulted, but I'm thinkin' it may have been a one-off. I suggested she start takin' a cab, rather than the tube, and I ask that you keep a sharp eye out—call us if you see anythin' or anyone who arouses suspicion."

"I see dodgy people every hour," the fellow replied with no small irony. "It's my job."

"And everyone is grateful; you do good work," Doyle said with all sincerity. "I don't know where these patients would be without you."

Softened by this accolade, the fellow unbent enough to say, "I'll watch out, but I have to be careful; our patients may hang back, if the police are always being called on-site."

"A good point," Doyle agreed. "Your first priority has to be the patients. But we can't allow the doctors to be assaulted, either, or there'll be no one to treat them."

"That's true," he conceded. "And we're already short-handed, after Dr. Benardi was killed."

A small alarm sounded in Doyle's head, and she raised her brows in surprise. "One of your volunteers was *killed*? Dr. Okafor made no mention of it."

Holding up his hands, the fellow disclaimed, "No—no; sorry to give you a start. Dr. Benardi was killed in his offices in Harley Street–some sort of domestic dispute. He was a regular volunteer here, though."

"A shame," Doyle agreed, and then, in the tone of someone who was not inclined to follow-up on these matters, she added, "Good luck, then."

But the nurse had turned to answer the phone, and only waved a cursory hand in farewell.

Thoughtfully, Doyle rang up the driving service, and then waited outside on the pavement, taking a casual survey of the CCTV cameras positioned on the street. It was all very strange, and didn't make a lot of sense, but it did warrant a following-up by the fair Doyle, if for no other reason than Dr. Okafor's black eye. Evidence of assault should be enough, one would think, to warrant the opening of a case-file investigation.

The driving-service limousine pulled up, and the driver smiled a greeting as he leapt out to open the door for her. Since Doyle wasn't the best driver, her husband—ever the worrywart—had insisted that she be ferried about by the driving-service, an amenity that was provided by their fancy residential building. When she'd first married Acton, Doyle had been almost ashamed to be seen riding about in such luxury, but now she was reconciled; there was no harm to having a few minutes of quiet reflection, after all, and it did make her life miles easier.

As the driver checked his mirror and pulled into traffic, Doyle asked, "What's happened to Mr. Tansi, then?" Her usual driver was a Nigerian man, and Doyle was disappointed that he wasn't at his post today, because she'd been hoping to glean some insights about this whole soul-eater business.

The new driver glanced up at her in the mirror. "He's gone, ma'am. I think no one is certain what's happened to him."

Doyle raised her brows. "Well, there's a surprise. He's been a fixture."

"Yes—it does seem unlike him, not to show up."

Idly, Doyle watched out the window. "Mayhap it was immigration troubles."

"That might explain it, ma'am," the driver agreed, and the remainder of the journey back to headquarters passed in silence.

CHAPTER 2

*B*ack at headquarters, Doyle was making her soul-eaters report to Inspector Habib, who listened, as one might expect, with an air of deep surprise. The Pakistani man was her supervisor, and was thus tasked with trying to decide if any further action on the matter would be warranted.

"This is very unexpected," he conceded with a small frown. "What was your assessment of the witness?"

"She did seem sincere to me, sir, even though her tale was so outlandish. No question that she'd been roughed up, and was thoroughly spooked–she claimed to be in fear for her life, and fully expected more of the same."

Habib ducked his chin to his chest, mulling this over. As a by-product of the law enforcement business, the Met tended to see many people who claimed to be in fear for their lives with little reason other than it brought attention to them—the kook detail, they called it—and so the witness' profession of fear didn't necessarily mean much. On the other hand, since the victim was a medical doctor and sported a shiner, she'd more credibility than the usual.

Doyle continued, "She said the victims were children, and that it was always the last patient of the day, and so I thought I'd take a peek at the street-level CCTV feed and see what there was to see." London was awash in closed-circuit security cameras, and it was hard to go anywhere in their fair city without being caught on film.

"Yes—do this first," he decided. "I am reluctant to make further inquiries absent collaborating evidence. We do not wish another clinic to be forced to close, in that area."

Doyle nodded her agreement. "Exactly; they said they're already short-handed, bein' as they'd already lost one of their volunteers–some doctor who was killed on Harley Street."

Habib lifted his gaze, remembering. "Dr. Benardi, I believe. It is DI Williams' case, and so I do not know the details." Coming to a decision, he nodded. "Yes. If you would, DS Doyle, please review CCTV film for corroboration of the doctor's story."

Doyle joked, "I'm not exactly sure what a soul-eater looks like, sir."

The Pakistani man tilted his head, and admitted, "There is something similar, in my culture. *Vetala.*"

In turn, Doyle confessed, "In Ireland, they're called the *Sluagh.*"

"It is all nonsense, of course," Habib pronounced, and Doyle duly noted that the man did not necessarily believe this was true. Being as she was the last person to criticize superstitious beliefs, however, Doyle only nodded in agreement. Her mobile pinged, but she didn't look at it, because she knew it was her husband, wondering whether she was coming home soon–she was supposed to be home a half-hour ago.

He's all on end, the tiresome knocker, Doyle acknowledged to herself, as she gathered up her rucksack to leave. And the fault for that can be laid squarely at Tommy's door, even though Tommy was approximately the size of a coffee bean. Doyle was newly-pregnant, and her already over-anxious husband had ramped up his over-anxiousness to new and impressive levels, owing to the fact there was now a bun in the oven. She should probably count her blessings that it only meant he was constantly checking-in on her, because if he truly had his way, she'd be wrapped-up in cotton-wool and tucked away on a high shelf, somewhere.

He'd behaved similarly during her first pregnancy with Edward, but Doyle had half-hoped that Acton would have mellowed-out a bit, what with having to practice the general flexibility that was necessary to survive with an energetic toddler underfoot. However, with this new pregnancy he'd immediately swung back to being over-cautious, and so his poor wife was left with the choice of either making the best of it, or ditching the man to go back to Dublin, which wouldn't be of much help because he'd probably just pitch a tent outside her door.

Doyle had married her boss, Chief Inspector Acton, one fine day when she'd been minding her own business, completely unaware that her life was about to be turned completely on its head. Whilst they were investigating a homicide, he'd proposed marriage out of the clear blue sky, and she'd married him in a willing whirlwind, only to discover that he was rather—well, he wasn't exactly what one would call normal; not by any stretch.

Acton was renowned at the Met for being reclusive and

brilliant—the rank-and-file called him "Holmes" behind his back—but she'd realized rather quickly that the renowned Chief Inspector also had some rather alarming tendencies, when it came to homicide cases. In short, he was often impatient with the careful protocols that were put in place with respect to the admission of evidence, and so he'd simply manipulate the evidence to suit his own ends, and make certain the right people went to prison—or didn't, depending upon his desired outcome. And—even more alarming—if he became convinced that the best-case resolution would be to skip the evidence-manipulating altogether, and instead cause the suspect to meet with an untimely death, that was not a problem for him, either.

It was a massive problem for his wife, however, once she figured out what he was up to, and so she strove mightily to convince him that—although imperfect—the justice system was miles better than having free-lance vigilantes, roaming about in the upper echelons of Scotland Yard. It didn't help matters that Acton held an ancient title, so that he was more or less bullet-proof, when it came to people suspecting him of dark doings. For reasons Doyle couldn't quite fathom, people admired aristocrats, and invested a great deal of good-will in them, based on their bloodlines alone.

Fortunately, she was not without influence, in that another symptom of Acton's complicated neurosis was an almost obsessive fixation on the red-headed support officer who was now his wife. The man loved her madly—with an emphasis on the "mad" part—and so she was uniquely able to persuade him to mend his ways, once she managed to catch wind of whatever-it-was that he was planning.

Sometimes it worked, sometimes it didn't, but all in all, it had been a blessing; she loved her husband and was—slowly but surely—trying to steer him away from his darker inclinations. Unfortunately, now that she was pregnant again, his alarming tendencies had resurfaced with a vengeance, and he'd gone into hyper-vigilant mode which was a bit nettlesome, truth to tell. At least she could comfort herself with the knowledge that it would ease off again, once the new baby was born. Please God, amen.

So that he didn't decide to send-in a SWAT team to extract her, she rang him up as she walked back to her cubicle. "I'm comin'," she said. "I'd a bit of a wrinkle on a case, and so I had to speak with Habib about how best to go forward." Not that he didn't know this; as part of the whole hyper-vigilant thing, he kept track of her movements through her mobile phone.

"What sort of wrinkle? I would be happy to help, if I may."

The offer was extended because the poor man felt guilty about pinging her up, but it was appreciated, nonetheless. "That would be grand, Michael, but brace yourself; it's an odd one."

"Shall I ask Reynolds to prepare luncheon?"

"You shall," she teased, imitating his posh accent. "I'll be home in two shakes; tell Mary I will feed Edward, if she can hold him off that long."

"I am afraid Mary is ill, today. Reynolds has offered to retrieve Gemma from school, so that Mary may stay home."

Mary, their nanny, was also pregnant, and was suffering mightily from it. Doyle could relate, as she was dreading the morning sickness she'd experienced with Edward, which had —thankfully—not as yet reared its ugly head. Gemma was the nanny's little girl, who usually came along with Mary when she came to their flat to look after Edward. This arrangement worked-out to everyone's satisfaction, since Gemma attended a local preschool in the mornings, and could be easily walked to and fro.

Picturing Acton at home with two small children underfoot, Doyle smiled into the phone. "You'll need reinforcements, then—herd them into a corner and try to hold them at bay; I'll be there as soon as I may."

"Code thirty," he replied, which was police code meaning an officer needed emergency assistance as soon as possible.

With a chuckle, she rang off, and glanced around her desk to make certain she had everything she needed; when she'd gone back to work after Edward was born, the powers-that-be had agreed to allow her to work from home two afternoons each week, and this was one of those afternoons. Originally, Acton had hoped she'd stay at home full-time with Edward, but he didn't even bring up the idea anymore; he knew she loved her work, and—due to her truth-detecting ability—she'd solved many a thorny case. They were a good team, she and Acton, and the villains in London's Metro area were suffering mightily for it.

After hoisting her rucksack over her shoulder, she made her way over to the lift. Acton sounded a bit better, today—that, or he was putting up a brave front. She truly hoped he wouldn't fret himself into a near-paralysis, like he had that one time when he'd entertained fanciful notions that she was at risk, for some reason. Faith, the poor man should remember that she was well-able to take care of herself, and had two flippin' commendations to show for it.

As she emerged onto the building's front pavement, she saw that the new fellow from the driving service was already waiting—Acton must have called him, even before she had. "Thank you," she said, and then, because she couldn't remember if she already knew, "I may have forgot your name."

"Adrian, ma'am," he replied in a friendly fashion, and shut the door behind her.

CHAPTER 3

*D*oyle was having lunch with her husband at home, eating at the kitchen table with both Gemma and Edward—Doyle having to remind Acton to take off his tie before sitting next to his son, who considered it rare sport to seize it in a butter-soaked grip.

It was a far cry from Acton's old life; before he'd married the fair Doyle, he'd lived in this elegant flat by himself, in expensive simplicity and entertaining no threats whatsoever to his fine silk ties. But all that had changed in a blink, so that now the man was forced to deal with an impetuous and rather headstrong wife, a toddler, a nanny, the nanny's child, and–last but not least–a full-time butler, so as to round out the assorted entourage.

It's quite the sea-change, Doyle acknowledged, but I don't believe he truly minds it–although I'd never have believed it of him, when we were first married. I think, in a strange way, that all the continuing chaos rather helps him to stay out of himself, if that makes any sense. He has no time to make brooding plots, since he's always half-exhausted from having to man the fortress.

Reynolds served-up the luncheon plates, and then retreated back into the kitchen, which gave Doyle the opportunity to relate the strange tale of Dr. Okafor and the soul-eaters.

"She seemed sincere?" Acton asked, with a glance at her. He was asking if the witness had been telling the truth, but couldn't do it outright, not with Reynolds hovering nearby.

"Yes. She was truly frightened." Doyle paused, and then corrected herself. "No—not frightened so much as—as *reconciled*, I suppose. She didn't think she would be allowed to survive, if she squeaked to the police, and she'd decided that she didn't much care." Thinking about this, she added, "She's deeply religious, and seemed rather fatalistic about it all."

He considered this, his dark brows drawn. "Did you have the sense she was impaired?"

Doyle shook her head. "No–I didn't, but on the other hand, if she's pilferin' drugs, she's probably good at hidin' the symptoms. I'm reluctant to start askin' questions of the staff, though, without somethin' more."

He nodded in acknowledgement—the fact that the inner-city communities were always short of decent doctors was a factor to be weighed-in with all investigative decisions. Unfortunately, the villains were well-aware of this constraint, and often took advantage, knowing the police would be reluctant to be too disruptive. He suggested, "Perhaps McGonigal should be consulted."

Quickly, Doyle thwarted Edward's latest attempt to grab a handful of her hair in lieu of Acton's tie. "Aye, that's a good idea. I keep forgettin' that we've a back-channel."

Dr. Timothy McGonigal was one of Acton's oldest friends, and he was also a member of *The Curing League*, donating his surgery services on a regular basis. Indeed, he was the one who'd tipped her off in the first place about these assaults, and, thus reminded, she added, "Mayhap he can ID another doctor who's been attacked. Habib's reluctant to go chargin' in like the cavalry without a solid case, since the clinic won't appreciate the police scarin' off the customers. I was goin' to take a peek at CCTV this afternoon, to see if anythin' tracks."

Reminded, she leaned to call out to Reynolds, "I'll be wantin' to use my desk this afternoon, Reynolds; just so you don't set-up Gemma." When Gemma was visiting, she tended to use Doyle's desk to do her schoolwork.

The servant nodded. "Very good, madam. Instead, we will work here at the table. And since the weather is cooperating, perhaps we will take the opportunity to walk to the park, when Master Edward wakes from his nap."

Suddenly struck, Doyle paused. "Wait—isn't today a school day? And a Russian lesson, too?"

Smoothly, Reynolds replied, "I was concerned that Miss Gemma is coming down with a cold, madam, and so I suggested that she stay in with us, today."

Doyle nodded, hiding a smile because—interestingly enough—this explanation wasn't exactly true. Instead, Reynolds must have decided that it was a good day to play hooky, and so he'd made-up a tale to take advantage of the rare good weather. Hard to believe, that the deferential butler would take hold of the reins in such a way, but everyone had their weaknesses, and Reynolds' weakness was little Gemma.

He could hardly be blamed; it was an extraordinary turn of events, and the sort of tale that would be declared too fanciful, if it were contained in a fiction-story. Mary-the-nanny had taken-in her stepdaughter because the little girl had literally nowhere else to go—Mary's husband had been killed, and there was no one else to claim her.

But, as it turned out, Gemma was a descendant of the Russian Romanov dynasty—indeed, one of the old regime's few survivors. For her protection, she'd been hidden away in England by a group of Russian monarchists, who were hoping, someday, to bring her back to her home country in triumph, and in the process overthrow the current Russian government.

The group had carefully concealed the little girl's true identity—too carefully, as a matter of fact, because an unfortunate series of events had buried her trail, so that those who'd hidden her could no longer find her. Gemma, through no fault of her own, was the subject of intense interest, both by the group who longed to see a monarchy restored to Russia, and by contrast, by those who already held power there, and who would not wish to relinquish their grip to anyone with such a hereditary claim.

She'd been finally tracked-down by Colonel Kolchak, who'd decided—along with Acton—that it would be best to keep her in England for a time, staying with Mary and her new husband, and keeping a low-profile under the protective wing of the House of Acton. As part of this agreed-upon arrangement, the Colonel had been conducting Russian lessons with Gemma, twice a week after preschool, so as to allow her to practice her native language and prepare for her rightful place in history.

Reynolds had decided to take Russian lessons himself on-line, so as to help Gemma practice; the top-lofty butler's enormous gratification in serving someone with an imperial bloodline had grown into to a sincere and touching devotion to the little girl herself, and in turn, Gemma was very attached to Reynolds.

Small blame to her; I'm very attached to him, myself, Doyle thought, as Reynolds brought over a towel so that she could mop-up Edward's impatient little hands. He's mighty long-headed, is our Reynolds, and a crackin' boon to someone like me, who's not very long-headed at all. Of course, Acton carries off the palm—when it comes to long-headedness—but there are those times when I need someone to explain things to me on the side, so as to thwart the schemes of the aforesaid long-headed husband. Reynolds, thankfully, fills that bill.

Doyle hoisted Edward up to carry him over to the sink for a final wash-off. "Are you headin' back, Michael? Anythin' of interest goin' on?"

"An inter-Unit meeting," her husband replied.

She grimaced in sympathy, because there were few things more wretched than an inter-Unit meeting, which was a nothing more than a miserable time-suck so that the brass could check a box and keep the bureaucrats happy. Faith, small wonder that Acton ran amok doing his vigilante-act, when you considered that such meetings necessarily took up a large portion of his working-life.

"Good luck, my friend. I'll put Edward down, and get some work done."

As he rose, Acton said, "If you would hold, just a moment; this may be an opportune time to show the lift's security system to you both."

Willingly, Doyle shifted Edward to her hip and followed him through the kitchen. Because they were fast running out of room, they'd purchased the flat below theirs, and the renovations to connect the two floors had just finished-up. A wide staircase would span the two levels, along with a lift, which seemed an extravagance to Doyle, but Acton had pointed out that it would make Reynolds' life that much easier, especially because they'd rather not have more than one servant, underfoot. The lift would also double as a "safe room" in the event of an emergency, and it was this aspect that Acton was anxious to show her—which of course he was, the over-protective knocker.

With Reynolds and Gemma in tow, they paused before the new lift—tucked away on the far side of the kitchen—and Acton pressed the button which opened the doors. Naturally, Edward took one look at the lift's interior buttons and began fighting like a dockman to push them, and so Acton lifted the squirming child from Doyle to hold him firmly against his shoulder. With a gesture, he indicated a toggle switch, positioned at a fair height above the other controls, and out of the reach of children. "Here is the emergency switch, and if it is triggered, the doors will immediately close and the lift will descend about four feet, to remain in-between the floors until the security code is entered. An audible alarm will sound, and an alarm will also sound at the Concierge desk."

"That is excellent," said Doyle, with as much enthusiasm as she could muster. If such a thing helped ease his worries, she'd gladly play along. It went without saying that their building had all the security of a fortress, already.

"Is it fire-safe, sir?" asked Reynolds.

"Yes. And the shaft is ventilated. The receiver allows two-way communication to the Concierge desk from within."

"Very good, sir," the servant nodded. "An excellent precaution."

"Very excellent," Doyle dutifully agreed. "Don't tell Mary about this, or she'll want to nip inside, so as to escape the children." This, said in obvious jest, because the gentle nanny was the least-likely person in the world to shirk her obligations.

With a hint of disapproval at this attempt at levity, Reynolds offered, "I will inform Miss Mary of these features when next she is here, sir."

"If you would."

"Are we worried about Edward's pushin' the buttons?" Doyle asked, as the boy made one last lunge for them before the doors slid shut. They'd already been forced to affix child-safe covers over every electrical outlet, being as toddlers were apparently very much interested in trying to electrocute themselves.

"The security code must be punched, first," Acton explained. "Another safety feature."

"We're brimful of them," Doyle agreed, which earned her a look from her husband.

CHAPTER 4

*a*fter settling-in Edward for his nap, Doyle went over to her desk, which was located in the old master bedroom—now a guest room, not that they ever had any guests to speak of—and pulled up the Met's link to the CCTV cameras which recorded nearly everything that went on in London. She wished, for a moment, that she'd thought to ask Acton to set-up the feed to the correct camera before he'd left; Acton was a wizard at knowing exactly which camera would have the best view, and exactly where it was—as though he'd the whole flippin' layout memorized in that impressive brain of his, which he probably did. No matter; she'd figure it out.

The graphic map appeared, displaying the intersection she'd asked for, and she chose the numbered camera that kept a street-level view, outside the clinic.

Reviewing CCTV tape was always hideously tedious, and therefore normally reserved for first-years, but she'd an advantage, in this instance, because she would look only at the last patients of the day, since that would be the fastest way to verify what Dr. Okafor had told her. Since the clinic was open until ten o'clock at night, she honed in on a last-hour search.

She watched the last patients who came into the clinic for the previous thirty days, and found only one child amongst them, bundled in a blanket and carried in by what looked to be a worried father, who then left about a half-hour later, again carrying the child.

Doesn't look suspicious, to me, thought Doyle, but she duly marked down the date and the time. And—now that she was watching the feed—the doctor's tale seemed less and less likely; surely it would be very noticeable, if soul-eaters were marching children in and out at such a late hour? Someone would take note, one would think.

Frowning, she paused. Unless—unless the villains were using a modicum of villain-sense, and weren't bringing-in their victims by the front door.

Chastising herself for being a knocker, Doyle pulled up the graphic-map so as to determine which CCTV camera would be positioned to see the back of the clinic—there had to be a back-way in, after all. She then pulled up that camera's feed, only to discover that it had been reported as disabled. The unit report showed that there had been multiple attempts at repair, but it appeared that a new underground connection might be required.

Doyle's scalp prickled, as it always did when her intuition was making a leap, and she immediately went back to the graphic-map to decide which camera had the second-best shot of the back entry-way. There—that one, probably. She pulled up the feed only to discover that the shot was askew, and focused on the sky rather than on the alleyway behind the clinic.

Thoroughly frustrated, she switched to the third-best feed, which was two blocks away but which might nonetheless show something useful, as it had a view straight up the alleyway.

There; she couldn't see the clinic clearly, but she could see the area behind it, even though it was at a distance. She applied her search criteria for nine to ten at night, and then began watching the feed, skimming through the days quickly.

Wait; what was that? She paused, and leaned forward. A van had pulled up, and someone in a lab coat—a woman, it looked to be—came forward to pull open the sliding door and help another woman with a child step down. A little girl? It was hard to tell, at this distance. The person who was leading her held her hand, and took her forward—not in an unfriendly fashion, but firmly, nonetheless—

Oh, Doyle thought; suddenly closing the screen. Oh—I can't watch this. Holy Mother, she's right; these people are evil.

She stared at the blank screen for a moment, shaken to the core, and then mustered up her courage so as to turn the shot back on, forcing herself to look for clues. No identifying plates, and it was too far away to get a decent description of the two adults. She'd the time and date, though, which was at least a place to start.

Now what? She rested her head in her hands for a moment, thoroughly dismayed. If what Dr. Okafor had said was true—that something nefarious was going on, with these late-night children—it was very unlikely there would be any record of it. The fair Doyle should make the attempt to get at the records, though, if for no other reason than to rule-out a legitimate doctor visit. It wasn't; Doyle knew—in the way that she knew things—that there was something terrible afoot, but she couldn't very well call-in a field unit to raid the place based on nothing more than her intuition and Dr. Okafor's unbelievable tale about soul-eaters—she needed something more. Besides, she didn't want to do anything to tip-off these people, so that they could scuttle off somewhere else.

Coming to a decision, she lifted her head. Best discuss it with Acton; Acton knew to take her intuition seriously, and he was a genius at figuring-out how best to trap unsuspecting blacklegs.

Glancing at the time, she considered pulling him out of his stupid meeting, but then decided she already knew what he would suggest as the next course of action—indeed, he'd suggested it already. Therefore, she pulled her mobile phone and rang-up Timothy McGonigal, hoping he wasn't with a patient.

Fortunately, he answered immediately. "Kathleen," he said. "How nice to hear from you."

"I was wonderin' if we could meet-up, Tim. Are you very busy?"

"I've an opening in a half-hour; a patient cancelled."

"I'll be there, then. Thanks so much."

"Are you in need of gift-advice?" he teased. Doyle had once met with McGonigal to discuss buying a piano for Acton, and it was just as well she hadn't followed through; he seemed very fond of the one he'd managed on his own.

"No, Tim; I'm afraid it's a professional question."

"Oh—oh, right."

That's interesting, she thought, as she rang off; he's uneasy. He must have his own suspicions.

Reynolds and Gemma were doing the girl's schoolwork at the kitchen table, and Doyle announced, "Don't get up, Reynolds; I'm off on an errand. I don't think it will take very long, and here's hopin' I'll be back in time for your walk, after our Edward wakes."

"Very good, madam."

Doyle smiled to herself, as she left through the front door, because beneath his fine show of servant-respect, Reynolds was actually somewhat disappointed that the lady of the house was going to join them on the anticipated outing. Small blame to him, after all; nothing like going to the park with your boss in tow, to bring down the general mood.

As she waited for the building's lift, she called Acton to leave a message, because even though he was hip-deep in bureaucratic nonsense, he'd notice she was out and about in the wild, and would wonder why.

She'd expected to leave a message but wasn't overly-surprised when he answered in a quiet voice. "Yes?"

She could hear voices in the background and so said softly, "I've found somethin' troublin' on CCTV, and now I'm off to meet with Tim. Just so you are aware."

"I will be there as soon as I may," he replied. "An hour, perhaps."

Frettin', the man is, she reflected as she rang off. It seems I'm to be surrounded by a basketful of frettin' men, between my certifiable husband, and Reynolds, and even McGonigal. Everyone's a bundle of nerves, save the new driver, who apparently doesn't know enough, yet, to be worried.

She crossed through their building's lobby on the ground floor, and the usual doorman smiled in greeting, as he hurried over to open the door for her. With an answering smile, she mentally added him to the short list of unworried men–instead, he was one who always just seemed happy to be happy, and the world needed more of them. This poor, fallen world, according to Dr. Okafor.

She slid into the limousine, and the happy doorman carefully closed the door behind her.

CHAPTER 5

"*T*hanks so much for lettin' me shoehorn myself in," Doyle said to Dr. Timothy McGonigal, as she sat across his desk from him. "I went over to the free clinic this mornin' to follow-up on your tip, and it's like pullin' teeth to get anyone to cooperate."

"I'm sorry to hear it," he offered, a bit flustered. "Perhaps I shouldn't have said anything."

It was very much in keeping that McGonigal would feel that he was at fault, somehow. He was a shy, kindly sort of person, and he tended to see the best in everyone, whether it was warranted or not. He'd gone to university with Acton, and stood as his oldest friend, having gone through some rather harrowing life events with the man.

Doyle assured him, "No—no, you did the right thing, Tim; we can't have people bustin' up doctors on the street. And I did manage to speak with Dr. Okafor."

She watched carefully for his reaction, but he only raised

his brows in surprise. "Was Dr. Okafor assaulted? Oh, dear; I did not know—what did she say?"

This presented something of a dilemma, and so Doyle tactfully offered, "She seemed a bit—well, a bit shaken-up; she seems to think that there are supernatural forces at work."

He nodded, considering this with a knit brow. "The African personnel often see things through a different prism," he explained. "It is an interesting mix of tradition and science."

"Yes, well, I suppose that could account for it."

"Not that there's anything wrong with it," he hastily amended. "Often they will offer a traditional cure as a cover for a medical remedy. As long as the patients are willing to be treated, we can't complain."

Doyle decided they were wandering off-topic, and so she gently prompted, "She did seem to think that somethin' criminal was bein' covered up—which is why she'd been assaulted. Have you heard any whispers?"

He sighed, and lowered his gaze to fiddle with the brass clock on his desk. "I've decided to resign from *The Curing League*, Kathleen. I'd already heard rumors of financial improprieties, and then there was Dr. Benardi's death." With some significance, he met her eyes.

Doyle blinked. "Oh—oh; was Dr. Benardi a member of *The Curin' League*, too?"

"Yes; he was the one who suggested I join, as a matter of fact–he had offices in this very building." With a conscious glance at her, he shook his head, slightly. "I began to wonder, a bit, about his ethics—he seemed to be involved in quackery, and boasted that he was making a great deal of money. His death was shocking, of course—and very much unexpected."

A bit perplexed by this disjointed narrative, Doyle ventured, "D'you think his death is connected to the clinic attacks, somehow? Or to the *League*'s shady finances?"

Her companion frowned. "No—no, it does not seem so. The authorities believe he was killed by a spurned lover—a man," he added, in clarification. "It's a bit strange; I never had the sense he was so-inclined."

"Some people fish from both sides of the river," Doyle duly noted. "Which means it may have been a 'revelation' murder, where the spurned lover wanted to take his revenge, and expose all the victim's secrets in the process."

"Perhaps," McGonigal agreed with little conviction. "But he always seemed to be—well, to be quite the Jack-the-lad, if you know what I mean. I suppose he could have been overcompensating, with his pursuit of attractive women. In fact, he seemed quite keen on Martina Betancourt, and asked me how I was acquainted with her."

There was a long pause. Now I've truly gone down the rabbit-hole, Doyle thought in bewilderment. "Martian Betancourt? How did Dr. Benardi know Martina Betancourt, Tim?"

Her companion raised his brows in surprise. "Oh—oh; she's been volunteering at the clinic. Sorry; she mentions you often, and so I thought you knew."

"Oh—oh, right," Doyle said slowly. "I remember now—she did say that she was wantin' to volunteer."

This information, however, only raised a grave disquiet in Doyle's breast. They'd tangled with Martina Betancourt before—rather recently—and the experience hadn't sat very well with the fair Doyle's esteemed husband. The young woman had proved to be a member of an ancient religious

Order out of Spain, an Order that considered itself an enforcement wing of the Roman Catholic Church.

And—as it turned out—the Order of Santiago had been covertly watching Acton, because Acton had been— inadvertently—skimming money from the Vatican. Well, not exactly inadvertently, since nothing Acton did was ever inadvertent; instead he hadn't been aware that the Vatican was losing money as a result of one of his Acton-schemes.

In the end, he'd managed to get off with a warning from these Santiago people—in no small part due to Doyle's making a plea to Martina Betancourt on his behalf—but Acton was not the sort of person to take such a rebuke in good part, and Doyle had already warned him that he'd best leave well enough alone; no good would come of trying to cross swords with such a group. Her mother used to say there wasn't a hair's breadth of difference twixt a zealot and the devil, and whilst this may have seemed unnecessarily harsh, there was something to be said in avoiding a battle with people who were all-too-willing to take on a martyr's crown.

And now—*surely* it couldn't be a coincidence, that Dr. Okafor was telling her that evil was afoot, that Martina's wretched Order was taking an interest in *The Curing League*, and that a soon-to-to-murdered doctor was asking McGonigal what he knew about the young woman.

I've got to tell Acton, Doyle decided with resignation; he's got to be made aware of all this. Because no matter how righteous the cause, we can't allow vigilante groups to go about killing people, willy-nilly, which is a rare irony, because while I'm at it, I've also got to persuade him that he shouldn't use this opportunity to wreak some vengeance of his own on the vengeance-takers.

Whilst she contemplated this rather disheartening

realization, McGonigal continued, "I did warn him off, a bit—I warned Dr. Benardi about Martina, I mean. I have the impression she is seeing Mr. Savoie, and I wouldn't want to cross Mr. Savoie."

Doyle stared at him in astonishment. "Mother a' *mercy;* I'm goin' to fall out of my chair, Tim." Philippe Savoie was an underworld figure—a French kingpin who'd figured largely in many a Doyle-adventure—and who was now living in London. Living in London, and—apparently—pitching in to help out the occasional Holy Order.

It shouldn't come as such a shock, perhaps; she'd already known that the notorious Savoie had some sort of past connection with Martina Betancourt, but his willingness to openly support the woman seemed very much out-of-keeping with what she knew of the man.

"Oh," the good doctor said in some distress. "I've done it again, haven't I? I shouldn't be gossiping, and let this be a lesson."

Doyle immediately assured him, "Of course, you should, Tim; it's the only reason the poor police manage to solve a single case—God bless the gossipers."

"I can't say for certain," he cautioned, "But Mr. Savoie tends to escort Martina home, when her shift is over."

Again, Doyle stared in abject astonishment. "Never say that Savoie himself is volunteerin' at a free clinic? It's nothin' less than the crack o' doom, Tim."

"No—no; he doesn't come on premises himself, Kathleen. Mainly, he seems to be helping out with Martina's efforts." In a confidential manner, he leaned in to disclose, "If we are short on supplies, she will ask him to expedite, and he provides. We are careful not to look into it too closely."

"Holy saints," breathed Doyle in wonder. "Is there any

chance that Savoie is the one who's been pilferin' funds?" This was a logical conclusion, and it would create quite the dilemma for her husband, being as he tended to enlist Savoie in his own questionable schemes. For Acton to arrest Savoie would be akin to the pot arresting the kettle.

But the doctor slowly shook his head. "Oh—I doubt it, Kathleen; there have been rumors for quite a while, actually —well before Savoie became involved. And Martina surely wouldn't be a part of any wrongdoing; she's very religious-minded."

"That she is," said Doyle, trying to come to grips with these various revelations. "That she is, my friend."

CHAPTER 6

*a*t this juncture, the office manager buzzed McGonigal to announce that Acton was in the foyer.

"Do send him in," the doctor replied, but Doyle—seeing him take a surreptitious glance at the clock—rose, instead.

"Rather than take up your time, I'll fill him in, Tim. If he's got more questions, he'll follow-up."

McGonigal nodded, and then escorted her out to the office lobby, where Doyle beheld Acton, engaged in a friendly conversation with the office manager.

"Tim," said Acton, turning to shake his hand. "So good to see you."

"I can't take up any more of his time," Doyle explained. "I'll give you a recap in the car."

They made their farewells, and then exited out the door and down the posh, carpeted hallway in silence, until Doyle observed, "So; it turns out you've a weakness for office managers. I can't say I'm surprised, what with all that efficiency, and such."

"It would not hurt to cultivate her," her husband replied in a mild tone.

"Because?" she prompted, curious. That Acton had no real interest in the young woman went without saying.

"Because she is well-situated to observe what happens in the building."

She gave him a speculative look. "Are we talkin' about Dr. Benardi's murder?"

"We are. You are right; there is something here that I do not like." He glanced down at her. "Shall we take a little walk, before we head back?"

"All right," she agreed, with poor grace.

"If you are hungry, I've an apple."

"All right," she said again, crossly. Acton tended to gently bully her into exercising whilst pregnant, and he'd also decided that she needed more fruit in her diet, and didn't seem to think that the store-bought fruit pies she favored should count. Which was ridiculous, of course; the only way a piece of fruit could be tolerated was if it was thoroughly smothered in pastry crust and syrup.

They exited through the building's entry door onto the broad pavement, which featured well-tended trees placed in wrought-iron enclosures. After a few steps, he lifted her hand and tucked it into the crook of his arm, "Note that I didn't ask how you were feeling."

"A small victory, and much appreciated." With a show of stoicism, she bit into the wretched apple. "I'm feelin' fine, Michael—truly. I'm sorry I'm so out-of-sorts, but it's been that kind of day."

"Let's hear it."

She blew out a breath. "The CCTV tape at the clinic was

botched—the back-entrance camera needed repair, and the secondary camera was directed toward the sky. I went to a third feed—it was at a distance, of course, and so it was hard to see—but there was indeed a late-night delivery of a child to the back door." She paused, sobering with the memory. "Somethin' evil is afoot, Michael, I'm sure of it. And I remembered that Timothy was uneasy about his work with *The Curin' League,* and so I came over to do a bit of probin'." With some reluctance, she took another bite of the stupid apple.

"And what did he say?"

She glanced up at him. "You know Tim, Michael—he's reluctant to start rockin' any boats. But he did mention there were rumors of financial improprieties in the *League,* and so he's decided to quit." She chewed on the apple for a moment, thinking it over. "He also seemed to think there was somethin' fishy about Dr. Benardi's murder—he was in the *League,* too. Thinks it's unlikely the man had a male lover."

Acton tilted his head, and pointed out, "It would be in keeping, though; I believe Williams has concluded that his was a revelation murder."

This was a fair point; a revelation murder was designed to expose secrets, and a spurned lover was often the perpetuator. Someone—usually a very angry someone—was willing to commit a murder, so as to expose the victim's secrets.

"Aye, I suppose that's true. Does he have a suspect in hand?"

"I do not believe he has, as yet. After all, the victim would keep such a connection well-hidden."

Doyle nodded, and took another bite, wondering how

many more bites would be deemed acceptable before she could ditch it in the nearest flower bed. "Well, Tim was skeptical; he said the victim was somethin' of a ladies' man—oh—oh, faith, that reminds me—here's somethin', and hold on to your hat; Tim seems to think that Martina Betancourt and Philippe Savoie are an item."

Acton bent his head, considering this, and then offered, "That seems unlikely, surely? She is RC, and is still married."

This was a fair point; Martina's husband was also a member of the Holy Order, but he'd been reported as killed until he'd shown up, posing as—of all things—the man who ran the news kiosk near their flat.

Since it seemed clear that the woman's husband hadn't let her know that he was only pretending to be dead, Doyle noted fairly, "Mayhap Martina's havin' a bit of revenge on her wayward husband, by steppin' out with Savoie. And who's to blame her? Faith, if you'd done somethin' like that to me, I'd be half-inclined to make the whole husband's-been-murdered tale a true one. And recall that there's some sort of history betwixt them—between Martina and Savoie."

"Perhaps," he conceded, although he didn't seem convinced. "And speaking of which, I've discovered something rather surprising; Reynolds has been in contact with Philippe Savoie."

She stopped walking to stare at him, thoroughly surprised. "*Reynolds* has? Truly? Faith, Michael; whatever for?" On past occasions, their servant had always seemed to regard the Frenchman with a hint of distaste; someone as by-the-book as Reynolds was not the sort to tolerate criminal masterminds. Of course, he worked for one, all unknowing, but that was neither here nor there.

Acton gently pulled so that she continued walking, and

replied, "I do not know. Neither man has mentioned it to me."

"It must be the money," Doyle guessed, falling into step beside him again. "Savoie offered to pay Reynolds for takin' care of his son last summer, and Reynolds was all affronted, and refused to take it. Mayhap he's changed his mind, then, and wants the cash. How interestin'."

"Very," Acton agreed.

Glancing up at him, she ventured, "D'you think Reynolds is underwater, and in need of a bit o' dosh? Should we offer him a bonus, or somethin'?"

"I am reluctant to reveal that I am aware of the contact," Acton replied.

Doyle nodded at the wisdom of this, and thought it interesting that Acton was monitoring the servant's contacts —but it was part and parcel of his paranoia, just now, and there wasn't much she could do, except keep reassuring him that all was well. Unless, of course, it wasn't—

With some alarm, she met his eyes. "Holy saints and angels, Michael; between cozyin' up to Reynolds, and the Martina Betancourt wrinkle, d'you think Savoie is plottin' somethin', behind your back?"

"Unlikely," he replied, and it seemed clear he'd already considered this aspect. "And surely, Reynolds would never acquiesce to such a plan."

Doyle took a guess at what "acquiesce" meant, and could only agree, relaxing her grip in relief. No; no—of course not; Reynolds is loyal to the bone. 'Twas a foolish notion, to even be thinkin' such a thing."

"I must return to work, I'm afraid. You should go home and rest, perhaps."

"I will, not to worry. I'll have a lie-down, and I'll eat a

bushelful of apples, too. There'll be a mountain of cores, by the time you come home."

With some amusement, he bent to kiss her head. "Good mother," he said.

CHAPTER 7

$\mathcal{D}$oyle returned to the flat—quietly creeping in, because Edward was still napping—and saw that Mary-the-nanny was at the kitchen table, looking a bit wan but determined, as she made tissue-paper rosettes with Gemma.

"How are you feelin'?" Doyle asked in a low voice, as she joined them at the table. "Or d'you hate bein' asked?"

"I feel much better, Lady Acton," Mary lied. "It feels good to be up and about; I had to go over to St. Margaret's for Gemma's teacher-conference, anyway."

"Well, if you need to go below and have a lie-down, there's no shame to it," Doyle offered. "Reynolds and I will take-up the mantle."

Reynolds took this opportunity to bring over a steaming cup of tea, and set it beside Mary. "Ginger tea, Miss Mary. It may help, somewhat."

"Oh—thank you, Reynolds. You are very kind."

Doyle eyed him. "Where's my coffee?"

"Quite, madam."

Reynolds returned to the kitchen—making no move toward the coffee-maker—and Doyle watched him sourly. No doubt he'd got the word from the master of the house that coffee should be discouraged, which seemed ridiculously unfair—people had been drinking coffee and havin' babies for thousands of years. Well, mayhap not thousands, but a very long time, nevertheless. Who's to say that coffee was worse for you than apples, for the love o' Mike? Apples didn't do a single blessed thing to restore one's mood, which —when all was said and done—was a very important consideration, when it came to pregnant people.

To take her mind from her cravings, Doyle watched Gemma frown in concentration, as she glued her tissue-flower onto a card. "Very pretty, Gemma," she offered. "And the butterfly's lovely."

Gemma looked up. "It's for the new baby," she explained in her soft voice.

"Will you make another, for our new baby?" asked Doyle, and the little girl nodded with a shy smile.

As the two women watched her begin another flower, Mary said in a low aside, "Her teacher says she doesn't say much, but they think she is very intelligent. Apparently, she notices *everything*."

Grand, thought Doyle; another Acton. Katy bar the door.

"Nigel is so proud of her."

"As well he should be. Mary."

Nigel Howard was Gemma's stepfather, a rising political star who'd taken one look at Doyle's nanny and had fallen irrevocably in love. The two had married, and—even though Howard was now an MP—Mary had continued on as Doyle's nanny.

From the first time she'd met the serene young woman, Doyle had known—in the way that she knew things—that her own future and Mary's were bound together, even though it had seemed very unlikely, at the time. They'd met when Doyle had interviewed Mary as a witness—back when the woman was living in the projects, and struggling to make ends meet; no easy task, with a stepdaughter and a ne'er-do-well husband.

Although technically, Bill Blakney wasn't truly Mary's husband, since the two had never married. And Gemma wasn't technically Mary's step-daughter, since—as it turned out—she was the missing Romanov who'd only been hidden away in Blakney's household as a temporary measure. But the temporary measure had turned out to be not-so-temporary, because Blakney had managed to get himself killed, and the House of Acton had stepped-in to hire the young woman as Edward's nanny, unaware that the missing little girl had created international ripples of alarm.

Faith, Doyle thought; when you thought about it, Mary's story was like a modern-day fairy tale, what with a secret princess of sorts, and with Mary now married to an MP, and about to embark on her own happy family. Not that she didn't consider Gemma her own, of course—in fact, it was one of the qualities that had drawn Doyle to her; Mary had accepted Gemma into her home without hesitation, and had loved her without condition. It's a bit like that Bible story, Doyle thought; where that woman stayed on to take care of her mother-in-law, even though she wasn't obligated to, and then wound up with her own fairy-tale ending.

Mary's fairy tale had a catch, though—and a hard one, at that. The Howards hadn't been allowed to adopt the girl, mainly because Colonel Kolchak had been resistant to such an idea on behalf of his fellow monarchists. It wouldn't do, apparently, to have a pretender to the Russian throne under the legal control of a British Member of Parliament, which was probably a fair point.

Nevertheless, since Mary was the only mother Gemma had ever known—and the situation in Russia seemed unlikely to favor the monarchists, any time soon—she'd been allowed to stay in place, with Acton and the Colonel working together to monitor the situation. It was only a temporary solution, though; the Howards had no real control over their daughter's fate, because Gemma's heritage was too significant, and to too many people. Doyle hated to think of Mary's coming heartbreak, and couldn't help but compare it to how she'd feel if anyone tried to take Edward away from her.

Doyle watched Gemma's efforts for a few moments, and then—unable to resist–began to fold her own tissue flower. My own story's a modern-day fairy tale, too, she acknowledged; although there's been some bumps on the road to happily-ever-after, most notably a husband who tends to sail a little too close to the wind when it comes to illegal enterprises. And not to mention that he tends to over-react, when his foolish wife finds herself in hot water—a common occurrence, unfortunately—and thus feels compelled to go all scorched-earth, on her behalf. And, of course, there were those times when he was like a hound at the point; standing very still, and carefully sniffing the air. Exactly as he was behaving at present, as a matter of fact.

Her hands stilled for a moment, as she reluctantly turned over this unwelcome thought in her mind. She'd presumed that Acton was overreacting to her pregnancy—much as he'd done the last time—but there was something in his manner, something that made her uneasy. She'd the sense—she'd the sense that her husband wasn't telling her all he knew—which shouldn't be so surprising, since such was the natural state of affairs from the first moment she'd met the man. No; he'd something up his sleeve, and, if past was prelude, it was some scheme that would be certain to turn her red hair grey. The last thing Acton wanted to do, after all, was to discreetly flirt with an office manager. And it seemed a bit strange that Dr. Benardi's death had been determined to be a revelation murder, when they didn't even have a male lover in hand, as a suspect.

Doyle pressed her flower onto a card a bit harder than was necessary, and unhappily considered the possibility that yet another disaster was fast-approaching. "Faith, I've had my fill of disasters," she said crossly, and didn't realize she'd spoken aloud until Gemma looked up in surprise.

"Oh—oh sorry, Gemma; I'm nowhere near as good at this as your mum, I'm afraid."

"It's very pretty," Gemma offered kindly. "We could give it to Emile."

This was of interest, and Doyle raised her brows. "Will you be seein' Emile, then?" Emile was Philippe Savoie's young son—a few years older than Gemma—and he'd spent much of the previous summer here at the flat, the two children often playing together.

"Oh," said Mary. "I forgot to mention, Lady Acton; Mr. Savoie asked if Emile could join us on our walk, this afternoon."

With a small smile, Doyle glanced up at Reynolds. "Are your loins girded, Reynolds?"

"Of course, madam. I quite enjoy Master Emile."

This was not exactly true, but Doyle forgave him—Emile

was not necessarily a trial, but he had a great deal of energy in the time-honored manner of small boys, and so he was rather exhausting to be around.

"With your permission, of course," Reynolds continued smoothly.

"Full steam ahead, my friend," Doyle replied easily, and immediately speculated that the servant's willingness to take-on Emile stemmed from his secret communications with Savoie; mayhap money was to exchange hands in the process. She'd keep an eye out, all quiet-like, and report her findings back to Acton.

CHAPTER 8

Two down; two to go.

After Edward woke, the outing-party got organized and made their way down to the lobby. They'd called the Concierge, asking him to take Edward's pushchair out of storage, and so the doorman had it waiting for them on the pavement, and jauntily saluted Edward, much to the toddler's delight.

Trenton, who acted as the House of Acton's private security, hovered in the background and didn't seem much amused by the byplay. Doyle wondered if perhaps the impassive Trenton was a bit jealous; Trenton was not one to clown-about with children, and probably didn't realize that the main attraction for Edward was the doorman's patent-leather hat.

"Where's our Emile?" Doyle asked Reynolds, as they were underway, with Reynolds managing Edward's pushchair.

"Master Emile will meet-up with us at the park, madam.

51

It is my understanding that his father took him on a fishing expedition."

"Is that so? Unlikely they've had any luck, unless the fish around here are deaf."

"Yes, madam," the servant readily agreed. "Although I will point out that oftentimes, the point of fishing is not necessarily to catch fish."

Doyle smiled at this proffered wisdom. "I suppose that's true, my friend; there used to be a group of old men, who fished off the banks of the River Liffey every day, smokin' and talkin'. I'd the strong sense that the fishin' poles served as an excuse for all the smokin' and talkin'."

"Exactly, madam."

Mary held Gemma's hand when they crossed at the corner, and, as they fell into step behind them, Reynolds asked Doyle, "Have you any travel plans this weekend, madam?"

Since they never had any travel plans, this appeared to be an attempt by the servant to gain information, and so Doyle eyed him curiously. "Not that I'm aware. What's afoot?"

Reynolds offered, "Mr. Hudson checked-in with me to ask whether Lord Acton intended to attend the funeral, this weekend, and I told him I hadn't yet been informed of any plans."

Hudson was the steward at Acton's estate, and so Doyle asked in mock-astonishment, "Never say someone's finally up and murdered Acton's mother? A good riddance, I'd say."

With discreet disapproval that such a subject would serve as a means for levity, the servant informed her in a wooden tone, "Apparently one of the Trestles footmen was killed in a hunting accident, madam."

Immediately contrite, Doyle exclaimed, "Oh—that *is* a

shame, and I shouldn't be jokin'. Although I might have to point out that the last thing I ever thought I'd be doin' was listenin' to my butler tell me that one of my footmen was killed in a hunting accident. I am *truly* through the lookin'-glass."

"Quite, madam. But Mr. Hudson must know whether to make preparations."

"I'll ask Acton," she replied. "Although if he hasn't mentioned it to either one of us, it seems unlikely that we're goin' to go."

"Oh, look—there's Emile," Gemma called out excitedly, and indeed the boy could be seen approaching them on the pathway ahead, accompanied by his father, who carried a long canvas carry-bag on a strap slung over his shoulder.

The boy bounded up the path to greet them with a great deal of enthusiasm. "Hallo Lady Acton; hallo Mr. Reynolds; hallo Miss Mary."

"Ho, Emile," said Doyle. "You've grown a foot, you have."

"I went fishing in the pond with my Papa, Gemma," he announced importantly. "Have you ever been fishing?"

"No," said Gemma, wide-eyed and suitably impressed.

"Maybe you can come, next time," the boy said generously. He turned to his father, who'd walked up to join the group. "May we bring Gemma, next time?"

"*Bien sûr,*" said Savoie, bowing his head. "If she wishes to come."

"I don't know how," Gemma confessed.

"I'll teach you. I told Papa that I was going to marry you, Gemma," Emile announced importantly.

"Now, isn't that grand?" Doyle remarked. "I can't *wait* to tell Colonel Kolchak."

Mary laughed. "It's very sweet," she insisted, and then said to Emile, "I think that's a very good idea, Emile."

They all greeted each other, and Doyle watched to see if she could discern any consciousness of plottings hatched between Reynolds and Savoie. It was hard to tell, because the impassive Frenchman always seemed as though he was secretly amused, and he seemed so now. The two didn't appear to be over-friendly; Reynolds bowed his head in stiff acknowledgment, whilst Mary warmly offered her hand, with Savoie gravely taking it in his own.

He never shakes my hand, Doyle realized, which is probably just as well, since my husband's on a hair-trigger. No need to spark off a prairie-fire, after all.

"Catch me," Emile said to Gemma, and then he took off, running madly down the path with the little girl in close pursuit.

As the adults followed at a more sedate pace, Doyle fell into step beside Savoie. "Faith, it feels like old times, to have Emile dashin' madly about."

The Frenchman watched his son with a benign eye. "Yes. I take him to *l'ecole*; he is happy there—he has many friends."

"I'm glad it all worked out," she said diplomatically, and decided not to inquire into the particulars, such as whether he'd forged any documents so as to enroll the boy. Best stay away from that tangle-patch; St. Margaret's was not the sort of school that would take kindly to false witness. Although no doubt Savoie had greased the skids with a generous donation, and that sort of thing tended to wash one's robes clean.

Faith, when you thought about it, it was the eighth wonder of the world, that someone like Philippe Savoie had turned out to be such a doting father, but still waters ran deep, and Doyle need look no further than her own doting husband to see proof of this. Savoie was one of those emingnas–or whatever the word was–and in keeping with his mysteriousness, he was not an easy person for Doyle to read. Cynical and aloof, he'd been a notorious criminal with the reputation for being rather ruthless, but then he'd willingly risked his life to come to Doyle's rescue, and on more than one occasion. It was true that they were friends, of sorts, and Doyle had the impression he didn't make friends easily.

And then, in the strangest twist of all, Savoie had taken-in a loose-end child, to raise as his own. He'd taken-in Emile without hesitation, and as though it was the most natural thing in the world. Which is rather like what Mary did with Gemma, Doyle realized; no wonder he shakes her hand–they have something very much in common.

And it was certainly possible that Savoie's newfound devotion to his son had caused him to turn over a new leaf, as unlikely as that seemed. After all, he'd moved from Paris to London, and then had moved heaven and earth to enroll Emile in St. Margaret's, where Gemma attended preschool. Not to mention he was shoveling money to Reynolds, and volunteering at the free clinic. Or, not exactly volunteering, perhaps, but offering his aid.

Reminded, Doyle eyed him sidelong, and teased, "I hear you're doin' good works, my friend."

"*Mais oui*," Savoie agreed, and—as usual—appeared to be very much amused.

Because he seemed disinclined to say anything further, Doyle continued, "It's not that I'm cynical, Philippe, but I hope you're not dallyin' with poor Martina. I think she's still cut-up about her wretched husband's leadin' her on a may-dance, and she doesn't need another helpin' of heartache, just now."

"*Non*," he replied. "Me, I do not do the dally."

This was true—although it wasn't clear if he was aware of the meaning of the word–and so as to clarify, she ventured delicately, "D'you know if she's heard from Antonio?"

"I do not ask," he replied, with a Gallic shrug. "I am the friend, only—the St. Bernard."

Interestingly enough, this was also true, and so Doyle was left to ponder the extraordinary idea that Philippe Savoie—of *all* people—was willing to help Martina Betancourt do good deeds without hope of gaining carnal knowledge of the woman. It was the ninth wonder of the world–if you were counting–although when you thought about it, the world was a pretty wonderous place, and so nothing should be too surprising.

Reynolds offered, "Would you like to stow your fishing pole under the pushchair, Mr. Savoie?"

"*Merci*," Savoie said, and swung down the canvas carrier so as to tuck it on the rack beneath.

Oh-ho; Doyle thought; unless I very much miss my guess, this fishing-pole carrier is going to find its way into our flat, and it no doubt has some cash, stashed away within. Strange, that our Reynolds would go to such lengths—he must have need of funds for some unexpected reason, and doesn't want to approach us, out of embarrassment. Much better to contact Savoie, who'd already offered him a fat envelope of cash, and who'd be happy to pass it along without making any awkward inquiries. Not to mention that it would also explain why she'd caught the impression that Savoie was amused, when she'd teased him about doing good works.

I'll tell Acton, she thought; although I don't think we

should let on that we know; Reynolds' feelings should probably be respected, and it's not as though he can't be trusted.

As he dashed toward the playground ahead, Emile called out, "I'm going to climb to the top of the bars and jump, Papa —you can catch me."

"Don't you be watchin' this, Edward," Doyle cautioned, and Mary laughed.

CHAPTER 9

*W*hen they returned to the flat, Doyle was not at all surprised to note that Savoie had "forgot" to retrieve his fishing kit, and so Reynolds carried it up to the flat with them, declining the Concierge's offer to stow it at his desk

"D'you have Savoie's number?" Doyle asked him innocently. "I'm sure Acton has it, somewhere."

"I will see to it, madam," the butler assured her, and Doyle noted that he casually stowed the canvas carrier in the hall closet.

Acton texted to say he would be home late, and so—after Doyle's thoughtful gaze rested on this message for a few moments—she took the opportunity to text Detective Inspector Williams.

Thomas Williams stood as her dearest friend, a fellow-student in her class at the Crime Academy who'd advanced through the ranks rapidly, mainly because he served as Acton's right-hand-man in doing off-the-books Acton-deeds.

Oftentimes, this pitched him into a divided-loyalties situation with Acton's disapproving wife, but they'd managed to maintain their friendship throughout, and it was warmly appreciated. Due to her perceptive abilities, Doyle had always had a hard time forming friendships, and it was a measure of her trust in Williams that he was the only person —save Acton, of course—who knew about her truth-detecting abilities.

She hadn't been seeing Williams as often as she used to—babies had a way of taking up all of one's spare time–and, in an unlooked-for turn of events, Williams had recently found himself married to a young woman who worked in the Forensics lab–although he maintained that it was a massive mistake, fueled by a massive bender, and that the marriage would be annulled at any minute, now. Doyle couldn't help but note that the minute seemed to have gone on for quite some time, now.

She texted, "Need contraband Code 5." The police code referred to a covert operation; since Acton took such a dim view of coffee-during-pregnancy, she'd taken to enlisting Williams to meet her for a quick half-cup on the sly, on the theory that it would be far worse for little Tommy-to-be if his poor mother went through complete withdrawal, and wound up a danger to herself and others. Besides, it would give her an opportunity to quiz Williams about the Dr. Benardi revelation murder—the one that didn't seem to be much of a revelation, at all.

"Now?" Williams texted.

Busy, the man is, she thought with a small smile, and typed her reply. "Tomorrow, change Code 1." Code 1 meant it was not urgent.

"Good–will text in am."

She put the mobile down, and gazed out the window at the streetlights below, thinking about the cases on her docket, and the work she'd be addressing in the morning. She'd report to Habib about the CCTV at the clinic, but she couldn't very well tell him that she was certain there was evil afoot, which was why she'd told Acton, who was much more inclined to respect his wife's fanciful conclusions.

It would be interesting to see how Acton handled it; if they sent someone over to repair the cameras, one would think the villains would immediately realize the gig was up, and fold their tents. So; more likely he'd set-up personnel to conduct surveillance, instead, and wait for the next poor victim to be led within.

She closed her eyes, briefly. It was a hard, hard fact of law enforcement that the police couldn't act in a protective capacity for anyone; they had to have enough evidence in hand to show that a crime had been already committed, before they could step in for an arrest.

So; if someone was afraid because they'd been threatened, or stalked, the most that person could do would be to apply to the civil courts for a restraining order—and even that was no easy task to accomplish, since otherwise the courts could be used as a handy weapon by every disgruntled ex-lover. It was a hard thing, to know that children were at risk, and that nothing could be done about it, as yet.

Reminded, she looked over at Reynolds, who was doing the end-of-day tidying up in the kitchen, and not behaving at all as though he'd a sackful o' dosh waiting for him in the hall closet. "What d'you know about soul-eaters, Reynolds?"

The servant paused, understandably surprised. "Soul-eaters, madam?"

"Aye. I'd a witness who was worried that soul-eaters were

preyin' on children."

The servant considered this. "Was the witness African, perhaps?"

"Well, yes. But I can't cast any stones, because the Irish have somethin' similar. So do the Pakistanish, apparently."

"I believe you mean Pakistani, madam."

"Whatever," Doyle said crossly. "The point is this; why soul-eaters? It seems an odd thing to conclude—an odd thing for anyone to conclude, and yet there it is, across all cultures."

Reynolds thought about this, and then offered, "I imagine the origin stems from the Greek story of Lycaon, madam."

Doyle considered him with a frown. "Does it? I suppose that's not much of a surprise—those wretched Greeks have a lot to answer for, they do. What's the tale about?"

"It's rather a distasteful story, madam," the servant cautioned.

"Well, I've seen distasteful things aplenty–some that would make your hair stand on end, Reynolds. Spill."

"Lycaon was rumored to eat the flesh of children, madam."

In rank disgust, Doyle exclaimed, "Oh—oh, that's *truly* horrifyin' Reynolds. And everyone seems to think that the Greeks were all so admiral."

"I believe you mean admirable, madam."

With some heat, she retorted, "Yes; well, thank *you*. Can't have me sayin' the wrong word, even though it sounds *exactly* the same."

With a flare of alarm, the servant soothed, "A very good point, and I do beg your pardon, madam."

Cradling her head in her hands, Doyle groused, "Sorry, Reynolds. Holy Mother of God, but I'd sell my soul for a pot o' coffee."

Reading her aright, the servant ventured, "Perhaps a small measure, then, madam; it would be our little secret."

Whilst this was being hastily prepared, he continued, "It is generally believed that tales of werewolves—and zombies —had their origin in the Greek story."

"Is that so?" With a knit brow, Doyle lifted her head to stare out the window again. "Well, I'm not one for werewolves or zombies, but I do think there's somethin' evil afoot."

"Oftentimes, the supernatural serves as a means to explain-away human failings," the servant noted.

But Doyle frowned. "I'm not sure it can be explained-away like that, Reynolds. I do think there is evil in the world —and good, too, of course. We're told that good will prevail, but sometimes it does seem as though the good side is takin' the long route, whilst the evil side is racketin' about at will, and layin' waste."

"Very distressing, madam." Reynolds handed her the coffee in a travel-flask, apparently as a subterfuge in the event the master of the house caught him in the act.

Doyle popped open the top, and breathed in the aroma like a sailor coming home to sea. "It might be distressin' to you and me, but my African witness didn't seem to think so —she was more or less resigned, bein' as we're livin' in a fallen world." With much pleasure, she savored a sip. "I suppose all we can do is keep fightin' the good fight."

"Indeed, madam."

A few minutes later, when Acton's card could be heard in the key-slot, Reynolds deftly lifted the travel-flask from the table and deposited it in the sink before hurrying over to take his coat and valise.

"Ho, husband," Doyle called out. "Reynolds and I were just talkin' about how the world is a fallen place."

"Unfortunate," Acton agreed. "Although it does pay the bills."

"Aye; we do live hand-to-mouth," said Doyle, with heavy irony.

"I will heat-up your dinner, sir," Reynolds offered as he retreated into the kitchen.

"Thank you, Reynolds." Acton leaned to kiss Doyle, and immediately murmured, "Coffee?" with a hint of reproach.

Unrepentant, Doyle quirked her mouth. "Just a tad, Michael, and no harm done. I browbeat Reynolds into it, because I was in a mood, I was, and snappin' at the poor man. I'm much better, now, and I think I'll have an apple." She smiled brightly. "An apple sounds delicious."

And so, Doyle gamely nibbled on a plate of sliced apples as Acton began his meal. He made no mention of why he'd come in late, and Doyle did not ask, because she didn't want to force him to shade the truth, so as to come up with something he was willing to tell her. There was definitely something afoot, and he was hiding whatever-it-was very carefully. Faith, she would not be at all surprised to discover that it had something to do with the smitten office manager, and Acton's attempts to winkle information about the Dr. Benardi murder. And if that was the case, then the fair Doyle's coffee-meeting with Williams wasn't coming a moment too soon.

Her husband remarked, "I am sorry to have missed Edward's bedtime. How went the park outing?"

"Grand," she replied, and was forced to refrain from mentioning the fishing-bag, because Reynolds remained in earshot. "Although if Edward or Tommy winds up with half of Emile's energy, we've troubled waters ahead, my friend. We'll have a runnin' account with the emergency care center."

"You alarm me," he replied, and cut another bite of beefsteak. He then said to Reynolds, "Thank you, Reynolds; it is late, and we will do the washing-up."

"Very good, sir."

As Reynold took the hint to make himself scarce, Doyle eyed her husband in amusement. "That'll be the day; when the likes of you does the washin'-up."

He tilted his head. "You underestimate my abilities, I think."

"Not your abilities as much as your willingness, which brings me to next topic; what have you decided to do about the clinic?"

"I put in an order for covert surveillance," he replied. "There is an empty office across the alley, and we are setting up on the second floor."

She blew out a relieved breath. "Thank God fastin'—I'm not ashamed to say I've been that fashed about it."

But this was the wrong thing to say to her over-anxious husband, and he paused to meet her eyes, and cover her hand with his. "You must not distress yourself, Kathleen. I'll have your promise."

"I'm not, I'm not; I do promise. It's truly awful, though, to think of those poor children–"

She realized she was headed down a fretful train of thought, and so quickly changed the subject. "Speaking of such, we may have to put up some sort of gate for the stairs; Edwards thinks its grand sport to try to get to them before I can catch him, and he's goin' to come a cropper, if he's not careful."

"By all means, then."

"He's a slippery little boyo," she observed fondly.

"Just be careful," he cautioned. "You mustn't exert yourself."

"My favorite Dutch aunt," she pronounced, and leaned to invite his kiss. "Exactly what a lass looks for in a husband."

With a small smile, he kissed her, and then paused to pull his tie loose, which allowed her a glimpse of the base of this throat.

There's nothing like raging hormones and a handsome husband, she decided, to set one off at the drop of a hat. Resting her chin on his shoulder, she murmured into his ear, "Shall I show you what a lass truly looks for, in a husband?"

Reading her aright, he bent his head to bring it to rest against hers. "To fetch another apple?"

Nuzzling his cheek, she giggled. "You're mixed-up, Michael; it's the wife, who offers the apple to the husband, and the next thing you know—bang--we've a fallen world."

"I shall withdraw the offer, then."

In a provocative tone, she suggested, "I'll take a bite out of you, instead."

He teased, "May I finish, first?"

"No," she decided, and pulled up on his tie so as to make him rise. "Best strike whilst the iron is hot, my friend. Any minute now, I'll be turnin' green about the gills, and be completely untempted by that fine body of yours."

"Then by all means," he said, as he tossed his napkin on the table. "I am very fond of that hot iron."

"What about the washin'-up?" she teased, her arms clinging about his waist, as they turned toward the stairway.

"Later," he promised, and she giggled again, because it was a lie.

CHAPTER 10

*T*hat night, Doyle had one of her dreams.

She had them, occasionally; they were not your normal, run-of-the-mill dreams, but instead they were very vivid, and rather disturbing, truth to tell—not that they were nightmares, exactly, but they were disturbing, nonetheless.

As part and parcel of their disturbing nature, the dreams usually featured someone who was dead, and who wanted to convey some sort of message to her—a warning, usually, even though the message was never very clear.

Doyle had learned long ago to pay close attention, because she'd realized that the warnings always had merit, and indeed, often seemed to have the purpose of exposing one of her husband's questionable schemes—as though the ghosts were aiding and abetting her attempts to save the man from his darker inclinations. And—because some of those darker inclinations could easily land him in prison—Doyle had learned to be grateful for the warnings, despite their unsettling nature.

Sometimes she knew the ghost who confronted her, and sometimes she didn't, but it was always someone completely unexpected, and this time was no different.

"Oh," she said, upon beholding the man in his late thirties, who stood before her. "Oh; hallo, again."

"Cheers," said Bill Blakney, in his gruff manner.

There was a small silence. "You look very fine," she offered.

He was dressed in formal clothes, which seemed out-of-keeping, and they were standing in the anteroom of an ancient building, judging by the worn, stone floors and walls. It was very still, and almost unnaturally quiet, which was quite a change from her previous messenger-dreams, which tended to be windy, and located atop some sort of rocky outcropping.

Blakney had been a suspect in a homicide case, some time ago—one arising from a murdered trainer at the local racecourse; a tale of race-fixing, amongst the Russian underworld. He'd owned a pawnshop, and was briefly considered a suspect, because he stood as ex-husband to one of the murder victims.

Then later, the man had circled back into Doyle's life because he was Mary-the-nanny's ne'er-do-well first husband —or husband by common law, anyways—who'd managed to get himself killed in an unfortunate turn of events, and thus leave Mary and Gemma to fend for themselves.

The ghost didn't offer any explanation for his presence in her dream, and Doyle had the impression he wasn't paying attention to her as much as he was listening—waiting, and listening for something—a bit anxiously, it seemed to her.

After deciding that she'd best get on with it, she ventured, "Is this about the soul-eaters, then?"

His attention thus recalled to her, Blakney leaned to spit on the ground with some fervor. "Fookin' Russians."

Startled by this behavior—quite unexpected, in this formal setting–Doyle tried to soothe the ghost down. "I don't know as anyone who's involved in this mare's-nest is Russian, Mr. Blakney."

He eyed her with a full measure of scorn. "Huh. A lot you know."

"I didn't notice any Russians," she insisted. "Although I wouldn't be surprised, since we've got just about everythin else; African, of course—and Benardi was Italian."

"Yeah," he nodded. "Like Rizzo."

She stared at him in surprise. "Why—why yes; Rizzo was Italian." Doyle paused, and then ventured, "I'm not sure as that's relevant, Mr. Blakney." Rizzo was a famous footballer, recently a murder victim in an unrelated case.

"Huh," he repeated. "A lot you know."

Doyle frowned, as this implication made little sense. "I think the Rizzo case has been put to bed—or as much as we can put it to bed, all things considered. Except I've got to find out how killed poor Tommy, of course." Tommy Dryden was a loose-end from the Rizzo case; a kindly and impoverished painter, who'd been murdered for reasons that were as yet unclear.

Blakney nodded. "Yeah—Tommy. He'd come into my shop, from time to time; bringing in some bits and pieces— nothing much, of course. Nice enough bloke; a shame about what happened to 'im."

There was a small pause. "I've got to find out what happened to Tommy," Doyle agreed slowly. "Thank you for remindin' me, Mr. Blakney."

Again, she'd the sense her companion wasn't listening as

much as he was waiting for something. With a touch of anxiety, he glanced over his shoulder toward a wooden doorway that was behind him, and when he turned his head, she caught a glimpse of the tattoos that decorated his neck, looking very much out-of-place beneath the starched white collar of his formal suit.

He turned back to her, and lowered his brow in a slightly menacing manner. "You keep your nose out of it," he warned.

Doyle blinked in surprise. "I can't," she explained. "I'm a copper."

"You're a mother, first."

She stared at him, puzzled. "Surely there's no difference, between?"

But she wasn't to receive an answer, as she was suddenly wide-awake, and staring into the darkness of their bedroom.

CHAPTER 11

*B*ecause Williams had texted to say he could meet her before work—which was much appreciated, as a dram o' coffee would fortify her for the busy day ahead— Doyle asked the driving service to drop her off at the local Deli, where he was already waiting at a table with two cups at the ready. With a guilty conscience, she'd briefly considered cancelling—since she'd already had some of the forbidden brew the night before—but then decided that she may as well be hung for a sheep as a lamb, so to speak, and surely another half-cup would do no harm. Besides, her ghostly visitor was prompting her to do a bit of information-winkling, and this seemed the perfect opportunity.

Williams had once carried a torch for her—before she'd married Acton—but now their relationship had settled into a warm friendship, and she trusted him completely; there was no finer person to have alongside in a tight corner, as she'd well-learned from many a tight corner.

It was oftentimes a delicate balance, however, because Williams entertained the same alarming views as Acton–when it came to serving-up the occasional round of vigilante justice–and he often stood as Acton's henchman in the course of her husband's questionable activities. In this instance, however, his knowledge of Acton's questionable activities might actually be helpful, for a change, and so she hoped to pick up a clue or two about what was brewing—and why she'd a ghostly visitor who seemed to be bringing up a lot of unconnected subjects.

Of course, she'd have to be as subtle as a serpent about it, since she didn't want to pitch poor Williams into yet another divided-loyalties situation; a shame, it was, since subtlety wasn't exactly her strong suit.

After slinging her rucksack over her chair, she sat down across from him. "Thank you, Thomas; you're the next thing to a saint."

"Don't rat me out," he teased.

"Never—I'll be tortured, instead." After taking a tentative sip, she set the cup down again because it was still too hot. "Acton's drivin' me mad, now that there's another bun in the oven. The poor man's deathly afraid I'll dash my foot against a stone."

Williams smiled in acknowledgment. "I think the first clue was the private driver."

Unable to resist, Doyle attempted another sip and then promptly burned her tongue. "No—it's still the concierge service, from my building. You're confused because Mr. Tansi isn't drivin' anymore; instead it's a new fellow."

Williams raised a brow in surprise. "But isn't he from Trestles?"

Trestles was Acton's estate, and, surprised in turn, Doyle paused. "The new driver? No—I don't think so."

"Oh." Losing interest, Williams returned to his coffee. "I just caught a glimpse, but he reminded me of one of the servants at Trestles—the one who helped me move the nursery furniture. Jamaican fellow, I think."

She teased, "Next you'll be telling me that all 'threes' look alike, and I'll have to report you to Personnel for sensitivity trainin'."

The police used numbered codes to identify ethnicities, although this practice was viewed with no small alarm by the reformers, who were worried about the police's profiling of ethnic groups. The brass at the Met had to constantly explain that it was very hard to describe a perp without mentioning his or her ethnicity, but such explanations tended to fall on deaf ears.

Hiding her avid curiosity behind a show of casual interest, Doyle asked, "How are things at home?" It was a delicate subject; Williams had recently and unexpectedly married Lizzy Mathis—although he didn't truly remember much about it, being as he was on a bender at the time. Since then, he'd several times expressed his intention to seek an annulment without delay, but this expressed intention did not seem to jibe with what was actually happening.

"I still have to sort it out—we're both so busy," he explained a bit vaguely. "And I don't want to embarrass her, so I may wait a bit longer."

"Aye, that," said Doyle in a solemn tone, and then smiled into her coffee cup.

"In fact, I'm glad you called, because I wanted to ask your advice."

Doyle lowered her cup whilst hiding her alarm—the last thing needful thing was to have Williams seek out the fair Doyle for marriage advice, but she'd best cooperate, and hope that she could somehow wind the conversation around to what she wanted to find out. "Let's hear it, then."

Williams let out a breath. "Martina rang me up; she wanted to apologize, and hoped we could be friends."

This was rather unexpected, as Martina Betancourt-of-the-Holy-Order was the very reason Williams had gone on the aforementioned bender. He'd been romancing the young woman, but then discovered that she was using him rather ruthlessly to achieve her own ends. In particular, she'd used him as a dupe so as to that she could pursue her Order's objective, and—to add insult to injury—whilst she was dating Williams, she'd neglected to mention that she was married to a missing husband.

Since Williams was unaware of the whole Holy Order angle, Doyle quickly reviewed in her mind what she should and should not say. "Oh—oh, I see; and what did you tell her?"

Williams said rather heavily, "I don't think she can be trusted, even as a friend."

"Small blame to you," Doyle agreed, and left it at that. As she'd said to Acton, there was little point in expecting earthly loyalty from a zealot, and Martina had already proved to be rather ruthless in achieving her aims. On the other hand, Doyle could sense that her companion was torn; the reason he'd needed advice was because he would very much like to hear an explanation from his former light o' love. It was very like Thomas Williams–to want to tie everything up in a neat package–and it was a crackin' shame that life was so very messy.

Thinking to further steer her companion along a better path, she added, "I spoke with Tim McGonigal yesterday, and he seems to think Martina is keepin' company with Philippe Savoie, of all people."

Williams' gaze was suddenly intent upon hers. "Yes—I know. Do you think it is Acton's doing?"

At sea, Doyle lowered her cup. "Acton's doin' what?"

"Putting Savoie with Martina."

She stared at him in surprise, and came to the sudden realization that she wasn't the only one to have ulterior motives for this little coffee-meeting. Slowly shaking her head, she replied honestly, "I truly don't know—but I doubt it, Thomas. I don't think Savoie answers to Acton; he'd not be willin' to do such a thing, solely on Acton's say-so."

He nodded, and lowered his gaze. "No, I suppose that's true. It was just a thought."

He suspects something, she thought as she watched him; he suspects something, and he was hoping I could confirm whatever-it-is that he suspects. And—come to think of it— small blame to him. Martina Betancourt was the last person to feel remorseful, and seek-out William's forgiveness for the way she'd treated him; instead, she must be up to something, herself, in asking to meet with him. And Savoie was an emigna—or amigma, or whatever-the-word was, so there was no telling what he was up to, either.

She offered, "I don't know much about Martina's doin's, but I did see Savoie at the park, yesterday–just like an ordinary da, takin' his son to the park. Mayhap he *is* turnin' over a new leaf, and doin' charitable works. Stranger things have happened, I suppose."

Again, the blue eyes were suddenly sharp upon hers. "Do you believe it?"

"I—I don't know," she offered slowly. "He truly loves Emile, and so mayhap he's tryin' to be a better person, for his son's sake. He's very pleased that Emile's at St. Margaret's—where Gemma is, too—and so mayhap he's makin' an attempt to walk the line."

"I suppose it's possible," Williams agreed in a skeptical tone.

Doyle quirked her mouth. "And then again, mayhap Martina can't resist tryin' to redeem a sinner who's so very sunk in sin."

With a slight edge to his tone, Williams observed, "Since she's still married, she'd be sunk in sin, herself."

"An excellent point."

Best change the topic, Doyle thought quickly, and decided it was past time to do a bit of winkling of her own. "I was talkin' to McGonigal about the Benardi murder—it happened in his buildin', so naturally he's a bit spooked. He seemed a bit surprised that the CID thinks it's a revelation murder; he'd no idea there was a male lover, lurkin' about in the background."

But Williams only shrugged. "That's usually the case though, isn't it? The point of a revelation murder is to expose something no one else knows."

Doyle persisted, "Have we a suspect, then?"

Her companion nodded. "Yes. Acton is coordinating with Vice. It has to be discreetly handled, of course, since Benardi was a respected surgeon, and he did a lot of high-profile volunteer work."

"That he did." Doyle tipped-up her cup so as to savor the dregs, and thought it very interesting that the husband of her bosom hadn't mentioned he was monitoring a suspect in coordination with Vice. Although it almost went without saying that if Benardi was in fact a murky doctor doing murky deeds for *The Curing League*, it could very well be that Acton was covering-up for the doctor-killer, which was a sad state of affairs, but not wholly unexpected. After all, if Benardi was one of the soul-eaters, Acton would think Benardi's death a job well-done, and would be happy to close the books on it.

Recalled to her original purpose, Doyle ventured, "You know, Thomas, I was thinkin' about a loose-end in the Rizzo case; Tommy Dryden."

Williams glanced at her in surprise. "The suspect? I don't think that's much of a loose-end, Kath."

"We can't be sure he was the killer," she insisted stubbornly, and tried to decide what to say—quite the minefield, because Doyle knew for a certainty that Tommy Dryden was not, in fact, Rizzo's killer, but Williams was not privy to this information. "It just doesn't seem in keepin'— the murder was too well thought-out, for the likes of someone like him."

But her companion only shrugged. "A lot of 'unsound minds' are pretty devious, Kath. And there was the church angle."

This was true; "unsound mind" as a motivation for murder was self-explanatory; the killer was not right in the head, and they taught you at the Crime Academy that whenever there was an unexplained murder in a religious institution—like Rizzo's murder in St. Michael's Church— you had to first rule-out "unsound mind" as the motivation. And what Williams said was true—oftentimes, the killer's mental impairment led to a carefully-orchestrated murder, even if the motivation, at its root, was madness. Although there were always the more straightforward manifestations; for example, they'd once had a killer who'd decided he was going to methodically kill everyone named "Sarah" in the phone listings.

Since she couldn't very well tell her companion that a ghost was steering her down this Tommy-path, she said only, "It's botherin' me, for some reason. We don't have a firm time-of-death for Tommy Dryden, which seems a bit too convenient." With a glance at him, she added in a casual tone, "I know he used a pawn shop in Fremont from time to time; mayhap we could look into their records."

"How am I going to put that in the budget?" Williams asked, turning up his palms. "I can't justify the man-hours."

It appeared that it was time to make a clean breast, and so Doyle offered slowly, "I don't think Tommy killed Rizzo—instead, I think he was made the scapegoat, since he's conveniently dead. And I think Acton knows who killed Tommy, but he's not sayin', for some reason."

After a surprised pause, Williams slowly shook his head. "I don't know anything about it, if that's what you're asking."

"Sorry to be probin'," she apologized. But it's botherin' me—I think it's important. Mayhap I'll have a look at the pawnshop, off-the-record."

With a grave expression, he nodded. "I'll tell you if I hear anything."

She rose, and shouldered her rucksack. "And in return, I'll tell you if I learn anything about the Savoie-and-Martina wrinkle."

"Thanks. I'll give you a lift to headquarters. Want to order anything to-go?"

"No—Reynolds already made me a crackin' good breakfast."

As they walked toward the door, Williams remarked, "I will say it's nice to have someone cooking at home."

"Don't I know it," she agreed, and again, hid a smile.

CHAPTER 12

$\mathcal{D}$oyle and Williams parted in the lobby at headquarters, and now she was making her way to the lifts, so as to descend to her floor and start on a busy day's work.

Her discussion with Williams had touched off a troubling train of thought, and Doyle almost wished she could return home so as to have a peek at the fishing kit that was resting in the hall closet. Martina Betancourt had been known to leave listening devices about, and it was possible that Savoie had been enlisted in this cause—mayhap the hand-over of cash to Reynolds was merely a subterfuge to smuggle-in a listening device. It seemed very unlikely, but then again, Savoie's keeping company with Martina in the first place was very unlikely, and Doyle harbored an uneasy feeling about the whole thing.

It was hard to even imagine—that Savoie would betray them—but in this business, she'd too often seen the lengths that men would go for love—or for lust–to discount this possibility. She shouldn't be foolish, and had best shake her stumps and investigate; there were too many strange things going on, and all of them happening at once.

Hard on this thought, her mobile pinged and she saw that it was Martina Betancourt, herself. Speak o' the devil and up she pops, Doyle thought, although I suppose she'd be very unhappy to be compared to Auld Nick.

"Hallo, Kathleen," Martina said. "I hope you are not busy."

"Not at all," said Doyle. "How goes the battle of the righteous?"

With a trace of amusement in her voice, the young woman replied, "I know you're joking, but that's exactly what I wanted to talk to you about. I'd love a bit of advice, and I think you'd be honest with me."

Fancy that, thought Doyle; everyone's wanting my advice, all of a sudden. "Of course," she replied. "Always happy to share any deep insights."

"Is there any chance it could be today?"

Since today was rapidly booking up, Doyle countered, "How's about breakfast, tomorrow mornin'?"

"Oh—sorry, but I'm afraid I'll be busy, tomorrow morning."

Doyle offered, "I'm due to work from home this afternoon; when Edward goes down for a nap, I can meet you at the local café for tea—it's a few blocks away from the flat."

"Perfect. I do appreciate it—text me when you start out."

Interesting, she thought, as she rang off; Martina's been trying to sweeten-up Williams, and now she's trying to sweeten-up me. I wonder what her aim is; Martina Betancourt is not at all the sweetening-up type.

She texted Acton, "Need 2 touch base soon."

He texted back immediately. "Code 5 home?"

With a smile, she paused to text, "Not that kind of touch base." On occasion, they'd taken to sneaking off to their downstairs suite at home for a hurried session of discreet sex.

"A shame. My office in 45?"

So; it seemed he was in the middle of something, and so she replied, "Can wait. Will meet w/Habib then come up."

"See you then."

Doyle made her way to Habib's cubicle, where he brightened upon spotting her approach. "DS Doyle, I have good news. DCI Acton has asked me to set-up surveillance for the clinic. It seems he has heard something, also."

"That is indeed good news, sir." Best not to mention that what Acton had heard was his wife, wringing her fanciful hands. "I hope we can catch the soul-eaters red-handed, the filthy beasts."

Habib nodded. "DCI Acton has requested that Officer Shandera head-up the surveillance team, and I have been assigned as the CSM."

This was of interest; Officer Jerry Shandera was a TDC—a Trainee Detective Constable who was attending the Crime Academy, and studying to be a detective. It seemed a bit odd that a lowly TDC was heading-up a surveillance operation, and it gave her pause, mainly because Officer Shandera had been shown to be trustworthy in the past, when it came to off-the-record Acton operations.

Therefore, one could suspicion that his presence indicated that this may be yet another off-the-record Acton operation, which was rather alarming—what was Acton up to, when it came to the soul-eaters? Did he know something he wasn't telling her? Not to mention that under normal circumstances, any and all off-the-record operations were headed-up by Williams, who was Acton's trusted henchman for these types of things. In this instance, however, Williams had been passed over, for some reason.

Habib's voice interrupted this rather unsettling train of thought. "Since DCI Acton has taken an interest, I wonder if we should bring-in the witness to swear-out a statement. I would not wish to jeopardize the surveillance operation by doing so, however."

Doyle frowned, thinking this over. "I think it's wiser to wait, sir. When I went over there yesterday, I played it off as a routine robbery—a one-off—and I'd be worried that if we pulled the doctor in for something more formal, the suspects may catch wind."

"Yes," Habib agreed with a precise nod. "I will tell DCI Acton that we will stand down, and wait for word."

He'd turned back to his computer, but Doyle ventured, "I wanted to ask, sir—is the Rizzo case considered closed?"

Habib turned to face her again. "It has now been designated as a Class B cold case, DS Doyle, because the prime suspect is no longer alive."

"Don't I know it," Doyle agreed. "So; we've no resources assigned?"

He paused to regard her. "No—not at the present time. Why do you ask?"

"I was just wonderin', sir. I suppose it's best to move on."

"Indeed," her supervisor agreed, and pressed his thin lips together. Habib had been sorely wounded by the famous footballer's death, and hated to dwell upon it, which—come to think of it—was something that had probably been exploited by Doyle's wily husband, who was bent on sweeping the whole Rizzo-case under the rug.

"I'm due to report to DCI Acton, sir," she advised a bit grimly and, as she turned to leave, decided that it may be more accurate to say that the wretched man was due to report to her.

CHAPTER 13

When Doyle arrived upstairs at Acton's office, she was informed by Nazy, his assistant, that he'd not yet returned, but was due back at any moment.

"Oh," said Doyle, a bit surprised, because her husband hadn't indicated that he was off-campus. On the other hand, his absence gave her a prime opportunity to do a bit of extra winkling, and so she immediately leapt to take advantage—Nazy was a young Persian woman who tended to be even more naïve than Doyle, if such a thing was possible. Although when you thought about it, such a person would be completely suitable for Acton's purposes, since she'd be easily hoodwinked by plausible explanations that didn't hold water. Much as I used to be, thought Doyle, rather nostalgically; faith, those were the days.

With a casual air, Doyle began, "I was just askin' DI Habib if the Rizzo case was closed—the mills of justice seem to have ground to a miserable halt."

Nazy nodded. "The activation status has been changed to

'cold case', Officer Doyle. I don't believe there are any resources allotted at present."

Doyle teased, "It's such a shame, Nazy; how can you romance Sir Vikili, if you're not deliverin' required-disclosure docs to his office?" The young woman harbored a mighty crush on one of the Inns of Court's top defense solicitors—not that she had the remotest chance of fixing the man's interest, of course, but an office crush made the day-to-day routine seem a bit more bearable, something which the fair Doyle herself had discovered in spades.

With some excitement, Nazy lowered her voice and confided, "Sir Vikili's brother, Mr. Javid, has been arrested; did you know?"

"I'd heard," Doyle agreed, and decided not to offer any more information, being as she didn't want the poor girl to fall out of her chair. It had turned out that the famous solicitor's brother was involved in a massive criminal enterprise, and if that didn't make family gatherings crackin' awkward, nothing would.

Nazy continued breathlessly, "Sir Vikili is representing him."

With a small smile, Doyle offered, "Can you imagine? A younger brother now has the upper hand over the elder. Sir Vikili must remember every time Mr. Javid wrestled him down to muss up his hair, and have to restrain himself from takin' his revenge."

Nazy laughed, but shook her head. "No, no, Officer Doyle; Sir Vikili has seen to it that Mr. Javid is out on bail, already."

Doyle raised her brows. "Has he? Well, Sir Vikili's a bigger man than I am—his older brother's a nasty piece of work, and prison's too good for him."

At this juncture, Acton could be seen exiting the lift at the end of the hall, and so Doyle straightened up to greet him as he approached. "Ho, sir; I've been distractin' Nazy from her work."

"I am sorry that I am late," he apologized. "A meeting took longer than I'd anticipated."

"Here are your messages, sir," Nazy said, as she handed him a sheaf. "I have prioritized them."

"Excellent—thank you, Ms. Chaudhry," he replied, as he held the door for Doyle.

"You're busy as a bee," Doyle remarked, after he'd closed the door and promptly kissed her in greeting. "I'll keep it as short as I'm able—Martina Betancourt phoned, and wants to meet-up with me."

"Does she indeed?" He leaned back against his desk and glanced through his messages, but Doyle noted that he started from the bottom of the stack, with what Nazy had decided were low-priority. After flicking through a few, he set the messages aside, and then reached to take her hands in his. "And what did you tell her?"

Doyle continued, "I told her I'd walk over to the café for tea this afternoon, but I figured I'd first check-in with you. She's not the ladies-who-meet-for-tea type, so I figure somethin's up."

He nodded in agreement. "No doubt. Shall I accompany you?"

"No," Doyle said bluntly. "You'd only glare at each other."

With a tilt of his head, he disclaimed, "You wound me; surely I would not be so ill-mannered."

Laughing, she leaned in to invite another kiss. "You forgot to say 'tut-tut'."

"I hope I don't have to warn you to be careful, Kathleen."

"Oh, I'll be careful, my friend, but I have to say that I'm curious. I know you're not a Martina-fan, Michael—and with good reason, of course—but she did do you a massive favor, even though you're not someone who likes to be beholden. She could have very easily made things very uncomfortable for you, and let this be a lesson to mend your wicked ways."

She paused, knowing that he didn't want to be reminded of that little episode, and so concluded, "But despite all that, I know she's no threat to me; instead, she sees me as a fellow-traveler, wieldin' a sword of righteousness."

With a small smile, he laced his fingers through hers. "And are you?"

"No," she said bluntly. "I'm one who thinks that God doesn't need much help, in the metin'-out-justice department. Instead, I think He's got it covered, and who am I to second-guess." Since this observation hit close to home, she paused to eye him with some significance.

But her husband, as always, had a ready answer. "How do you know God is not working though Martina?"

She laughed aloud. "Now, there's a startlin' thought—you've stumped me. But I suppose that's exactly what the likes of you would say—you're both the same, in a way, and you should have married Martina; you'd both be rulin' the world, by now."

He leaned to kiss her again. "I like you much better."

"Good to know."

"Trenton will be close at hand, if he is needed."

"That goes without sayin' my friend—you're a bundle of nerves, lately." She contemplated her hands in his for a moment, and then decided to offer with all sincerity, "It's a hardy banner I am, Michael; truly. This birthin' babies business is as simple as pie—simpler, in fact, since I've no idea how to bake a pie, and I've already baked myself one healthy boyo."

"Yes," he said, and drew her to him in an embrace that was tinged with remorse. "I am sorry if I have made you feel uncomfortable, Kathleen. You know that I struggle with it."

This, of course, was quite the understatement; faith, if he'd his way, his free-range wife would be kept home all day, safe in her luxury chicken-coop.

Choosing her words carefully, she fiddled with one of his buttons. "It's not that I don't understand, Michael—and you're miles better than you were at the beginnin'. I think we're copin' just fine—aside from my havin' to eat apples, and such. But it's just—well, I think you're tryin' to hide your worries, and I wish you weren't tryin' so hard." She lifted her face to meet his eyes. "Bein' as I'm a gabbler, I always think it's better to talk things out, but you're the opposite, and so you tend to rope yourself off. Mayhap we could come to a compromise, of sorts."

"I don't know if that is possible," he replied with some regret, and it was true.

She sighed in acknowledgement; indeed, he'd tried to confront his demons once upon a time, and the process had not gone well at all. Perhaps she should just count it a victory that the demons had been beaten back, and were not as much in evidence, nowadays.

"Sorry," she apologized. "I've no business venturin' into these deep waters in the midst of a work-day, and shame on me, for steppin' into that tangle-patch."

He made no response, and she decided that—since the direct approach didn't seem to be working—she'd best move on to the indirect approach. "And speakin' of tangle-patches,

Williams says you've a suspect, in the Benardi case. Why didn't you mention it to me?"

But he shook his head with regret. "No longer; I decided I could not file a viable case, based on the evidence."

"Oh. Which brings me to the next topic; Habib says the Rizzo case has been put to bed."

She felt his chest rise and fall. "Can you blame me?"

In resigned acknowledgment, she blew out her own breath. "No, I suppose not. But I do feel a bit sorry for that poor painter, who will bear the stain of a murder he didn't commit."

"He is dead," Acton gently pointed out. "And so it hardly matters, does it?"

Now, there speaks someone who doesn't have various ghosts, racketing-about in his dreams, thought Doyle, but then she was suddenly struck, because in a strange way, it was true—it hadn't mattered to Tommy-the-ghost that he was being framed for his football idol's death. Instead, Tommy had seemed much more worried that his murder wasn't being put to good use, somehow.

Doyle teetered on the edge of asking her husband if he knew who'd actually killed Tommy Dryden, but then drew back; she'd yet another ghost who was leading her somewhere, and instead of taking the bull by the horns with Acton—never a winning proposition, only see how the "deep waters" conversation had gone—instead, she'd go visit that ghost's pawn shop, and see what there was to see.

And for these same reasons, she decided not to ask why Williams was out, and Officer Shandera was in, when it came to the surveillance operation on the free clinic. There were too many strange things going on, she thought yet again; and all of them happening at once.

"I'll leave you to it," she said, and straightened up. "Thank you for puttin' surveillance on the clinic, Michael—I hope it's not a wild goose chase."

"Nothing as yet," he admitted.

"Friday night's when we should see somethin'," she said. "Here's hopin'."

With a mental sigh, she walked to the door with him whilst acknowledging to herself that she'd sacrifice a week's pay to take a peek through the last couple of messages in Acton's stack. She'd best step carefully, though; if there was an Acton-scheme afoot, it would be better to reconnoiter the ground, first. A shame, it was, that her best detecting always seemed to be done in thankless pursuit of her wayward husband.

"Keep me posted," he said as he ushered her out the door.

"Always," she replied, and regrettably knew it was not true.

CHAPTER 14

$\mathcal{D}$oyle phoned the driving service, and then briefly contemplated "accidentally" leaving her mobile phone on Nazy's desk. Even in normal times, Acton tended to keep track of her whereabouts using her mobile, and it was likely he'd redoubled his efforts, with how hyper-cautious he'd been, recently. On the other hand, if the limo driver was indeed an Acton-plant, as Williams had thought, her husband would hear all about her little excursion anyways, so better to think up a plausible tale for her side-trip to a Fremont pawn-shop, even though it may strain her abilities to do so.

The new driver smiled his greeting, and after they were underway, Doyle asked, "I meant to ask you, Adrian—aren't you from Trestles?"

"I am," he replied readily, and glanced up at her in the rearview mirror. "I was a groundskeeper, there."

Making a wry mouth, she apologized, "Sorry; I should have recognized you—shame on me."

"No—no worries, ma'am; I don't think we've ever met."

Naturally, she thought; and if Williams hadn't caught a glimpse, I'd be none the wiser. "How'd you come to be here in London, then?"

"I've lived in Meryton all my life, ma'am, and so I decided I'd try to live here in the city, just to see what it was like."

"I did much the same," she admitted. "D'you like it, so far?"

"I do," he said, and this was not exactly true. "It's an adjustment, of course."

"Aye, that," she agreed, in a massive understatement. "Although I suppose—in an ironic turn of events—you may be safer here in London than at Trestles; I understand that a footman was killed." This, to let him know that she was keeping track of lady-of-the-manor types of things.

The driver nodded, somber. "Yes. A terrible shame."

Surprisingly enough, this was not true, and for a few moments Doyle was so astonished she wasn't certain what to say. Perhaps the dead man had been this fellow's rival, back at Trestles, but it seemed so out-of-keeping—the driver didn't seem the type to wish for death on his rivals. He seemed very —very innocutous, or whatever the word was.

She made a show of looking idly out the window, and asked, "So; did you parents immigrate to England? There's another fine example of gatherin' up your courage, and strikin' out for a new place."

With a smile, he glanced at her again in the rear-view mirror. "No ma'am. We go back a long way, in fact. So long ago that my ancestors were brought over as indentured servants, but the then-Lord Acton gave them their freedom. We've settled in the area, ever since."

So; another loyal foot soldier, thought Doyle. It was all very interesting, and it was also plain-as-a-pikestaff that his fellow was security, despite all that polite innocutous-ness. Ah well, she shouldn't complain; if it made Acton rest easier, it was no hardship to her.

But this also meant she'd best think up a crackin' good reason for her pawn-shop visit; Acton would know that it wasn't connected to any case on her docket, and so she'd best begin spinning a tale.

In an airy tone, she advised, "It shouldn't take more than a few minutes, if you don't mind waitin'. I've got to go check on a secret project I'm workin' on—somethin' for Acton's birthday."

"I'll be happy to wait, ma'am," the driver agreed.

When they arrived, though, the driver took one look at the questionable building—with it's security-caging across the front windows—and offered, "Perhaps I should come in with you, ma'am."

"It's all right," she said cheerfully. "It won't take but a minute, and recall that I'm a police officer."

"All right, ma'am," he said, but she noted that he parked at the kerb in front of the shop, even though it was a no-parking zone.

Doyle entered the dingy little shop, and wished she'd a better idea of what she was doing there—not to mention a better excuse to give Acton for this visit. Very unlikely she'd be looking here for his birthday present, but she wasn't very good at thinking on her feet, and so she'd best come up with a plausible gift.

The shopkeeper, who'd been leaning against the display case and looking at his mobile, straightened up upon seeing her. "What you got, miss?"

Faith, I must look like a lady who's in need of funds, she thought, and instead showed him her warrant card. "Police."

The man's attitude changed completely, of course, and he protested, "I run a clean shop, here."

This was not exactly true, but that was not exactly a surprise; pawn shops were notorious for fencing stolen goods. Since Doyle wasn't interested in rocking this particular boat, she explained, "Not to worry; I'm here on a tip, and I just need to see if you've a suspect in your records. I'm tryin' to place him in London, on a date certain."

His brows came together as he regarded her in surprise. "Tommy Dryden?"

It was Doyle's turn to be surprised. "Why—why yes; how did you know?"

The man shrugged. "You're too late; someone's been here before you, and took those records into custody. Took my CCTV film, too. It was that famous detective-fellow—you know the one."

Indeed, I do, thought Doyle, trying to hold fast onto her temper. Indeed, I do.

A bit smugly, the shopkeeper cocked a brow. "You lot need to get on the same page."

Mustering up a rueful smile, Doyle said in her best imitation of a maiden in distress, "Oh; I hope I don't get into trouble."

"They won't hear about it from me," the fellow laughed.

"Thank you," said Doyle. "I must say, I feel a bit stupid." Truer words, never spoken.

The shopkeeper lowered his voice and offered, "No worries; you can pretend you were checking-in about the necklace."

"The necklace?" asked Doyle, at sea.

The man jerked his head over to the jewelry display cabinet. "That one—the sapphire necklace."

Doyle turned to see the very same sapphire necklace that had figured largely in the Rizzo case, now displayed in the rather jumbled cabinet that held a wide array of pawned jewelry. A necklace that—as far as she was aware—now belonged to Acton.

I've truly gone down the rabbit-hole, she thought, staring at it blankly; it's a crackin' amazement I haven't gone barkin' mad.

Watching her reaction, the shopkeeper chuckled. "They do keep you in the dark, don't they?"

"Indeed, they do," said Doyle, a bit grimly.

With an easy gesture, the man explained, "It's paste, of course. It'd be worth more than the store, if it was real. I'm to try to get fingerprints from the man who comes in to claim it." He winked. "I do the coppers a favor, I get a few favors in return."

With a mighty effort, Doyle pulled herself together. "Right. I should go, I suppose, before I waste any more time." In a conspiratorial manner, she smiled at him. "Promise you won't squeak on me."

He grinned. "Mum's the word."

CHAPTER 15

*O*nce back in the car, Doyle was very much inclined to confront Acton about the assorted underhanded tricks he was in the process of pulling, but decided she needed to think it all over, first. She was a leaper-to-conclusions by nature, and—combined with her uncertain temper—it hadn't always served her well. For example, the fact that her husband had quietly substituted-in his own driver wasn't a huge transgression, certainly; he hadn't told her because he knew she didn't like to feel spied-upon, and so it was as much her fault as his that he'd felt the need to be so secretive.

And speaking of which, she should probably use this opportunity to winkle-out a bit more information from the driver, but this seemed beyond her powers at the moment, since she'd no idea what it was she should be trying to winkle.

In an attempt to gather-in her bewildered thoughts, she firmly instructed herself to start at the beginning—start a timeline, just as they taught you at the Crime Academy. The sapphire necklace was owned by—it had been originally owned by Sir Vikili, the famous solicitor, and it was old and valuable—some sort of family heirloom. It had been used to bait a trap for Acton, but Acton—as always, and to give the man his due—had outfoxed everyone, sidestepped the trap, and then had kept the necklace for good measure.

So; Acton wanted the pawnshop-owner to try to get prints, which meant Acton must be baiting his own trip with the stupid necklace, and it just went to show you that Acton had a wicked sense of humor, despite all appearances to the contrary.

But who was the trap for? Sir Vikili, trying to track down and reclaim his family heirloom? Unlikely that the famous solicitor would be dumb enough to leave his prints at a pawnshop, though, and besides, Acton had a great deal of respect for Sir Vikili, despite the fact they were often on opposite sides of a criminal trial. Very unlikely Acton was setting-up a pawnshop-trap for the man; instead—if he truly wanted to arrest him—Acton would be all polite, and such, and ask Sir Vikili if he would be kind enough to report to Detention.

It must be someone else, then; someone who would be very interested to discover that an incriminating necklace from the Rizzo case was sitting in a Fremont pawnshop, minding its own business.

Could the trap be set for Savoie? There were a couple of alarming things going on with Savoie, just now—his Martina-devotion, and his communicating on the sly with Reynolds, of all people. It was almost as though the man was cozying-up to persons who knew a great deal about the workings of the House of Acton, which certainly raised a red flag.

Mulling this over, Doyle found she had a hard time believing such a thing, although she shouldn't; after all, the Frenchman knew about the necklace's existence, which would seem to be an important consideration, if this whole set-up was indeed a trap. On the other hand, it seemed unlikely that Acton would go to such lengths to set a trap for Savoie, since Savoie was his partner-in-crime. No doubt her husband already had bushels-full of evidence in hand, if he truly wanted to send the Frenchman to prison. Not to mention the most important consideration of all; if Acton thought Savoie was betraying him, the last thing he'd do would be to set-up an evidence-trap so as to send the man to prison. Instead, Savoie would simply disappear, with no one the wiser—she knew her husband's tendencies well, unfortunately.

Her scalp started prickling, as it did when her instinct was prodding her to pay attention, and so she frowned, trying to decide why it would. Of *course* this Acton-trap wasn't intended for Savoie—despite the red flags—because the Chief Inspector's vengeance in such a situation would be nowhere near this convoluted, nor kind. Savoie would just sink from sight, never to be heard from again–not to mention the last thing Acton would want would be for Savoie to be taken into custody, and start grassing-out Acton's own transgressions.

So; it wasn't a trap for Savoie, then. Who?

Thinking it over, she came up empty. I'm that flummoxed, she decided, and blew out a breath. And then there was the other angle, here—was the necklace connected, somehow, to Tommy Dryden's murder? It seemed a huge coincidence, that Acton had swept-up Tommy's pawn records, and that the necklace had been left to bait a trap at the very same place. He was up to something—something big, and she'd bet her teeth that Acton had been checking his phone messages for word from this very shopkeeper.

So; what was he up to, the wretched man? The records-seizing was easily explained; Doyle had little doubt that the dates on the pawn records showed that Tommy Dryden could not have killed Rizzo, but that inconvenient little fact couldn't be allowed to interfere with the illustrious Chief Inspector's plans to sweep the Rizzo murder case under the rug. Tommy was Acton's decoy—framed for Rizzo's murder—and now conveniently dead, himself, so that there were no loose ends, and no need to assign any further CID resources to the Rizzo case. The case had been thoroughly shelved, save for the one loose end that no one else knew about; Tommy's ghost had shown up in Doyle's dreams, earnestly explaining that he shouldn't be Acton's "decoy", but that instead, he should be Acton's "assist" in helping him solve a crime.

Doyle closed her eyes in frustration, because here was yet another piece of the puzzle that seemed to fit nowhere—there were no Rizzo-related crimes that Acton needed an "assist" to solve—or at least, not so far as she could tell. Instead, Acton was carefully laying all Rizzo-related crimes to bed, and just as carefully covering all tracks, so that the famous footballer's case went cold.

Her mobile pinged, and she didn't even bother to look, because she knew it was her husband, who was no doubt aware that he was slated to receive the rough end of a jack-saw, courtesy of his wife. I'll let the man stew for a bit, she thought a bit grimly. It's nothing more than he deserves, the conniving *sassanach*.

So; what was the connection, betwixt the trap Acton was setting, and Tommy Dryden's pawn records? She closed her eyes for a minute, knowing—in the way that she knew things

—that there *was* a connection, but was unable to catch a glimpse of what it might be.

I'm that frustrated, she admitted to herself; I've the sense that if I'd half-a-brain-and-a-cork-eye, I'd figure it out. Although in my defense, whilst there are a lot of strange things happening lately, nothing seems to tie-in with anything else, and—to top it off—I've a ghost telling me to mind my own business, for a change.

This gave her pause, because she hadn't really thought about this, but it did seem very much out-of-keeping. Usually, she'd ghosts who were trying to point her in the right direction, but Bill Blakney was warning her off, and in no uncertain terms.

He knows what's afoot, she thought slowly. He's the one who sent me over to the pawn shop in the first place, so he wants me to find out that Acton is up to something. Yet at the same time, he wants me to stay out of it–which makes no sense, whatsoever; what's the point of sending me over, if he wants me to stay out of it? And how is any of this connected to the fact that I'm a mother, before I'm a police officer? Why would that make a difference?

Since they'd arrived at the residential building, she decided to give it up for the time being, and instead spend a happy and mindless hour with little Edward, who wasn't running any sort of counter-play with international implications—or at least, not as far as she was aware. He was his father's son, after all.

CHAPTER 16

*O*nce back at the flat, Doyle was met at the door by Mary, who was minding Edward—the boy beaming upon beholding his mother, and lifting his arms in a demand to be held.

Doyle obliged, and gave her son a great smacking kiss, which made him giggle and duck his head into her shoulder. She saw that Gemma was standing on a stool in the kitchen, helping Reynolds prepare lunch, and so she asked Mary with some concern, "Is Gemma still not feelin' well?"

The nanny explained, "Reynolds thought we should hold her back for one more day. She did cough a few times this morning, and he was worried that she might infect the other children."

"We'll give her an easy day, then," Doyle agreed. "She can nap when Edward does." As she hung her coat in the hall closet, Doyle took a quick look, and duly noted that the fishing-pole case was no longer in evidence.

Mary continued, "I took Edward for a nice walk this

morning, when Gemma worked on her lessons; he was a bit restless, and Mr. Reynolds thought he could use some air."

"That's to the good, then—at least I'm off the hook."

Mary laughed, being as she was well-aware that the master of the house was prodding his unenthused wife to exercise. "I'll set the table, if we're ready for lunch."

"We are," Doyle agreed, and wandered into the kitchen to watch Reynolds and Gemma, as they strategically placed garnishes on the plates. "I'll give you fair warnin' Reynolds; I wouldn't be surprised if Acton made an appearance."

The butler looked up in surprise. "Lord Acton hasn't said, madam."

"Just a feelin' I have," she explained, and didn't mention that this feeling was based on the certain conviction that her husband would be in a pelter to see how much she'd gleaned at the pawn shop, which—unfortunately—wasn't much at all. It was a shame she wasn't better at bluffing, but she could console herself with the fact that Acton was not one to be bluffed, in the first place.

I know how that man operates, she thought, as she quickly thwarted Edward's attempt to grasp at the edge of a plate—Reynolds insisted on china, and Edward had already taken quite a toll on the serving set. It was a shame, almost— that she knew Acton so well; it would be nice to be adrift in blissful ignorance, for a change.

As it had in the car, her scalp started prickling, which seemed a bit strange. What was so startling about that? Indeed, she knew how her husband's mind worked, given her long experience with catching him out at his schemes and all-around masterminding. It was exhausting, truly; she wasn't cut out to catch-out masterminds—that was much more Acton's stock-in-trade.

Again, her scalp prickled, and—exasperated—she decided to ignore it, and instead help Mary and Gemma set the table.

As they carried the napkins over, Doyle offered, "I'm that sorry you're not feelin' well, Gemma."

As if on cue, the little girl paused to cough in a contrived manner, and Doyle hid a smile; apparently Gemma was shamming an illness to skip school, which was a time-honored tradition that Doyle well-appreciated. And it certainly helped that the girl had an indulgent mother, as Doyle had. It was almost a shame, truly; Doyle had fond memories of roasting potatoes in the fireplace grate, bundled with her mother in a quilt against the cold. Gemma, being Russian royalty, would necessarily have to miss out on the finer things.

And speaking of the finer things, Doyle looked over to where Reynolds was standing at the counter, slicing fruit—no doubt slated for the fair Doyle's wretched plate—and called out to him in an offhand manner, "Did Savoie fetch his kit, Reynolds?"

"He did, madam," the butler replied smoothly, and not at all like someone who'd just socked away a sackful of cash. "Mr. Savoie came by this morning."

At Doyle's elbow, Gemma said in her soft voice, "The gun-man."

Mary and Doyle immediately exchanged alarmed looks across the table, and Mary leaned forward to say in a low tone, "Now, Gemma, you mustn't say anything; if Mr. Savoie carries a gun, I suppose that's none of our business."

Her eyes wide, Gemma nodded in understanding as Doyle tried not to look conscious. She carried her own illegal gun in an ankle holster as a matter of course, being as her certifiable husband was certifiable; indeed, it was the first thing he'd ever given her. Lately, with Edward toddling about, she'd taken to locking it up in the gun safe when she was at home, which meant—truth to tell—that she occasionally forgot to put it back on when she went out again.

I should tie a string 'round my finger, or something, she thought; Acton would be most unhappy to know that I forget it, sometimes, and I suppose if it makes him relax a tad more, then it's no hardship for me. Not to mention that it has come in handy, on more than one best-be-forgotten occasion.

"Edward's going over to the stairs, Lady Acton," Gemma warned, and Doyle raced to snatch-up the toddler before he made his goal, which was apparently to take a massive tumble down the steps.

"No," Doyle warned her squirming and unrepentant son. "Faith, I'm going to have to tie you out to a peg in the ground."

"Lord Acton has requested that a stairway gate be installed," Reynolds informed her, as he helped her fasten Edward into his seat.

"Yes; I suppose we've little choice," Doyle offered unenthusiastically. She was having trouble enough, mastering the child-proof locks that now adorned all the doors and cupboards. A shame, that there wasn't a device to keep one's husband out of trouble, just as easily. Although—come to think of it—she was the equivalent of Acton's safety-gate, which was an interesting way of looking at it.

They began their luncheon—a hit-or-miss procedure, with Edward learning to use his utensils—and Doyle duly noted that poor Mary could only manage to push her food around on her plate. "You have to eat, Mary," she scolded. "Here, have some of my horrid fruit."

"I feel much better today," Mary lied, accepting an orange slice. "I think it's easing off."

"It will be all be worth it," Doyle assured her, and diplomatically didn't mention that when one was in labor, one wasn't at all certain that this was the case.

The concierge buzzed, and Reynolds announced, "Colonel Kolchak is downstairs, madam."

"Oh—oh, send him up, of course."

This was unexpected, and Doyle asked Reynolds with some trepidation, "Does he know the Russian lesson was cancelled?" The Colonel was the kind of person who liked to be kept abreast, and not at all the kind of person who would skip school so as to roast potatoes in the grate.

"He does, madam. I am always careful to keep him informed of Miss Gemma's status."

Doyle made a face. "He's a worry-wart, though; I hope he's not bringin' along a full slate of doctors with him."

The Colonel tended to be overly-protective when it came to Gemma, being as the girl represented the hopes and dreams of the Russian loyalists who wanted to restore the monarchy. Although her identity was under wraps for now, no doubt they'd plans to push her forward, at some point, and this scheme would be in ashes and ruins if Gemma didn't stay healthy.

Upon entering, and seeing that they were assembled at the table, the Russian man immediately apologized, and declined Reynolds' offer to take his coat. "Please forgive me for this intrusion, Lady Acton, but I could not be easy."

"Not a'tall," said Doyle, gesturing to the table. "Come and have lunch, we've plenty."

"No, no—thank you all the same; I was concerned about Georgievna, but I can see that she seems to be recovering."

"She'd a bit of a cough," Doyle explained, so as to spare the girl another feigned performance. "But I imagine she'll be hale as a harrier by mornin', and back to normal."

The man deferentially approached and bowed to take the little girl's hand in a respectful, old-world manner. He asked her something in Russian, and Gemma readily replied in the same language.

With a fond smile, the older man straightened up, and released her hand. "She is doing very well, with her lessons."

It was on the tip of Doyle's tongue to mention that Reynolds had been taking Russian lessons so as to allow the girl to practice with him, but she drew back; there seemed to be an odd sort of possessiveness—or perhaps more correctly, an odd sort of guardedness—when it came to the Colonel's attitude toward Gemma, and small blame to him; it was thanks to his dogged efforts that Gemma had been found again, and plucked out of obscurity. Not to mention, of course, that he considered Gemma to be some sort of exalted being in an almost false-idol sort of way, and so he probably wouldn't be best pleased to hear that she rubbed elbows with a servant as much as she did. After all, Reynolds was a very savvy fellow—when it came to reading people—and if Reynolds himself hadn't mentioned his Russian lessons, it was probably wisest that Doyle follow suit.

The Colonel bowed in Doyle's direction. "Forgive my foolishness, Lady Acton. We will resume our lessons tomorrow, then."

"Very good, sir," said Reynolds respectfully, as he escorted the Colonel to the door.

Reynolds doesn't think it's very good at all, Doyle thought in amusement; Reynolds is like a dog with a bone, when it comes to Gemma. Ah well; someday I'll be waving Edward off at the preschool, and I can hardly bear even thinking about it.

As Reynolds held the door for the Colonel, Acton appeared on the threshold, and the two men greeted each other with what Doyle characterized as aristo-speak, which always seemed to her Irish ears to be overly-polite and devoid of any discernable feeling. She flashed Reynolds an I-told-you-so look, and then carried Edward over to the sink so as to wash him down.

Mary rose to assist in clearing off the plates, but Doyle instructed, "Go lie-down with your poor self, Mary; we'll put Edward and Gemma to bed for a nap, and no one will miss you for a moment."

With a wan smile, the nanny left for the downstairs suite, and Acton came into the kitchen as Doyle sat Edward on the counter to dry him off—no easy task, with his father's tie within grabbing distance.

Acton offered, "If you've already dined, shall we take a walk?"

"All right," she groused. "Although I think you're just tryin' to make sure I've no crockery at hand to throw at you."

"There is that," he admitted. "And I wouldn't want to wake the children."

"I'll 'wake' you one, I will," she advised in an ominous tone, and handed Edward off to Reynolds.

CHAPTER 17

$\mathcal{T}$he doorman hurried over to man the lobby door, as Doyle accompanied her husband outside so as to begin their walk. As they struck out along the pavement, Acton asked, "Where shall we go? Do you have a preference?"

But Doyle was in no mood for polite chit-chat. "If I'd my druthers I'd be marchin' you straight into the Thames, my friend. I will hear your explanation, and with no bark on it—what are you about?"

But in true Acton-style, he answered her question with another question. "Why did you go to the shop?"

It was never a good idea to tell Acton about the ghosts, being as he didn't seem to think they were ghosts as much as some sort of manifestation that his wife was a madwoman. Whilst he was a great respecter of her intuition, apparently ghosts were a bridge too far, and so she replied, "I wanted to follow-up on Tommy Dryden's murder. It's a loose end, in the

Rizzo case, since you'll never convince me that Rizzo's killer is the same one who killed Tommy."

"No," he agreed.

She glanced up at him. "D'you know who killed Tommy, then?"

"I can guess, mainly because Dryden's pawn tickets were claimed by Antonio D'Angelo."

She halted to stare at him in astonishment, at a momentary loss for words. D'Angelo was Martina Betancourt's estranged husband, who'd supposedly been infiltrating the money-laundering rig on behalf of the Holy Order. "Oh—oh, Michael; Mother a' Mercy, but isn't *that* a wrinkle. All this time he's been supposedly missin', but instead he's thrown-in with the blacklegs."

"So it would seem. "

Her brow knit, Doyle resumed walking. "I can't say as I'm all that surprised, I suppose. He's a bit dodgy, what with pretendin' to be dead, and not even lettin' his wife know that it was all a misdirection play."

"It was not the action of an honorable man, certainly."

They walked a few steps in silence, and then she shook her head in wonder. "So—instead of takin' down the villains, D'Angelo joined them, and then killed poor Tommy, for good measure."

In response, Acton observed, "It would not be the first time someone who started out with good intentions could not withstand temptation."

Having witnessed the results of this sort of thing many a time in her professional career, Doyle could only agree. "Aye; and it's not like we haven't seen it amongst the coppers, too. There's so much money to be had, if you just bend your principles a tad, and pretty soon you're bendin' them completely in half. But *murder*—murder is a whole 'nother level of evildoin' Michael. Shame on D'Angelo, for pretendin' to be righteous with one hand, whilst doin' such evil deeds with the other."

The penny dropped, and she lifted her face to him. "And that must be what he saw—what Tommy saw, that he wasn't supposed to see. Tommy was paintin' at the church, and he must have seen D'Angelo doin' somethin' shady, like transferrin' stolen goods. That's why D'Angelo had to kill him–after all, he couldn't allow this painter-fellow to expose him as one of the black-hats when he was supposed to be one of the white-hats."

"Very likely."

Thinking this over, she returned her gaze to the pavement, stretching ahead of them. "It's all kinds of ironic, Michael. D'Angelo probably thought he'd neatly resolved his little witness-problem, and then along comes the mighty Chief Inspector Acton, who decides that Tommy Dryden should be pinned for Rizzo's murder, and proceeds to shine a white-hot spotlight on this obscure little painter, and on all his doin's."

"Yes. I imagine the pawn tickets were on Dryden's body, and D'Angelo decided to claim the items in Dryden's name, so as to throw-off the date of death."

With a great deal of meaning, Doyle observed, "And you couldn't have that, husband, because you were already manipulatin' the timeline for poor Tommy's date-of-death so as to suit your own purposes."

As could be expected, he made no response, and so with great exasperation, she scolded, "This is *exactly* why honesty is the best policy, Michael; now we've got competin' cover-ups goin' on, and the devil take the hindmost." She eyed him sidelong, but he remained silent, and so she prompted, "So; what is it you've planned?"

"I am going to wait, and see what develops," he replied, and it was the truth.

She thought this over, as they walked a few steps in silence. "D'you know where D'Angelo is hidin' out? He's a bit slippery."

"I was hoping that perhaps you would discover what you can from his wife, today at tea."

Reminded, she lifted her brows. "Oh—oh, right, then. I'll do my best, but she may not know, Michael. Recall that she's a zealot—when all is said and done—and she'd never approve of all this wholesale sinning on the part of her better half. There's good reason he's left her out of the loop; he knows she'd rain down hellfire on his head."

"Nevertheless, if you could gently probe, perhaps."

Quirking her mouth, she offered, "I'll do my best, although I think we both know that I'm not much of a gentle-prober, my friend. I'm more along the lines of a blurter-outer."

"Nonsense; you are charming," he insisted, and pulled her closer so as to kiss the top of her head. "But it would pay to be careful about what you tell her. Say nothing of the painter, nor of the pawn tickets."

"No—don't worry," she agreed. "But on the other hand, she must want somethin' from me, or she wouldn't be settin' up this meetin', in the first place. So, there's competin' interests, all-around."

With this observation, her scalp started prickling, and she studied the trees for a moment, trying to decide why it would. It was no surprise that there were competing interests, surely? In Acton-world there were *always* competing interests, since the man never passed-up a chance to pull whatever strings needed pulling so as to suit his fancy. Faith, when you thought about it, it truly wasn't much of a competition for those poor competing interests, since Acton's interests always won-out over any other paltry interests, like the rule of law that they were supposedly sworn to uphold.

For example—and as an excellent case-in-point—her husband hadn't seen fit to mention the sapphire necklace that was sitting in the pawn shop, baiting a trap for a person or persons unknown. He's hoping I didn't find out about it, she admitted to herself with a mental sigh—not to mention he never answered my question about whether he knows where D'Angelo is hiding out. I'm getting miles better than I used to be, about noticing when he sends me off on another topic, instead of giving me a straight answer.

As if on cue, her husband deftly changed the subject. "Should we be concerned about Mary? Hire another nanny to assist her, perhaps?"

Blowing out a resigned breath, Doyle nodded. "I'm thinkin' we may have to, Michael. She's a brick, is our Mary, but I know from sad experience that it's hard to operate when you're feelin' so down-pin. And on top of that, she's got her own life to think of—she's due at a dinner party for Howard's Parliament committee tonight, and I think she feels she has to go, no matter what. It's a shame, but I suppose if you're a political wife, you've got to show up, and put on a good face."

It was on the tip of her tongue to say that Mary wasn't the sort of person who was cut-out to be a political wife, but she was held back by the realization that the exact same thing could be said about the fair Doyle, and the position in life where she'd wound up. Best not to second-guess, and instead assume that all was unfolding as it was supposed to—in all things, give thanks. Which reminded her that she should check-in with Dr. Okafor, and find out if she'd suffered any consequences from Doyle's visit to the clinic.

"I will begin to make inquiries, then."

She nodded, and they walked in silence for a few moments. It went without saying that Acton would be reluctant to allow another nanny into his tightly-controlled world, but there seemed little choice in the matter, and it was all his fault to begin with, for marrying his support officer before he'd considered the substantial ramifications that came along with snatching-up a wife in such a way.

Doyle said, "I can't begrudge Mary her own life, and her own family, but I'll miss her; I've always had the sense that our lives are bound together, in some strange way."

In sympathy, Acton squeezed her against his side. "It is not as though we will not see her. The children will play together, certainly."

Shaking off her sadness, Doyle smiled. "Of course, Michael. I'm just waxin' mopey, and you should pay me no mind."

He tilted his head down to hers. "At the risk of making it worse, do you think you could manage a trip to Trestles, over the week-end?"

"The funeral," she guessed. "Reynolds asked if we were goin'."

"We should," he explained, almost apologetically.

"Of course, Michael. And you mustn't think I don't want to go—it's a beautiful place, and I know you're very fond." Acton's hereditary estate was indeed beautiful—with its expansive grounds and timeless atmosphere, and Doyle knew that her husband very much enjoyed the time he spent there. Unfortunately for Doyle, the place was chock-full of ghosts, who hung about in the rafters and thought that the Irish Countess was the next best thing to a raree-show.

And an added disadvantage came in the form of the Dowager Lady Acton, Acton's mother, who was lurking like a spider in the Dower House, spinning her schemes. Although she may have run out of schemes to spin; Acton was not one to tolerate any slights to his wife, and so he'd ruthlessly moved his mother out of the main manor house, and the woman had been largely sidelined, ever since.

Indeed, the reality of the new pecking-order actually seemed to be improving the elderly woman's attitude slightly, and she appeared to be making a mighty effort to better mind her manners. It was just as well—Acton wouldn't hesitate to kick her out altogether, if she so much as looked sideways at the fair Doyle; as mentioned, the man didn't tolerate any slights to the wife of his bosom.

Fondly, Doyle leaned in to rest her head on his arm, and—roundly exasperated—tried to ignore the persistent prickling of her scalp.

CHAPTER 18

*a*cton returned straight to work, and Doyle tiptoed back into the flat, careful to be quiet because if Edward was shorted of his full nap, he became quite the crosspatch. "How's our Mary?" she whispered to Reynolds, who was waiting with the door propped open.

"Napping with Gemma," Reynolds replied in a low tone. "Everyone is asleep."

"I wish I was," Doyle groused. "I'm goin' to meet stupid Martina Betancourt for tea, and I'm not lookin' forward to it a'tall."

The butler carefully closed the door, a crease between his brows. "Then perhaps you should cancel the appointment, madam."

"I can't. It's actually work-related, more's the pity. Whilst I gird my loins, mayhap you could make me a go-cup of coffee? The café's coffee is a sorry excuse."

With a wooden expression, the butler suggested, "Perhaps you should lie down for a bit, instead, madam."

Doyle made a face. "I can't–I've no time, what with Acton walkin' me all about, like a plough-horse in the traces."

In mild disapproval, Reynolds offered, "I am certain Lord Acton is only thinking of your well-being, madam."

Much struck, she paused to stare at him. "That's just it, Reynolds. His idea of what's best for me tends to take it to the tenth level, and then some. He overdoes everything, when it comes to me; he over-contentates—"

"I believe you mean over-compensates, madam."

"Thank you; he overcompensates, when it comes to my well-bein'. I suppose I shouldn't mind, but sometimes it's a bit wearin', and I wish he'd take it down a notch or two."

She turned her gaze toward the windows, because this train of thought seemed to tie-in with the one she'd recently entertained on the walk—the one where her instinct was prodding her, for some reason. Acton was a bit nicked—and more than a bit nicked, when it came to his wedded wife— and because of this, he tended to *over*-champion, if that was a word, and go all scorched-earth on anyone who'd mistreated her, as the Dowager had learned to her sorrow.

Faith, there was a time when she'd been worried that he'd turn around and throat-punch anyone who jostled her on the pavement, but surely, he'd tempered his actions, since then? He was much better—and he'd definitely tempered the black moods that used to come over him; where he'd shut himself away, and drink heavily. Those black moods were few and far between, now, mainly because she'd learned how to head them off—he may be a complicated man, but she was a dedicated woman, when it came to easing his burdens. Strange, that she kept thinking about it, though.

I should make a list, she thought, closing her eyes briefly; there are a lot of strange things happening, and all of them at once–so many that it's hard to keep track. Between Savoie, and Williams, and the dead doctor who doesn't seem to have a male lover, and the necklace, and a ghost who wants me to mind my own business–

"I am sure Lord Acton means well, madam," the servant ventured, no doubt a bit alarmed by this glimpse of marital rebellion.

She brought her attention back to him, and with a rueful smile, disclaimed, "Fah; don't mind me, Reynolds, I'm just blowin' off some steam. And let's not forget he's thrown his mother out of the manor house, and not a moment too soon."

"Yes, madam," the butler soothed. "Although I imagine the Dowager Lady Acton will attend the funeral."

"Of course, she will; she'd never miss a chance to give-off airs."

The butler bowed his head but made no reply, since he was not one to criticize his betters.

In short order, Reynolds was again quietly opening the door as Doyle readied to take yet another tedious walk, this time to the stupid café where—to add to its sins—the coffee was only passing-fair, and Reynolds seemed to have forgot that he was supposed to make her a go-cup.

"Wish me luck," she whispered to the butler.

"Yes, madam. I will inform Trenton that you are on your way down."

Just crackin' grand, thought Doyle crossly; although here's another instance when I'm chafing where I shouldn't be. Trenton's been a huge help, and I need to get along with my sulking self, and muster up a better attitude. We see a lot of people, at the Met, who would have very much appreciated having their own security team, with poor Dr. Okafor serving as an excellent example.

The clerk who was manning the concierge desk offered a respectful greeting as she crossed through the lobby, and as she returned his smile, she noted that he'd a fishing pole, propped up against the wall behind him.

Pausing to stare at it, she asked, "Are you goin' fishin', then?"

The young man laughed. "Soon, I hope. I found it in the rubbish chute—it looks almost new."

"Oh? Just the bare pole? Fancy that; it wasn't in a carrier, of some sort?"

He shook his head. "No, just the pole. It got stuck sideways, and so when I had to reach into the chute so see what happened, I figured I may as well keep it."

"Lucky you," said Doyle, who knew with absolute certainty that this wasn't a coincidence—although—although *surely* it didn't make much sense; if Savoie had smuggled cash to Reynolds in the fishing kit, why would Reynolds take the pole out, and throw it down the chute without the carrier? Not to mention Reynolds wasn't the sort of person who'd throw away a perfectly good fishing pole. Mayhap Savoie was the one who'd pitched it? But again, why would he toss the pole, and keep the carrier? Perhaps it *was* just a strange coincidence.

No doubt because she was standing and gawping, the clerk ventured, "You won't need the car, Lady Acton? Because if you've changed your mind, I will be happy to call for it."

"No—no, thanks; I'm walkin', because I've got to exercise, else I'll get called to account. It's a mournful shame, but there it is."

"Oh," the fellow said, uncertain as to what reply would

best please. "Well, if you do get tired, you can always call for the car to bring you home."

"Right you are, and I shouldn't be grousin'." Reminded, she asked, "Did we ever hear what happened to Mr. Tansi? Not that the new driver's not a fine fellow; I'm just curious."

With a gesture of bewilderment, the clerk spread his hands. "We never heard from him. It's a little strange—you'd think he would know we were worried. I doubt he was in trouble with the law, or anything; he was very religious."

That does seem a bit odd, Doyle thought, as she made her way out the door. I hope he hasn't met with foul play—I should check the Met's database, just to be sure.

CHAPTER 19

*A*fter an uneventful walk, she arrived at the café to find that Martina had already secured a table inside —since the weather was a bit questionable—and as Doyle approached, the young woman rose to greet her. "Lady Acton."

"Kathleen," Doyle reminded her, as they sat down. "How have you been, Martina?"

This was asked with some trepidation, because her companion looked a bit pulled-about. Haunted, thought Doyle; that's the word. She looks a bit haunted—and small blame to her, what with a husband who's on the lam, and murdering witnesses, left and right. Not that I'm one to cast that stone, of course.

"It is well," Martina said quietly, and it was a lie. *"The righteous must still do right, and the holy still be holy."*

"Aye, that," said Doyle, a bit nonplussed. Remembering Acton's request, she ventured, "May I ask if you've heard from Antonio? If it's a sore subject, I'll say no more, and we'll speak of somethin' else."

"Yes; I have managed to contact him," the young woman replied, and pressed her lips together, briefly. "He is my husband—despite everything that has happened. And because he is, it is up to me to see that he remembers from where he has fallen, and repent."

Good luck with that, thought Doyle; he's not likely to be mending his ways any time soon, if he's committing murders to cover-up his own misdeeds. And it's obvious she doesn't have much influence over him, poor woman, since he's busy blotting his copybook like David-on-the-rooftop, despite the fact he knows she'd be devastated by it. It must be a hard blow, considering they used to roam around the world, persecuting the evildoers together.

Casting about for something comforting to say, Doyle offered, "He's fallen by the wayside, is all, Martina; redemption will be his savin' grace. We have to believe that love will prevail—it always does."

"Of course," the other woman replied with a small, sad smile. "And how are you, Kathleen?"

"Pregnant, again." Doyle paused, because she could suddenly feel a wave of acute misery, coming from across the table. Faith, I stepped in it, there, she thought; Martina is no doubt having to re-think any plans of starting a family of her own.

Quickly, Doyle added, "No mornin' sickness as yet, which is why I'm happy to eat somethin' hearty. I wonder if they've Irish butter, here?"

"I hope so," her companion said, making a mighty effort to recover her equilibrium. "I'll have whatever you're having."

You know, that's very strange, Doyle thought, as she pondered the menu. Martina Betancourt is being deferential, and I've no idea why—it's definitely not in her nature to be deferential to anyone, save God. Faith, I'm the one who should be deferential to her; after all she gave me fair warning that her righteous Order was coming after Acton, if he didn't mind himself.

Thinking to probe these matters, Doyle lifted her head to say with all sincerity, "Thank you again for your warnin', Martina. I looked into what you'd told me, and I put a stop to it."

"Think nothing of it, Kathleen. I know there were no ill-intentions."

Doyle quirked her mouth. "That's as may be, but it was a close-run thing, and I know I'll not be throwin' another dinner party, any time soon."

Martina unbent enough to chuckle. "It was a memorable evening, certainly—I'll not soon forget it, myself." In a casual manner, the young woman asked, "Did Javid ever finish Lord Acton's portrait?"

Doyle smiled, relieved at the harmless subject—the aforementioned dinner party had been held to unveil Doyle's formal portrait, painted by a famous female portrait-painter, with the plan being to have a matching portrait painted of Acton. "She did indeed, and Acton's hung both of them up at Trestles, alongside all the others in the long gallery. Faith, it's like livin' in a time-warp there, and I don't know as I'll ever grow accustomed. We're due to go for a funeral, this week-end."

With a nod, her companion lowered her gaze to study the menu, and Doyle was surprised to catch a sudden flare of raw, unhappy emotion. Doesn't like hearing about Trestles, either, Doyle thought; mental note–don't speak of babies nor of ancestral estates.

At this juncture, the waiter came, and Martina simply gave an order that matched Doyle's. She then asked, "Has the construction work been completed at St. Michael's?"

"It has—the place is as sound as a barrel," Doyle proclaimed. "And thank God fastin'; what a long and miserable slog that was, not to mention poor Rizzo's murder didn't help matters."

"A terrible time," her companion agreed, and quoted, *"And the great dragon was thrown down; he was thrown down to the earth, and his angels were thrown down with him."*

The pronouncement seemed a bit overly-dramatic, all things considered, and Doyle ventured a bit doubtfully, "I suppose. Small comfort for Rizzo's football team—I imagine they're still rendin' their robes asunder, and gnashin' their teeth at opportunities lost."

Martina's gaze met hers. "I believe Mr. Javid's trial is coming up—I must say that I am surprised he's out on bail."

The artist's husband, Mr. Javid, had also attended their ill-fated dinner party, and he was the one who was now in a great crackin' pot of legal hot water, thanks mainly to Martina and her Order. In response to her companion's implied disapproval, Doyle made a wry mouth. "Unfortunately, a lot of what happens in criminal justice depends on how well-connected the defendant is. It's not right, but there's no denyin' it, and because Mr. Javid's brother is a famous solicitor, they'll tread very carefully."

"Do you know where he is?"

Doyle regarded her in surprise. "Mr. Javid? I don't. I'm not assigned to the case, though, and so I'm not followin' it very closely."

Why, she's fishing for information, thought Doyle, as the waiter interrupted to set down their tea-sandwiches; but this particular pond was as empty as a pocket. That must be why she wanted to meet—she's hoping I can tell her what she wants to know–something to do with Javid-the-artist's awful husband, and the construction work at St. Michael's. It was all very puzzling, and Doyle decided it was past time to do a bit of probing of her own.

As they began to nibble on the offerings, Doyle said, "Philippe Savoie is helpin' out the free clinic, I understand. Now, there's a conversion that rivals St. Paul's on the road to Damascus."

Martina laughed, and her mood seemed to lighten somewhat. "Philippe has been very helpful—I truly think he has heard the call."

Not in love with Savoie, Doyle duly noted; she still loves the wretched husband. "Well, good on Savoie, then. *Some come into the vineyard in the late afternoon.*"

With a small smile, Martina quoted, *"And the armies in heaven, clothed in fine linen, white and clean, followed Him on white horses."*

Sister Luke would be very unhappy, if I couldn't come up with a rejoinder to all this war-talk, Doyle thought, and so she offered, *"And they shall beat their swords into plowshares, and their spears into pruning-hooks."*

Martina chuckled, but before she could frame a counter-response, Doyle's mobile pinged, and she saw that it was her supervisor, Habib. "Call in," it said.

"Oh," said Doyle. "I've got to take this, I'm afraid." She stood to walk outside, ringing up Habib as she did so. "Doyle here, sir."

"DS Doyle," he replied, and he could hear a flurry of

voices in the background. "Dispatch tells me a new homicide report has come in, at the free clinic."

"Oh—oh, *no*." Doyle closed her eyes for a moment; poor Dr. Okafor—it was all so unfair. "Right; I'll be over straightaway."

After taking a moment to recover her equilibrium, she returned to explain to Martina, "I must go—I'm that sorry."

"Of course; I'm sorry, too," the young woman replied, and as Doyle turned to leave, she had the sense—as strange as it seemed--that Martina wasn't truly sorry, at all.

CHAPTER 20

*H*ating her feeling of helplessness, Doyle nodded a greeting at the PC who was posted on the clinic's perimeter, and as he allowed her under the tape, she decided that it was this sort of feeling—this helplessness, coupled with rage—that inspired people like Acton to take matters into their own hands. It was so hard, at times like these, to trust God to sort everything out, because it truly didn't seem as though He was paying much attention, sometimes. Maybe Martina had the right of it, with her bloody-minded Bible verses.

Officer Shandera stood at the front desk, interviewing the charge nurse—who was much more subdued and shaken than the last time she'd seen him—and Doyle pulled the PC aside to ask, "Did you catch anythin' on tape?" It would be some modicum of comfort if the surveillance team that had been set-up across the alleyway had managed to film the killer, waltzing in to murder the good doctor and unaware that the CID was watching him, all the while. It wouldn't be much of a comfort, of course, but anything was better than this miserable knowledge that Dr. Okafor knew she was slated to die, and then did.

The West Indian man shook his head. "No—we must have just missed it; the killer was lucky."

"Aye," Doyle said absently. Either the killer was extraordinarily lucky, or he'd caught wind about the surveillance—there was always that troubling possibility. He'd caught wind, and thus had struck whilst he still could.

With a nod toward the back of the clinic, Shandera continued, "The victim is in the examination room on the left."

"I'll go back, then."

"Yes, ma'am."

Mentally bracing herself, Doyle walked down the narrow hallway to the examination room—where she could hear the SOCOs setting up their operations—and leaned into the doorway to take an initial survey. The woman's body lay on the examination table, still dressed in her doctor's coat; her eyes were closed, and between them was an entry wound from what looked to be a small-caliber bullet.

The most important take-away, however, was that the victim was a not a "three", like Dr. Okafor, but was instead a "one"—as white as white could be.

"Holy *Mother*," Doyle breathed in astonishment. "Where's Dr. Okafor?"

One of the SOCOs turned to look at her. "What was that, ma'am?"

Doyle pulled herself together. "Have we an ID? And have you a pair of gloves I could use?"

"Yes, ma'am," the woman replied as she offered Doyle her

box. "The charge nurse says this is Dr. Abigail James, one of their regular volunteers."

As she pulled on her gloves, Doyle carefully stepped into the room and gazed upon the dead woman's face. She seemed familiar, and Doyle realized that it looked like the woman who'd received the child from the van, in the CCTV tape she'd seen—the one who'd been wearing a lab coat. But that didn't make much sense; that woman was one of the soul-eaters, surely? Why would *she* be killed? Were the villains covering their tracks, mayhap, having caught wind of the surveillance?

"Ugly," the SOCO remarked. "Looks like torture."

Doyle scrutinized the body and nodded. There were small, circular burn marks on the woman's throat and forearms—probably cigarette burns. Someone had wanted the decedent to suffer, before she died.

"A spite-murder?" The woman suggested, as they looked over the body. "Or it may be an unsound-mind."

"We'll see what the Coroner says," Doyle replied, and took a moment to text Acton. "Coming?"

"On my way," he replied.

"Officer Doyle?" It was Officer Shandera, standing at the doorway. "There's a woman outside who'd like to speak with you—a doctor who works here."

"I should see her," Doyle said to the SOCO. "And DCI Acton is comin'; he'll be interested in hearin' a preliminary report."

"Thanks for the warning," the woman said dryly.

Doyle followed Shandera down the hall, and then came outside to behold Dr. Okafor, standing outside the perimeter and looking a bit anxious.

"Officer Doyle," the woman said. "What has happened?"

"I'm afraid Dr. James is dead."

In the grip of a strong emotion, the woman's jaw worked for a moment. *"For my angel will go before you, and completely destroy them,"* she whispered.

Faith, everyone's Bibling me, today, thought Doyle a bit crossly. "D'you have any ideas about who could have done it, Doctor? Did Dr. James have any enemies?"

Solemnly, the African woman nodded. "Yes, Officer Doyle. Her enemies were the righteous."

"Yes, well; be that as it may, I'd like to take a statement." She paused, and since her companion didn't seem much inclined to worry much about earthly justice, she added, "If there were people workin' with her—doin' the soul-eatin'— we'll need to know who they are, so that we can stop them from going elsewhere, and settin' up another soul-eatin' shop."

With complete confidence, the woman replied, "They will be dealt with. The Lord has heard my prayers."

Doyle nodded. "All very well and good, of course, but the Met should probably try to nab 'em, in any case."

But the woman didn't seem to be listening, as she rested her gaze in wonder on the clinic behind them. "I hope she repented, before she died. Heaven will not be closed to her, if she sincerely repented of her sins."

This seemed overly-generous, and with some cynicism, Doyle thought, I imagine the late doctor repented of a good many things–there's nothing like a spot of torture, to focus the mind.

Thinking to take a different tack, Doyle said, "We'll need a witness for the righteous, Dr. Okafor–so that others may see what's happened here, and repent of their own sins."

"Of course, I will witness," the woman replied, nodding. *"You are my witnesses, says the Lord."*

"Stay right here, then, and I'll arrange to have one of the PCs interview you."

Doyle returned to the front desk, where Shandera was hovering, awaiting further orders.

"I've a witness interview for you, Officer—Dr. Okafor is outside. Let's bring her into the waitin' room and make her comfortable, although I'll warn you that you may have to wade through a few religious references."

"Yes, ma'am," Shandera replied with a small smile. "It will be like speaking to my great-aunt."

"Who called it in?" In the Crime Academy, they always taught you to take a long look at whoever reported a homicide.

He replied, "The charge nurse, ma'am. The clinic wasn't supposed to be open today, but he came on the premises to let a repairman in. They noticed the smell, and found the body— quite a shock, of course, and so they locked up, and waited for the police."

Doyle nodded. "You've taken statements from them? Anything alarmin'?"

"No—it all checked out. It was easy, in fact, because I'd already checked-out the repairman—he was a witness from the Rizzo case, too. He was the same plaster-man who'd found the body at the church."

Doyle stared at him. "Is that so? D'you have a snap?"

Seeing her reaction, Shandera-the-detective-trainee drew his brows together in consternation. "Do you think it's not a coincidence, ma'am? When I interviewed the man in the Rizzo case, his story checked out, and there was nothing in his background to raise any alarms."

With a smile that was meant to reassure, Doyle said, "All I can tell you is DCI Acton doesn't believe in coincidences, even if the evidence says it is one. So, whenever you run across an amazin' coincidence, you should probably take a long, hard look."

"Yes, ma'am," the young officer replied, a bit chastened as he scrolled through his tablet. "Here—here he is."

He displayed the photo, and Doyle was hard-pressed to refrain from gasping aloud, because the plaster-man in question was Martina Betancourt's estranged husband, Antonio D'Angelo.

CHAPTER 21

"*I* was that surprised, Michael," Doyle said to her husband, as they stood in the examination-room doorway, and watched the Coroner's team do their methodical work. "I was certain the victim was goin' to be Dr. Okafor, and instead, it's one of the suspects. A huge relief, all-in-all."

"Yes," he agreed absently, because he was deep in thought, was Acton.

She waited a few minutes in silence, respecting the process. It was a tangle-patch of a case, because yet another unlikely coincidence was the timing—that the murder had happened just before surveillance had begun. Coupled with the D'Angelo connection, it seemed to indicate that the villains had twigged-on to the fact that the CID was closing in, and had decided to kill one of their own, for some reason; either because they were worried she was the weak link, or they wanted to send a warning to others who might be weak links, and who might decide it would behoove them to cooperate with the coppers.

But the nature of the death didn't fit this most-likely scenario; there was no point in making her suffer, or in leaving her here on-site, where evidence could be left behind to incriminate them. And it was interesting that D'Angelo was the one who'd led them to the crime, since one could presume that he was one of the people behind it.

If you didn't know anything else, Doyle mused, as she scrutinized the corpse on the table, you'd think this was a spite-murder, or a murder by a person with unsound mind— someone who was not thinking clearly, just as the SOCO suggested. It all didn't add up.

Acton spoke to the Coroner. "It does not appear that she was bound."

"No," the man agreed. "Bruising starting to appear on her arms and legs, though."

"Post-mortem?"

"It does not appear so; there are signs of inflammation."

Post-mortem bruises showed differently than bruises sustained whilst the victim was still alive, and this pointed to a helpful clue. "She must have been held down, whilst the burns were being applied," Doyle said. "And since she wasn't bound, that points to more than one killer."

"Yes," Acton agreed.

"D'you think the charge nurse was in on it, then?" she ventured. Upon arriving at the scene, one of the first things Acton had done was quietly instruct Shandera to make certain the charge nurse did not leave.

"I imagine he knows more than he is letting on," her husband replied. "It is interesting that he held the keys to the clinic, and was the person who decided who could come on-premises when the clinic was closed."

"Aye," she agreed, seeing what he meant. "That's not usually a nurse's role."

He nodded. "It speaks to a small group, so as to keep a lid on information."

She looked up at him. "Should we issue an All Ports Warnin' for Antonio D'Angelo?"

"Perhaps," he said. "Although I am reluctant to let him know we've seen through his disguise."

She blinked. "Aren't we goin' to arrest him for this murder, Michael? It *can't* be a coincidence—that he's wanderin' about, pretendin' to be a workman on two different homicide scenes."

But her husband only tilted his head. "We know for a fact that he did not kill Rizzo."

Frowning, she tried to follow his train of thought. "So--d'you think it may be the same case, here? He came on-premises to let the coppers know about the doctor's murder?" She eyed him with some skepticism. "That doesn't tie-in with the theory that he's a blackleg, and that he killed Tommy Dryden."

"No," he agreed. "Let's wait a bit; I will conduct some research, and determine upon a course of action."

There was a small pause, whilst Doyle tried to fight the certain conviction that her husband knew more about this than he was letting on. That D'Angelo was a suspect seemed well-established, so why wouldn't Acton want to roll him up, and throw him in the nick? People were dying, here.

"Did you have an opportunity to ask Martina about D'Angelo?"

Doyle nodded. "She said she'd been in touch with him, and was trying to get him to mend his sorry ways. Come to think of it, she asked about the construction work at St. Michael's, so she must be aware he was posin' as a workman, and wondered if we knew." She blew out a breath. "She's wracked, poor thing. And—if it's of any interest—she's definitely not in love with Savoie, nor havin' an affair with him."

"That is reassuring," he replied.

A bit startled, she kept her gaze on the scene before them and thought, well—there's a wrinkle; unless I very much miss my guess, he already knows that Martina's not in love with Savoie. So, either he's been meeting with the fair Martina on the sly, or he's hearing it from Savoie, himself—which no doubt means that Savoie is monitoring the woman on behalf of Acton, which makes *much* more sense than trying to believe that Savoie has turned over a new volunteering-out-of-the-kindness-of-his heart leaf. Faith, Williams had already guessed as much, and shame on me, for not reaching the same conclusion. After all, it would be the tenth—or eleventh? wonder of the world for that particular Savoie-leopard to change his spots.

"Anything else?" her husband asked.

Recalled to their conversation, Doyle offered, "She kept quoting the Book of Revelation, which seemed a bit strange, to me."

He raised his brows. "Apocalyptic teachings? It seems in keeping."

But she shook her head. "Not really, Michael; the RCs don't fuss about the Book of Revelation like the Evangelicals do—I think it's a bit too much hellfire-and-brimstone for the likes of us, and therefore it makes us very uneasy. And it's something new, too; she didn't used to quote Revelation–she didn't used to be so—so fatalistic, and so *grim*. I think she's that fashed about her wretched husband; he's playin' fast and loose with the Ten Commandments, and she's worried about all that hellfire, rainin' down on his head."

He considered this, and suggested, "It may be misdirected anger, with a touch of projection, for what he's done in abandoning her."

"Aye, that's true," she agreed. "Mayhap she can't admit to herself that she's been cast-off. I've the sense she continues to hold out hope that he'll repent, and come crawlin' back to her." Thinking about his, she quirked her mouth. "Which just goes to show that I should appreciate you more, Michael. Between Martina's husband and Javid's husband, you're a rare prize—Martina herself asked me about Mr. Javid, as a matter of fact."

He raised his brows. "Did she?"

"Aye that; she wanted to know about his criminal case, and how it was goin'." She grimaced. "Now, if there was ever a man who deserves to serve hard time, it's him, based on personality, alone. A shame, it is, that Sir Vikili will work his magic and probably keep him out of prison, somehow."

"You are harsh," said Acton in a mild tone.

"He just gave me the willies," she insisted. "There's nothin' worse than a man who browbeats his wife."

"You have such a lovely brow," he teased. "I don't dare."

The Coroner signaled to Acton, and he stepped aside to confer with the man, which was just as well, because yet again, Doyle had the sense that her husband was steering the conversation away—what with his lovely-brow-compliments, and such—and she'd the sense—she'd the sense there was something very important, in what they'd been speaking of. Mayhap he didn't want her to twig-on to the fact he'd assigned Savoie to infiltrate Martina's operation—too late, of course, but Acton didn't know that she'd already guessed.

And it truly wasn't much of a surprise, now that she realized it; Acton didn't like Martina—didn't like her at all—but that was no doubt because she'd granted him a boon, and Acton didn't like being beholden to anyone, let alone a rival vigilante who was crowding-in on his own turf. Faith, Doyle had even given her husband a lecture about reining-in his usual desire to turn the tables against Martina, which is what always happened when someone tried to best him. Acton didn't like to be bested.

But it appeared the fair Doyle's pleas had fallen on deaf ears, and shame on her again, for not seeing it sooner. Acton now had proof that D'Angelo was implicated in Tommy's death, but he wasn't moving on it; the wretched suspect was still at large, doing plaster-work and leading the police to homicide scenes, in his spare time. And the reason for Acton's strange reluctance had now become clear; he wasn't arresting D'Angelo for one simple reason—Acton now had leverage. The Order of Santiago contingent had leverage over him, and in Acton-world, such a thing was not to be tolerated; leave it to Acton to even the score, and create counter-leverage, or whatever you'd call it. Even if they wanted to, they didn't dare come after him now, since they'd their own skeletons, rattling around—literally, in this case.

Her scalp prickled, and she knew she was on the right track; here was why her intuition had been acting up—Acton, as usual, had decided to out-mastermind the masterminds, and now he was no longer at their mercy. It made complete sense, and all puzzles were now neatly solved.

Pausing, she suddenly realized that this wasn't exactly true—there still remained the mysterious necklace, sitting in the pawn shop, despite the fact Acton already had the goods on D'Angelo, and could lower the boom at any time. There must be another piece to this puzzle, then, and she'd best pay attention; Blakney wouldn't have steered her toward his pawn shop for no good reason.

CHAPTER 22

*T*he Coroner's team began preparing the body for transport to the morgue, and as they turned away from the doorway, Acton said to Doyle, "I'd like to question the charge nurse, if you don't mind, with you to listen-in."

"Aye, that. And sooner rather than later—he looks shook. Let's hope he's willin' to spill before he thinks the better of it, and calls in a solicitor."

"Yes," Acton agreed.

Doyle grimaced. "It's hard to imagine, that you'd want to cover for the kind of person who'd hold someone down and terrorize them before they died. It's crackin' evil, is what it is."

But Acton tilted his head. "Did you notice the burns, though?"

Since obviously Acton had noticed something, she frowned, trying to remember the details. "They weren't very big. Cigarette, I thought?"

He nodded. "Perhaps, but I saw no ashes in the room, and

it seems unlikely the killers would remove such evidence, considering they left the corpse behind. It was a flameless device, perhaps, and brought along for this very reason—to apply to the victim. Yet the burns weren't very large, and were few in number. It leads me to believe the intent was to gain information, rather than to torture for torture's sake."

She thought this over, and could see what he meant. "But if Dr. James was a fellow-villain, why would they do this to her? Mayhap she'd turned coat, and they wanted her to tell them who she'd squeaked to."

"A strong possibility," he agreed. "Although she hadn't spoken to the police, so it appears their fears were unjustified."

But—on reflection—this theory didn't make a lot of sense to Doyle, either. "Then why on earth would they kill her on-site, and then leave her here, for us to find? Why not take her somewhere to torture at their leisure, and then dispose of the body? Leavin' her here only throws a light on their murky doin's at the clinic."

"That is true," he agreed in a neutral tone.

He knows something, she thought crossly; something he's not telling me, wretched man. It's a crackin' wonder I haven't applied a cigarette or two, myself.

They came to the lobby area, where the charge nurse sat in one of the waiting-room chairs, a bit white about the lips, as he looked up at their approach.

"Do we read him the caution?" Doyle asked Acton in a low voice.

"Not as yet," Acton replied. "I'd like you to get a sense, first."

She nodded, as it was an unfortunate truism in police work that as soon as you reminded a suspect he'd the right to counsel, he tended to think this a very good idea. Since this man was a witness, though, it made it a bit easier, and no caution need be read until his answers started to show that he might be incriminating himself.

Acton introduced them, and then sat down beside the nurse, which was what an interrogator tended to do when he wanted to appear sympathetic, and not at all like an interrogator. "I am so sorry," he began. "A terrible tragedy."

"It's a shock," the nurse replied in a subdued tone. "The last thing you'd expect."

Doyle saw Acton glance toward her, but she kept her hands still; Dr. James' death was indeed the last thing the charge nurse expected to happen.

"Did you know her well?" Again, Acton's tone was all warm-sympathy.

"I suppose—we've worked together for over a year."

"Do you have any idea," Acton asked with just a tinge of outrage to his tone, "—any idea, who could have done such a thing?"

"No," the man said. Again, Acton glanced to Doyle but she stayed still. It was quite the surprise, all in all; the man truly had no idea, which meant that mayhap he wasn't a potential suspect, after all.

Acton continued, "This type of clinic often brings in questionable people. Did any of her patients threaten her, or seem angry? Do you remember any recent incidents?"

"No," the nurse said, shaking his head slightly. "And anyway, she was a pediatrician, and tended to treat children."

Doyle raised her hand to brush her trouser leg, briefly. Whilst what the witness said was technically true, he was suddenly uneasy about the topic, and she'd caught a stifled flare of alarm.

Acton paused for a moment, and then said apologetically, "I know it is a difficult subject, but do you know if she was involved in any—any illicit activities? I am sorry to bring it up, but I'm afraid the question must be asked."

"No," the charge nurse said, his gaze fixed on the floor. "No—she wouldn't do anything illegal."

As this was an out-and-out lie, Doyle brushed her hair from her forehead.

"Thank you," said Acton. "I am sorry for your loss."

They rose, and Doyle accompanied Acton as he walked over to confer with Officer Shandera.

Briefly, Acton bend his head, and then instructed, "I will send a team, and DI Habib will act as the Crime Scene Manager. Please call-in a field unit, and have them read the caution to this witness before bringing him in to Detention for a twenty-four hour hold."

Doyle blinked in surprise. "What's the charge, then?"

"I will think of one," her husband told her. "But for now, I'd like you to go home and rest, please."

"Done," she readily agreed. It had been a long and wearying day, and no less wearying because she knew her husband was yet again sifting through what he wanted to put into evidence, and what he did not, which did not bode well for the fair Doyle's piece of mind.

CHAPTER 23

$\mathcal{D}$oyle came home to discover that Mary and Gemma were preparing to leave for their own home, with Mary having a one last fortifying cup of Reynolds' ginger tea whilst the servant helped Gemma pack up her school rucksack.

Edward sat at the kitchen table beside Mary, helpfully offering the nanny a soggy saltine, which she accepted with all good will. Doyle kissed Edward on the head, and was rewarded with her own saltine, as she pulled up a chair beside him.

"Is the dinner party on, Mary?"

"It is," the nanny replied, and then added stoutly, "I tend to feel a bit better in the evenings, and besides, it's important to Nigel."

"Well, you'll have a respite tomorrow, and much-deserved. We're headin' off to Trestles for the week-end, as soon as Acton can get away from work. And with Gemma goin' to Russian lessons after school, you'll have a chance to catch a full day of rest, and best enjoy it; once the baby comes, havin' a restful day will seem like a distant memory."

Mary offered a wan smile. "Thank you, Lady Acton. A restful day sounds like heaven."

Doyle watched Reynolds hold the rucksack so that Gemma could put her arms through the straps, and idly asked, "Y'know, Mary, did Savoie ever offer to pay you, for takin' care of Emile last summer?"

The nanny raised her brows in surprise. "Why no; and why would he do such a thing? It was no hardship at all."

Doyle laughed. "Faith, you're a blessed saint, Mary. I can't hold a candle."

"He's a lively little boy, is all," the other insisted. "And Mr. Savoie has always been very good about seeking out my advice, when it comes to Emile—he's very conscientious."

"Very conscientious, for a 'gun-man'," Doyle added in a wry tone.

Mary laughed, and said, "My Gemma notices everything, even when she shouldn't."

But Doyle only shook her head. "Gemma may be a better judge than you, my friend. I don't know as there's another soul alive who'd describe the likes of Savoie as 'conscientious'."

"I think he's got hidden depths," Mary insisted. "Only see how much he loves Emile."

"Emile, who's going to marry Gemma," Doyle reminded her.

Again, Mary laughed. "Maybe that's it, Lady Acton; Mr. Savoie knows we'll be in-laws someday, and so he has to be kind, for Emile's sake."

"Better that he be kind to Colonel Kolchak, then, who would be a much harder sell than you are, Mary."

"I suppose that's true."

The young woman's mood came down a bit, and Doyle cursed herself for being so clumsy; all too soon, Gemma was going to be taken away, and there was little her loving step-mother could do to stop it. She'd little claim, after all, and it was only by Acton's mighty efforts that the girl was still in England, and living a quiet life with her step-parents. It was only a temporary situation, and Mary knew this better than anyone.

At this juncture, Reynolds brought Gemma forward, and explained to Mary, "Miss Gemma's homework is in her rucksack, and there is also a drawing she would like to present to her teacher, tomorrow."

"Thank you, Reynolds."

Poor Reynolds is a bit on-edge, Doyle thought, which is rare for the man; no doubt he'll appreciate having his own restful day, too.

"Have a lovely weekend, Lady Acton," Mary offered as she steered Gemma out the door. "I think we're due for nicer weather."

"That we are," Doyle agreed diplomatically, since it was supposed to rain steadily for a few days. Small matter; they'd be at Trestles, and Edward could work off his energy by tromping about in the halls. And there was always the hope—however faint—that the weather would curtail any lengthy walks outside, but just to be safe, she should probably forget to pack her wellies.

CHAPTER 24

*T*hat night, Doyle had another dream.

Yet again, she was standing in the quiet, stone-floored room and facing Bill Blakney, who continued to seem very much out-of-place, dressed in his formal clothes.

Doyle began, "He knows more than he's lettin' on, about the doctor's death. It makes me very uneasy."

Blakney shrugged his shoulders, which was not easy, in his fitted coat. "It's the same old song," the ghost replied. "Nothing changes, save the scenery."

But Doyle had to disagree, and slowly shook her head. "I don't know if that's true, Mr. Blakney. I think there's been a basketful of changes, lately, but I can't make heads-nor-tails of any of it. The footman at Trestles was killed, but the new driver isn't sorry—he's not sorry a'tall." She paused, and then added, "There's other things, too—so many that it's hard to keep track of them all. There's too many strange things happenin', and all of them at once."

But the ghost had turned his head toward the door, and

didn't seem to be paying attention to her as much as he was listening intently.

Watching him, Doyle found that she was a bit annoyed; if she was to be forced to stand and listen to vague warnings, the least a ghost could do was to pay attention. In a slightly louder voice, she complained, "It has me all on-end; I can feel the flutterin' of wings, but I can't see the birds."

Blakney glanced at her, briefly. "The same old song," he repeated, and seemed disinclined to discuss the matter further.

She prompted, "I went over to your pawn shop—seems a dicey place, I must say."

Ah—this got his attention, and he turned back to her. "That's where I met the fookin' Russians." As he had before, he spat on the ground in an angry gesture of contempt.

Frowning at him, Doyle ventured, "Was it the Russians, who killed the footman? That seems very unlikely, to me."

"Don't start guessing," he warned with a scowl. "You're to stay out of it."

"I'm afraid that's not in my nature," she confessed. "I see strange things happenin', and I always want to figure out why. When I feel the flutterin' wings, I tend to keep lookin' till I can see the birds."

"Not these birds," he warned in no uncertain terms. "Better if their necks are wrung."

"No one deserves to be murdered," she countered. "And you should know this, better than most." Blakney had met a bad end, due to his having been swept up in a best-be-forgotten double-crossing scheme.

He cocked a scornful brow, and added with a touch of belligerence, "Does that include the soul-eaters?"

A bit confused that he'd diverted to this subject, Doyle

nevertheless replied in a firm tone, "Yes, it does. There's a Commandment about it—you can't go about murderin' people. And you can't expect perfect justice, this side o' heaven."

She caught herself, as she belatedly realized that the heaven-subject may not be the best one to discuss with a ghost whose own status remained unclear, and so instead, she hurriedly concluded, "We can't allow everyone to go about usin' their own yardstick, else where will it end? In a free-for-all, with justice only in the eye of the beholder."

"You're one to talk," he scoffed. "For all your fine words."

This seemed to be a reference to the time Doyle had been forced to kill a man, and she explained, "Well, that didn't count as murder, it was self-defense. That's a whole different sort of thing."

He snorted, rather inelegantly.

There was a small silence, and then Doyle conceded, "I suppose it's all a bit confusin'–sortin' out when there's 'just cause', and when there's not. It's all very complicated, and the laws about it are hard to understand, sometimes." She paused, and then added, "Although I have to say that it never seems to be very complicated for Acton. There's one who definitely uses his own yardstick."

"That's exactly right," the ghost agreed with an emphatic nod. "You keep your nose out of it."

Much struck, Doyle ventured, "You know, Mr. Blakney, that's the opposite of what I usually hear, from—from people in your position." This was true; the various ghosts she'd encountered usually were attempting to steer her toward, rather than steer her away.

"Keep your nose out of it," the ghost repeated, and then turned his head so as to glance again toward the closed door.

"Who is it, that you're waitin' for?" she asked curiously. "Can you tell me?"

"The bride," he said briefly. "I hope she's coming."

Doyle blinked in confusion, because it seemed very unlikely that a ghost would be getting married, but on the other hand, it would explain why he was dressed in formal clothes. And since he seemed a bit uncertain about whether the wedding was actually going to go forward, poor man, she offered diplomatically, "Best wishes to you, then."

He turned back to her with a scowl. "Back off," he repeated.

CHAPTER 25

They drove to Trestles at mid-day, timing it so that
Edward could take his nap in his car seat. Since she
and Acton necessarily had to stay fairly quiet, it gave Doyle
time to puzzle over her dreams, and to try to make sense of
them—the dreams were always important, even though in
this one, the main message seemed to be that she should
stand down. Stand down from what, though? She couldn't
very well stand down, if she'd no idea what it was that she
was standing down from.

The strongest impression she'd gained from the ghost was
that he was not happy about the Russians, which seemed a
bolt from the blue—were there any Russians involved in
current events? She couldn't think of any—Dr. Benardi was
Italian, and Dr. James and the charge nurse were both
English. Dr. Okafor was Nigerian, of course, as was the
missing driver—but wait, she was wandering off-topic, and
should try to stay on frame. Why was the ghost barkin' on
about Russians? She could see no connection.

And aside from that, he seemed rather scornful of Doyle's principles, but this was only to be expected, considering he'd been a petty-criminal during his relatively short life on earth. He was warning her away—that much was clear—and heavily implying that certain murders were well-deserved. So; since the ghost had re-appeared just as she was heading out to Trestles for a funeral, this rather pointed to the idea that the footman's death was a murder, and not an accident, as everyone seemed to think. But surely Acton would be aware, if there was any hint of wrongdoing? And in any event, it seemed very unlikely that there were any Russians involved.

And aside from hating on the Russians, Blakney was also keen on wanting her to stay out of whatever-it-was, where the right people were getting themselves murdered. Naturally, this meant that Doyle was champing at the bit to puzzle-out what he was dropping hints about; she knew it was important—although not so important that the ghost wasn't getting married, in the meantime.

Which also seemed a bit strange; Blakney had been Mary's common-law husband, but the two had never married, and if a man was not willing to commit to sweet Mary, it seemed unlikely that he'd change this inclination in the afterlife. Perhaps he was given no choice, or something, which gave one a rather startling glimpse of how things were sorted-out in the hereafter.

With a mighty effort, Doyle gathered-in her scattered thoughts, and decided that she should probably start with the basics—the known-knowns, as they said in the Crime Academy. Why would Bill Blakney—of all people—be haunting her?

Best start with a timeline; she'd met Blakney when he was

a witness in a complicated homicide case, running his pawn shop whilst also running weapons for the Russian cartel, on the side—in fact, that very day was the first time she'd realized that her superior officer, the illustrious Chief Inspector Acton, was himself involved in murky doings, with gun-running serving as a prime example.

Blakney had then shown up again on Doyle's radar when she'd made Mary's acquaintance—both Mary and Gemma, actually, since Gemma had been stashed away with Blakney so as to hide her true identity. Faith, even Mary hadn't known her stepdaughter's true identity—it was kept that secret—and therefore it created all sorts of problems when Blakney was unexpectedly killed. Mary began working as Edward's nanny, and when she'd moved away, it meant that little Gemma was lost to the Russian faction, who were no doubt frantic that the focus of their re-conquest plan had gone missing. Missing, until Acton had started making inquiries, and those inquiries had led to the Colonel's reunion with Gemma.

Thinking over these known-knowns, Doyle could still see no sense to the ghost's rather belligerent warnings. Why would the man have gone sour, on his former cohorts? He'd been their partner in crime, after all, and they must have trusted him—trusted him to the extent that they'd left Gemma with him. And—according to Mary—he'd been genuinely fond of the little girl, although Mary tended to sugar-coat things—only see how she thought Savoie had hidden depths, for heaven's sake.

Her reverie was interrupted when Acton reached to take her hand, and say in a low voice, "We'll have a quiet dinner, and go to bed early."

He was worried, she could see, because she'd been silent

so long—silence wasn't her usual mode of operation. "I feel fine, Michael, I was just thinkin'." She pronounced it "foine" just to tease him. "When's the funeral?"

"Tomorrow morning, at the local church."

Thinking that perhaps she should try to probe these matters, she said, "Poor man—a wretched shame, it is. Had he a family?"

"None that we could find. He'll be buried at Trestles—it seemed the least we could do."

Doyle's scalp prickled, and she wondered why it would—after all, everything her husband had said was completely true. "Was he Russian?" she ventured.

He glanced at her, surprised. "No—or at least, not to my knowledge. Hispanic, I believe."

She nodded, wondering how much more she could probe without letting her better half know that she was entertaining a troubling sense of unease. "Is he another one, who's served the family from the cradle?"

"No—he'd been on staff for a few months, only."

With a show of idleness, she watched the wipers sweep the rain off the windscreen for a few moments, and then observed, "It's touching, really, that the House of Acton pulls itself together for this poor fellow's send-off. It's that 'noble-obliging' thing."

"*Noblesse oblige*, I believe you mean."

"Aye," she said. "But I think that's what funerals do—and weddin's, too; they pull you away from the day-to-day, so as to remind you about what's truly important."

"Indeed," he agreed.

Her scalp prickled, yet again, and she frowned slightly, surprised that it would; funerals and weddings did have a way of reminding you of what was important—why would such a thought be controversial, for the love o' Mike? Did it have anything to do with this particular funeral? Or mayhap the ghost's wedding?

Since her ghost had stopped fussing about Russians long enough to make a few pointed remarks about the soul-eaters, it was on the tip of her tongue to quiz Acton about the Dr. James crime scene–and the conclusions he'd drawn from it– but for some reason she held back. I don't know enough, she decided; not yet, at least, and I've a ghost who's warning me to tread carefully.

Instead, she decided to turn the conversation to slightly less-dire subjects. "Is your mum joinin' us for dinner?"

He squeezed her hand. "Only if you don't mind, Kathleen."

Doyle smiled. "I don't mind a'tall; she's been behavin' herself, lately–and she's Edward's gran, after all."

But her husband was not one to forgive and forget. "She has been unkind to you, and if you'd rather not see her, I will arrange for it."

She blew out a breath. "Faith, Michael; if it doesn't bother me, it shouldn't bother you. No need to be borrowin' trouble, where there is none." Famous last words, of course; her husband was hell-bent on slaying all dragons, will-she or nil-she.

"I've asked Hudson to assign one of the maidservants to mind Edward. She may be a candidate to assist Mary, in the near-term, and so you may wish to keep this in mind."

"I'll test her out, then." She hid a smile, because Acton, of course, was going to use his own judgment, whatever his wife thought about this potential assistant-nanny. Although mayhap she wasn't being fair; after all, Doyle had presented Mary as a nanny, even though he couldn't have been best-pleased with her choice, at the time. It just went to show that the fair Doyle had a doting husband—not to mention that she was a fair judge of character, herself.

And—speaking of such—she decided she may as well seize the opportunity to explore the topic, since it had conveniently come up. "I was thinkin' about Mary's life–how it was like a fairy tale, what with her goin' from strugglin', to a life of ease, and a lovin' husband."

"*The wheel is come full circle,*" he agreed.

Doubtfully, she replied, "Well, I don't know what it has to do with a *wheel,* Michael, but I suppose it's a silver-linin', that Bill Blakney managed to get himself killed. Otherwise, it wouldn't have worked out half so well as it did."

He tilted his head. "I imagine he would disagree."

Doyle knit her brow, and watched the rain come down. "That's a fair point, a' course. And we can't see what might have been, after all. I do think he was a decent fellow, underneath all his toughness."

"I remember that you thought as much, when we interviewed him."

"I still do," she mused.

"He is dead," he reminded her. "A casualty of the *Santero* case."

"Yes, I know," she agreed. "But I think he'd hidden depths, as Mary would say. She wouldn't have been living with him, else."

"Do I have hidden depths?" he teased.

"Faith, you take the palm," she replied readily. "Your depths are as deep as a collier's well, my friend; they keep me awake, sometimes, those depths of yours, and leave me at my wit's end."

With a small smile, he squeezed her hand. *"I do profess to be no less than I seem."*

"Well, you can profess whatever you want, but you've got deep, deep depths, and I've managed to fall into that well headlong, all unknowin'."

He lifted her hand to kiss its back. *"A chance which does redeem all sorrows that ever I have felt."*

She gave him a look. "That's very sweet, Michael—I think."

CHAPTER 26

hey were having a light dinner with the Dowager in the formal dining room—"light" meaning only three courses, since the kitchen was busy preparing for the funeral reception tomorrow.

Edward was absent, because his parents had been required to feed him a variety of snacks in the car once he awoke, with the result that he'd arrived sleepy instead of hungry, and the young maidservant who'd been assigned to him had cheerfully carried him off for his bath. It was just as well, actually; the Dowager may be on her best behavior, but Edward was a wild card, and had never met a utensil he didn't want to throw as far as he was able.

Doyle sat in her usual spot, across from the painting on the wall that featured a still-life of game birds who'd been shot and strung-up—some famous artist had painted it, Acton had said, but she couldn't remember his name. Not something you'd think you'd display in your dining room, but it just went to show you that aristocrats had a long, long

169

history of murder-in-the-blood, and probably thought it very soothing.

The Dowager took a precise bite of her capon. "Reynolds did not accompany you, this trip?"

"No, Mother," said Acton.

"A shame. You were very fortunate to have found him, I think."

"He's a treasure, ma'am," Doyle agreed. As one of his many butler-talents, Reynolds knew exactly how to flatter and soothe elderly harridans. "It's deservin' of a break, he is, though. Mary, too."

With a show of diplomacy, the Dowager made no remark, being as she'd previously expressed the opinion that Mary was not qualified to care for a future earl, and that a grave mistake was being made. With an inward smile, Doyle thought, I'd so love to be able to tell her that Mary's daughter outranks us all, but I'll probably never be given the opportunity, more's the pity.

"You are a very brave mother, my dear," the Dowager continued. "In my day, we'd never venture out without the servants."

Although her tone implied this was not exactly a compliment, Doyle accepted it at face value, being as even a semi-compliment was unexpected. "Thank you, ma'am. We're lucky we've so much help, here at Trestles."

She paused, because—come to think of it—it *was* a bit unusual, to have brought no reinforcements from home, this trip. Trenton had not accompanied them today—or at least, Acton hadn't mentioned it; nor had the driver who used to be a groundskeeper here—although he didn't much like the decedent, so mayhap he felt it would be hypocritical to show up for the man's funeral. And Reynolds and Mary were enjoying some time off–it was a lot to ask, to have the staff spend the weekend at the estate, when they'd much rather spend a bit of down-time on their own.

And, speaking of a little down-time, Doyle decided there was no time like the present, and smiled at Acton, who never wanted to tell his mother anything, and small blame to him. "We have some news, ma'am."

"Oh?" asked the woman, her hand pausing.

"Yes," said Acton. "Kathleen is expecting."

"Why, how wonderful. My deepest congratulations." She then added with what appeared to be an attempt at archness, "I must say I am not surprised."

Faith, she's trying to make a joke, Doyle thought in amazement, and laughed. "Yes, ma'am."

"Is the news public, as yet? May I say?"

"You may," said Doyle. "We are very happy to share it."

"A girl, this time," the Dowager pronounced. "I have a feeling."

"A wee lass would be welcome," said Doyle diplomatically. "We'll have to see."

With a dry smile, the Dowager re-addressed her meal, and remarked, "Speaking of happy news, Sir Stephen has met someone—did you know, Acton?"

Inwardly, Doyle braced herself, as Sir Stephen was a sore subject. The man was Acton's distant cousin, and had been technically his heir until Edward had come along. A bigger creep never put an arm through a coat, and Acton had actually manipulated events so that DI Williams could make a claim to the title if Acton was unexpectedly killed before he had a son; it only showed how little her husband trusted Sir Stephen.

Acton met this remark in silence, but the Dowager

persisted, "I do believe she's been a beneficial influence, and it is past time he settled down. She's from an honorable family, which must be seen as a good sign." Carefully, the older woman did not look at Doyle, and pressed her lips together for a moment to show that she was exercising great restraint.

Sensing her husband's flare of annoyance, Doyle chirped, "There's good news indeed, ma'am. Is it anyone Acton knows?" It went without saying that the fair Doyle would be unacquainted with anyone the Dowager would deem honorable.

"I do not believe he has had the pleasure; it is Lady Abby Rosings, out of Hunsford."

There was a small moment of silence. "Oh," said Doyle. "Oh, yes–we've met Lady Abby before, ma'am." Carefully, Doyle avoided looking at her husband, because Lady Abby— last Doyle had seen her—hadn't been behaving very honorably at all. Pretty and rather high-strung, the young woman had been engaged to marry Nigel Howard before the man had taken one look at Mary-the-nanny and fallen deeply in love, breaking off their engagement so as to marry Mary, instead. Needless to say, Lady Abby hadn't taken it very well.

I suppose that's the hazard of being a pretty aristocrat, Doyle thought; you don't handle defeat very well, having never made his acquaintance, before.

"I believe they plan to attend the funeral," the Dowager continued, and Doyle could sense that both of them braced themselves for Acton's reaction.

"Very well," he replied in a mild tone. "Although he may not sit in the family's box."

Oh-oh, thought Doyle; the family has a "box"; I'd better

be on my best behavior, or I'll be sent to sit in the dishonorable back of the church, alongside Sir Stephen.

"We've asked for a Roman Catholic priest to come in from Ashworth," the Dowager explained to Doyle. "The poor young man was Roman Catholic, and it seemed only fitting." She managed to convey the discreet conviction that it was a shame this failing had not been corrected, prior to the poor young man's unfortunate demise. After a small pause, she then offered with a show of generosity, "It will serve as a relief to you, my dear, to speak of Roman subjects with him."

"That's grand, ma'am," Doyle hastily replied, as she could sense her husband's displeasure. "I look forward to havin' a look at his rosary."

"You must rest, Kathleen," Acton said, and signaled to the servant. "I will meet with Hudson, but then I will join you shortly."

"If you'll excuse me, ma'am?" Doyle asked.

"Of course," the woman graciously replied, as though it were her house, and not Doyle's. Then–apparently recalled to her grandmotherly obligations–she added, "I quite look forward to seeing Edward again on the morrow."

"And he looks forward to seeing you, ma'am," Doyle replied, taking a shrewd guess that the Dowager was unaware that a person Edward's age didn't look forward to anything as much as he took life as it came, like a buccaneer. Which reminded her, she'd best check-in, to see how the maidservant was faring with the buccaneer's bath.

CHAPTER 27

*D*oyle arrived in time to help put Edward to bed, and the cheerful maidservant didn't seem much the worse for the bath experience—other than having had a soaking, of course. She bade Edward good night, and then left Doyle to adjust the lights—her son didn't like the pitch-dark. Doyle stayed to rub Edward's back for a minute, hoping he was tired enough that he'd slip right into sleep—it was touch-and-go, in a strange place.

She'd the sudden sense that she was not alone, and looked up into the corner of the nursery, where the Trestles knight leaned against the wall, idly watching them. She'd seem him many a time before, and he'd been instrumental, over past generations, in arranging things so that the estate wasn't lost to the House of Acton. As was his usual, he wore a worn, leather hauberk, and rested a hand on the hilt of a sword—the tip of the sword having been broken off, on a best-be-forgotten occasion.

Speaking of murder-in-the-blood, Doyle thought, as she

paused to carefully remove her hand from the sleeping child, the wretched knight had it, in spades, and she'd always had the impression he very much approved of Acton's bloody-minded doings, since it was nothing less than what he'd done, in his day. I'm lucky the two can't consult, she thought a bit crossly; I've enough on my plate, as it is.

"We're having another boy," she whispered to him. "Tommy, this one is." The knight had been working like a journeyman to secure the family's bloodline, but he seemed to have relaxed somewhat, in his ghostly maneuverings, since Edward had been born. Still, no doubt he'd appreciate the fact they'd have a back-up, so to speak, since in his day, the heirs didn't always survive childhood.

As was his usual, he made no response, but Doyle gained the impression he was well-content, for a change—similar to how he'd been right after Edward was born; as though he'd just won a hard-fought victory. His good mood was actually a relief, since it meant that the other ghosts that inhabited the place wouldn't be congregating in corners and trying to stay out of his way—he tended to be a short-tempered warlord, which probably went with the territory.

Acton carefully opened the door, and the knight disappeared. Doyle signaled that Edward was asleep, and she tiptoed out into the hallway as her husband softly closed the door behind her. "I turned the monitor on," she whispered. "Here's hopin' he sleeps through the night."

Acton tucked her under his arm. "Here's hoping we do."

"Same thing," she observed.

"What did you think of Callie?"

"Callie is a trump; she'll do fine, Michael."

They walked into their adjacent bedroom, where the sumptuous, canopied bed had already been turned down, and the heavy velvet curtains had already been pulled across the diamond-paned windows.

She paused. "D'you mind if I peek? I do like that view, in the moonlight."

He promptly steered her over to the draperies, and then lifted one to the side, so that they stood side-by-side, looking out on the moonlit garden, down below.

A time-warp, she thought, as she reviewed the formal garden and its neat pathways. I imagine this view looks very much at it has for hundreds of years. But not as far back as the knight's time—there'd been additions made to the main building, since the time when he held sway, and there was that whatever-his-name-was Brown person, who'd re-figured the grounds. But it was an amazing heritage, all the same, and I should appreciate it more than I do; after all, Acton loves it–almost as much as he loves me.

Fondly, she rested her head on his shoulder. "What's Hudson to say for himself?"

"All is in train for the funeral, tomorrow."

Glancing up at him, she teased, "Did you notice how your mum was behavin' herself?"

"I did, save for the fact she usurps your position, Kathleen."

As always, this was a sore point, in that the rather convoluted aristocratic protocols were important to him, and so he was quick to see an insult, and take up the cudgels in her defense. Not to mention he didn't like his mother much, and so was spoiling for a fight to begin with.

She ran a soothing hand along his back. "It truly doesn't bother me, a'tall, Michael, and for heaven's sake, I can't snub her—I'm not a born-and-bred nob, so I've no experience in deliverin' an elegant snub. Instead, I'd just do somethin' vulgar, like overturn the table, or smash the dead-birds paintin' over her head, and thereby prove that she's been right, all along. Best to leave well-enough alone."

"Yes; I suppose so," he agreed, and leaned to kiss her head.

"Speakin' of which, is there anythin' special I should know about tomorrow's events? No countess-rituals I will be called-upon to perform?"

Surprisingly, she caught a flare of emotion from him, quickly stifled, and she turned her head to look up at him in surprise. "Mother a' Mercy, Michael; never say there *is* a ritual?"

"No—no rituals," he assured her with a small smile. "I will say a few words, as is appropriate."

She nodded, and–after deciding that she must have got her wires crossed–she went back to admiring the view.

CHAPTER 28

*D*oyle stood amongst the congregation in the old church's courtyard, greeting the other attendees with subdued funeral-talk, and rather wishing her favorite buccaneer were present, so as to shake things up a bit.

The Anglican priest had introduced the Roman Catholic priest, and now the two clergymen stood beside Acton as the mourners filed in—leave it to the Anglicans to have a receiving line at a funeral, Doyle thought a bit cynically, and then chastised herself for being petty—the last needful thing was to start a religious war, although she'd the impression that no one around here was much of a zealot, when it came to such things.

Her scalp prickled, and before she could think of why this would be, the RC priest said in an aside to Doyle. "Would you care to join me, Lady Acton, in saying a Rosary for the departed?"

"Of course," Doyle replied. "After the service?"

"Oh—I was thinking perhaps this evening, after the

reception, instead," the priest replied in a bland manner. "I wouldn't want to intrude on the parish, here."

Doyle nodded in agreement and hid a smile; she knew her priests, and—although the man sincerely wanted to offer up prayers for the departed—he was also hoping to score another meal on the heels of the reception, being as such opportunities were few and far between.

"Did you know him well, Father?" Doyle asked politely.

The priest shook his head. "Not at all, actually, so he may have been lapsed—I'm the only RC clergy in the area. A shame—he'd quite a fine rosary, in his possession, and I wish I could find someone to send it to."

"I think Acton mentioned he was an immigrant," Doyle offered. "Mayhap he can make inquiries."

"That would be splendid," the man agreed. "His family should be made aware, certainly. Such a shame, to be taken so young."

Melinda then glided over to greet Doyle, bestowing air-kisses on both her cheeks. Melinda was the daughter from a neighboring estate, approximately Acton's age and quintessentially aristocratic; languid and completely indiscreet. "I'm on the search for a new husband," she whispered in Doyle's ear. "Keep a sharp eye out."

"Well, you can't have Acton," Doyle teased. Melinda and Acton had a youthful relationship, once upon a time.

"No, thanks—he'd be a handful. Although speaking of a handful, I do envy you the sex."

"Whist," Doyle chided, trying not to laugh. "There's to be no sex-talk at the funeral."

"Spoilsport," Melinda said without rancor, and then cast an eye over the others who were present. "Oh, *my*; who's that?"

Doyle followed her gaze, and was very much surprised to see DI Williams coming through the line, accompanied by Lizzy Mathis. Doyle realized that their attendance shouldn't have been entirely unexpected, because--although Mathis worked in the Forensics lab at the Met–she had secured that position through her connection to Acton. Lizzy Mathis was Hudson's great-niece, with her roots firmly established here at Trestles—yet another loyal retainer, going back generations. Or was she Lizzy Williams, now? Doyle had best wait for her cue.

To Melinda, she said, "That's Thomas Williams, from the Met, and I think he's here with Mathis, so you'd best not start a ruckus–she's not one to cross."

"As if I would," Melissa replied, with a small moue of distaste. "Too vulgar for words. And speaking of which, there's the prodigal son."

Doyle saw she referred to Sir Stephen, approaching Acton like a good penitent, with the two men shaking hands and exchanging a few words in a respectful manner.

Doesn't fool me for a moment, Doyle thought; Acton hates the fellow with the heat of a thousand suns.

And as the Dowager had foretold, Lady Abby indeed accompanied Sir Stephen, a very stylish hat aslant on her pretty head, and her manner humble and ingratiating. As Acton spoke to the young woman, Doyle wondered if Sir Stephen knew about the kerfuffle in Dublin, and rather crossly wished there wasn't so much to keep straight, about what should be said to whom, with secrets lying so thick on the ground that you had to wade through them. Faith, if this were an Irish funeral, all past grievances would be cleared up by a few bouts of fisticuffs, and then everyone would retreat to the nearest pub to hoist one up in honor of the departed.

"She's mad as a hatter," Melissa pronounced in a whisper. "She must be a pip in the bedroom, to make it all worthwhile."

"No sex-talk," Doyle reminded her.

"Oh—oh, right; sorry."

To show there were no hard feelings, Doyle offered, "I rather thought you might wind up with him."

"Sir Stephen? Oh, no," her companion said in her languid manner. "I know him too well."

Not exactly an accolade, Doyle thought, and then found she was shaking hands with Lady Abby, and agreeing that it was all a terrible shame, and that guns were indeed very dangerous.

That's odd, thought Doyle, much struck; she's the first person to make any reference to how the poor footman died; no one's mentioned the details.

Lady Abby's gaze strayed over toward the church's entry door. "Is Nigel here? I wanted to say hallo."

Nigel Howard was Mary's husband, and Lady Abby's former fiancé. A bit surprised, Doyle replied, "No—I don't think he's expected."

Startled, the young woman's eyes met Doyle's. "No? Didn't his wife come with you?"

"No; Mary stayed home, this time around." Best not to mention that Mary was feeling down-pin because they were expecting their first; Lady Abby was indeed a bit distraught, beneath her well-cultivated manner, and even if she wanted to mend fences, she couldn't be counted on not to say the wrong thing and upset poor Mary, all unknowing. For perhaps the millionth time, Doyle thanked all available saints and holy angels that she and Acton had managed to find each other; this love-and-longing business was fraught with peril, and thank God fastin' they'd managed to skip over that part entirely.

The Dowager arrived, dressed in her blacks and looking very regal, and this appeared to be the cue for the rest of them to enter the church, Acton coming forward to offer his arm to Doyle, even though it seemed clear that the Dowager had expected this courtesy from him. The Anglican priest quickly stepped into the breach—in his own way, he was just as adept at dealing with elderly harridans as Reynolds—and they thus started the procession to the family's box at the front of the church.

CHAPTER 29

*A*fter they'd returned to Trestles after the funeral,
Doyle noted that the reception's general atmosphere
was rather light for the occasion; not a surprise, perhaps,
since the decedent wasn't very well-known, and the
mourning was more pro-forma than grief-stricken.

As everyone helped themselves to the buffet, Doyle
wandered over to greet Williams, who was speaking with
Melissa whilst Mathis was helping Hudson direct the kitchen
staff.

"I'm chatting-up the heir," Melissa informed Doyle,
unabashed. "I have to look lively, and it's every woman for
herself."

"Williams is not the heir," Doyle reminded her, unsure of
whether she should also mention that Williams was married
—it didn't seem to be general knowledge, as yet. Not that it
would matter much to Melinda, truth to tell.

"Edward's eclipsed me," Williams agreed with a smile. "I

appreciate the attention, but I'm afraid there's nothing to be gained."

"I'll be the judge of that," Melinda replied in a suggestive tone, and Williams laughed.

Raising a hand to wiggle her fingers, Melinda moved away, and Doyle remarked, "It must be exhaustin', Thomas—havin' everyone throw themselves at you all the livelong day. Although I suppose you can't hold a candle to Acton's troubles on that front."

"Only because I missed out on the title," he teased. "I can only regret what might have been."

Doyle lowered her voice. "Lady Abby's here–speakin' of what might have been. A word to the wise, is all." Williams had been tasked with escorting the volatile young woman home from the aforesaid kerfuffle in Dublin, and so he was well-aware of the hazards presented by her presence.

"I saw her. She seems a bit more rational, which is a good thing."

"Everyone's behavin' themselves, all around," Doyle agreed, much struck. "Mark it down, because it's unlikely to ever happen again."

Williams chuckled, and Doyle's gaze rested on Acton, who was politely speaking with the two clergymen, the RC priest happily nibbling on a plate piled high with hors d'oeuvres. Her husband lifted his eyes to meet her gaze, and she sent him a smile of reassurance—he was worried she was overdoing it, and seemed to have forgot that the whole point of marrying hearty Irish peasant-stock was that they were well-used to overdoing it, and didn't tend to collapse in a heap.

Williams noted the exchange, and ventured, "Has Acton said anything?"

Recalled the fact that Williams was worried he was in Acton's black book—not a good place to be, as Williams well-knew—Doyle offered, "No, he hasn't, but I truly don't think you're in the dog-house, Thomas. You're just bein' fanciful."

He shrugged in concession. "Maybe. Acton might be testing-out some of the lower ranks, which is not a bad idea. I shouldn't be so territorial."

Doyle made a face, because the last thing the CID needed was more Acton-tested officers with a bent toward vigilantism. Remembering her sense that Acton wasn't saying what he knew about the case, she asked, "Have you heard whether they've any leads, in Dr. James' murder? Has Habib said?"

He shook his head. "No suspects as yet. The working-theory is that it may have been a retribution murder, by a parent. That would also explain what looks like half-hearted attempts at torture."

Doyle blinked. "A parent? D'you mean a parent of one of her patients?"

It was William's turn to be surprised. "Acton hasn't told you what's been going on, there?"

She stared at him. "He has not. Tell me, Thomas; I broke the case, after all."

He grimaced. "It's ugly, Kath. They were harvesting t-cells from kids—the younger the better—and they didn't much worry about whether the victim survived the process or not."

"Mother a' *Mercy*," Doyle breathed in horror. "'Soul-eaters'—so that's what she meant. And that's why Acton sent me home—he didn't want me to find out the particulars."

Watching her, Williams made a sound of regret. "I shouldn't have said, maybe."

Mentally, Doyle shook herself. "No; I'm a copper, and I

shouldn't be so queasy. But I think when you've your own children, this sort of thing does make you flinch."

"It's strictly greed, behind it. The t-cells are very valuable, and sold off-the-market for exorbitant prices."

"Pure evil," she pronounced, and then decided to change the subject. "Speakin' of pure evil, have you heard from Munoz?" Their co-worker had taken a holiday to Ireland, so as to meet her new in-laws.

"No, I haven't. And I'm not sure whether that's a good sign or a bad sign."

"Time will tell," Doyle agreed, and then ventured, "Speakin' of which, I see that you two came together—you and Lizzy."

He shrugged, slightly. "We're working things out, still—there's no real hurry. As a matter of fact, we're going to visit her parents, after this."

Doyle teased him, "Bein' all respectful and such, just like our Munoz. Faith, it's a sign of the apocalypse."

He smiled in acknowledgement. "We're living together; I should introduce myself."

"Well, technically, you're married," she pointed out cautiously. "That's a bit different."

Again, he shrugged. "With all due respect, Kath, that doesn't matter to a lot of people."

"Aye, that," she was forced to agree, and then was surprised when her scalp prickled. Marriage mattered a lot to someone—it mattered a whole lot. Who? Lizzy Mathis? No—Lizzy was playing a waiting game, and Doyle had the sense she'd the situation well in hand. Blakney the ghost? He was getting married, after all—but no; it was someone else. Someone who was rather frantic on the subject, in fact.

She closed her eyes for a moment, trying to catch at the

elusive thought, but was interrupted when Acton appeared at her elbow. "Do you need to sit, Kathleen?"

"No—no, I was just thinkin', is all—can you smell the wood burnin'?"

With an assessing eye, he continued, "Have you eaten, as yet? There is a very nice selection of fruit."

"There is, indeed," she said heartily. "I hardly know where to start."

"I'll go see how Lizzy is doing," Williams offered, mainly because he could see that the Dowager was bearing down on them.

As Williams made his escape, Doyle asked Acton bluntly, "Are you unhappy with Williams?"

"No," he replied, and it was true. But before he could expand on the subject, the Dowager commanded his attention, and Doyle took the opportunity to sidle away toward the fruit selection of the buffet, mentally girding her loins, and keeping an eye out for any stray cream-sauce that might be put to good use.

CHAPTER 30

$\mathcal{A}$s Doyle was casting an unenthusiastic eye over the offerings, the RC priest took the opportunity to come over and give his regards, being as they were both strangers in a strange land.

Only too happy to have her fruit-eating interrupted, Doyle offered, "Let me know when you're ready for the Rosary, Father; we can find a quiet room—mayhap the room where Acton keeps his piano."

"Oh—yes, thank you, Lady Acton." The priest set down his plate and dug into his cassock pocket. "I brought along the departed's own rosary for the occasion, since it seemed only fitting."

He pulled out the string of beads carefully, pooling it in his hands, and Doyle could only stare in surprise—it was beautifully-wrought; silver with blue stones—lapis—lapis something, and she'd seen something very similar, once before. Finding her voice, she said, "It's Spanish, I think." Mother a' Mercy, she thought in wonder—it *can't* be—can it?

The priest confessed, "If there's no one to claim it, I may send it to my mother; it's such a pretty thing."

Doyle nodded, thinking furiously. "I think that's a fine idea, Father—may as well put it to good use, after all."

Hesitant, he suggested, "I wouldn't want anyone to think I've stolen it, though; perhaps I should seek Lord Acton's permission?"

"No," said Doyle slowly. "There's no need a'tall."

He continued speaking to her, but Doyle wasn't listening. The dead footman's rosary was the exact same as the one that was connected to Martina Betancourt's Holy Order—the Order that was busy wreaking revenge on anyone who'd run afoul of the Vatican. The very same Order who'd focused their sights on Acton, once upon a time.

And Martina—Martina herself had been here at Trestles for a short while, posing as a maidservant. Had Doyle ever noticed her, speaking to this dead footman? She hadn't been paying attention, of course, and small blame to her—before she'd met Acton, she'd never come within calling distance of a sinister conspiracy, and now she tripped over one nearly every flippin' time she turned around.

But Doyle didn't need confirmation because she knew—in the way that she knew things—that the two had indeed been connected; that Martina and the footman had been spying on Acton's household. As part of their vengeance-doings, the Order had been spying on him without his knowledge, until the fair Doyle had convinced Martina to call off the dogs.

Which also explained the general air of contentment, at this funeral, and why no one was mentioning exactly how the decedent had died. There was no need, because everyone already knew; a castle invader had been exposed, and he'd been dealt with in the same way all castle invaders had been dealt with for nearly a thousand years—faith, it was a wonder they weren't displaying his head on a pike, right here in the great hall.

Doyle closed her eyes, making a mighty effort to pull herself together, and was unsurprised to find Acton at her side again, his mother rather impatiently trailing behind him. "Everything all right?"

"No," she said crossly. "It is not."

"Oh," said the priest, a bit flustered. "I beg your pardon, Lady Acton—"

But at this juncture, Acton's mobile pinged, and he glanced at the ID, and then lifted the phone to his ear. "Yes?"

Doyle could sense a flare of profound surprise from her husband, and then he held his hand over the phone to say, "I must take this call, I'm afraid. Please excuse me."

"Acton," the Dowager scolded in an imperious tone. "You must not bring your work home."

Trouble, Doyle thought immediately, watching him stride away; and an extra helping, at that, since it has to be something that would break-through a "no-calls" request.

Contrite, the priest ventured, "Perhaps you should indeed sit down, Lady Acton—I'm so sorry to have kept you standing so long–"

"No—no, please; Doyle explained, trying to muster up a smile whilst keeping a weather eye on her husband, as he stood outside the hall's entry doors, speaking quietly on his phone. "I'm perfectly fine, Father; Acton's just a worry-wart, when it comes to me."

"He'd never had need to worry, before," the Dowager noted, speaking to no one in particular.

The priest pivoted to ask the Dowager, "Would *you* care to sit down, Lady Acton?" Deferentially, he offered his arm.

"You must rest; everything has been arranged so beautifully, and you must be exhausted from all your efforts."

"I am, indeed," the older woman regally agreed, taking his proffered arm. "Thank you."

As they turned to go, Doyle explained, "We may have to wait for the Rosary, Father; it sounds like an emergency."

"Ridiculous, that he brings his mobile everywhere," the Dowager pronounced, very much affronted, and the priest offered sympathetically, "It is the times we live in, Lady Acton. Come; sit, and I will fetch you a petit-four."

As he led her away, Doyle decided they must give all priests basic-training in dealing with irritable old women, rather the same as how the coppers got basic-training in hand-to-hand. Basic survival, it was.

She noted that Acton had rung off, and now conferred in low tones with Hudson, the steward. Not good, Doyle thought, watching them. Now what?

Acton re-entered the hall and strode over to Doyle, his expression serious. "We must go, I'm afraid. Hudson will make our apologies." He then lifted his head, and Williams immediately materialized, as aware as Doyle that something serious must be afoot. "You will be needed, I'm afraid, and immediately."

"Yes, sir," said Williams, who was all-too-happy to be thus enlisted, and—as an added bonus—duck-out on meeting Lizzy's parents. He turned to his erstwhile wife in apology, but she said calmly, "Don't worry—we'll do it some other time. I will stay to help Hudson."

She's a patient woman, is Lizzy Mathis, thought Doyle—I should watch and learn.

But the lesson obviously hadn't taken hold as yet, because Doyle could hardly contain herself, as they emerged from the great hall, and into the foyer. "What's afoot?" she whispered urgently.

Her husband replied in a grave tone, "Colonel Kolchak has been killed—shot at St. Margaret's school, sometime yesterday afternoon."

CHAPTER 31

*D*oyle's heart leapt to her throat. "Is Gemma all right? I think they had lessons, yesterday."

Acton nodded. "Yes—Gemma was not present. The body was discovered this morning on the playing fields, and presumably it was not discovered sooner, due to the rain."

A footman brought the car around on the gravel drive, and Doyle stepped forward to take a still-sleepy Edward from Callie, and load him into his car seat. "Holy *Mother*, Michael; let me call Mary then, and see what she can tell us."

"Let's wait," her husband reminded her. "It is a pending homicide investigation."

"Aye—sorry," she agreed, after the barest hesitation. This was interesting; ordinarily, Acton didn't mind stepping all over the protocols, if it suited his fancy. He must be wary about this one, for some reason.

The footman shut the doors, and then they were away. Almost immediately, Acton's mobile pinged, and Doyle had the sense he was speaking to someone at the Home Office, mainly because his tone changed to what she characterized as his public-school voice, which he tended to use when amongst his own species.

"I am sorry to disturb you on a weekend," Acton began, "but the case has several troubling aspects, and we may need the diplomatic corps to have a look."

What sort of troubling aspects? thought Doyle in alarm, as she began to feed Edward his favorite fish-shaped biscuits, one-by-one, so as to keep him quiet during the call.

Acton listened for a moment. "Yes; of course, that is the presumption. But there are several elements that do not reflect well on the Crown—nor on myself—and so perhaps we should strategize on the subject."

The voice at the other end spoke for a few more moments, and then Acton said, "Very good. Allow me to gather-up what is known, and I will come by—I will text when I am on my way."

He rang off, and immediately phoned Williams. "I will meet you there—St. Margaret's. We will need to keep a tight lid, for diplomatic reasons, and I imagine the Home Office will be handling all communications."

He paused, listening to Williams' response. "There is a team there, already. They found my number in his mobile, and now everyone's on standby."

As he put down his phone, Doyle could sense his grimness, and she ventured, "Shall I start buildin' an ark, husband?"

There was a moment's silence, and she could see that he was trying to decide how much to tell her. "The victim's electronics paint a rather disturbing picture. It is possible the evidence was planted, however, and so we must proceed with caution."

She ventured, "I suppose the first thing you'd suspect is that the people runnin' Russia have decided they'd enough of the Colonel's little opposition party, and so shot him dead with no further ado."

"Yes," he agreed. "It was always a risk; his royalist movement is a threat to some very ruthless people. The diplomatic aspect is one of the reasons it will have to be handled very carefully, certainly."

Struck with an alarming thought, she asked, "D'you think the same ruthless people know who Gemma is? Mayhap they're lookin' to be rid of her, too."

"It is a concern," he agreed. "Royal Protection Officers have been dispatched to her home, as a precaution."

He paused, and she reached to shake his arm, gently but insistently. "Tell me, Michael; what's afoot?"

Slowly, he revealed, "The officers on the scene had a look into his electronics, so as to identify him, and found his connection to us, and to the Howards."

Puzzled by his grave tone, she ventured, "Surely, they don't think we're part of the Russian opposition group, do they?"

"No, but it seems apparent that the Colonel was planning on marriage to Gemma. It was part of the plan he'd hatched with his compatriots."

Astonished, Doyle could only stare at him for a moment, her mouth agape. "*Marriage* to Gemma? How can that be? She's but a wee lass."

Acton nodded. "Nevertheless. Their communications contain indications that he was planning to bring her back to Russia as his wife. Such a move would bolster the group's claim to power."

But Doyle was having trouble even contemplating such a thing. "He'd marry a *child*?"

"Not so very unusual, in his tradition."

The penny dropped, and, with a knit brow, Doyle turned to gaze out the windscreen. "And you're worried, because we don't want anyone thinkin' that we were aware of this plan, and thought it a good idea."

"Or that the Home Office did, for that matter. Recall they are aware of her identity, even though it was kept quiet. I imagine they are reaching out to the Russian government as we speak, and making assurances."

Bewildered, Doyle slowly shook her head. "I'll not believe the Colonel was a pedophile, Michael; he just seemed—well he seemed *reverent*, more than anything else."

But her husband only lifted a shoulder. "It does not look well."

"No, it doesn't," she had to admit. "And it's true that he seemed—well, he seemed *proprietary*, in a strange way—although I always put it down to his having whisked her out of harm's way." Frowning, she thought about it. "I don't think he's ever tried anythin'—with Gemma, I mean. We'd have been suspicious—or Mary would have. And Gemma shows none of the signs."

He nodded. "I agree. But it seems clear he was making plans for a marriage, and sooner rather than later. I imagine the object was to make certain no one else had the opportunity to claim jurisdiction over her."

With some heat, Doyle declared, "What is *wrong* with everyone? Holy saints and angels, Michael; this is exactly what you get when you glorify a bloodline in this way—everyone is willin' to do shameful things, so as to lash themselves to it."

Her husband, of course, was not one to refute this point, but only remarked, "The Colonel's death has a silver lining, then."

Exasperated, Doyle reminded him, "Murder is *never* the right answer, Michael; I've told you a *million* times."

"We may have to agree to disagree, then. In this instance, it seems the Colonel's enemies have performed a very valuable favor."

There was a small silence. "It was a revelation murder," she agreed, much struck. "And it's all sorts of ironic, because the killers didn't know it was goin' to be such; they were just hopin' to put a period to the coup-plannin'."

"Hence, a silver lining," he repeated in a mild tone, and in response, she pressed her lips firmly together, and counted to ten.

CHAPTER 32

$\mathcal{N}$ext, Acton called Howard, Gemma's stepfather, to inform him of the situation, and to further explain that the Royal Protection Officers were just a precaution, until more was known. "It has all the earmarks of a professional hit," he told the listening man. "Which raises a concern; we must make certain that Gemma is not in danger, and I would ask that she be kept at home for the time being."

Like me, thought Doyle, with a mental sigh; Acton's not going to want me at the scene, if he needs to shift things about so as to distance the House of Acton and the Home Office from this particular murder. Although to be fair, he was justly alarmed; the fair Doyle had taken that short-cut across the St. Margaret's playing fields many a time herself, and he was a cautious man, was Acton. Not that she could be mistaken for a Russian royalist, of course—this was one sinister conspiracy, at least, that she'd not brushed elbows with.

With a start, she realized that this latest conspiracy-murder had completely shoved aside the original conspiracy-murder, and that there was no time like the present to call Acton to account, since they were pulling caps on the subject, already.

And so, she passed another biscuit to Edward—the car seat would be a crackin' mess, but it was well-worth the boyo's contented silence, and when Acton rang off, she said in an ominous tone, "Brace yourself for another round, my friend. I've managed to twig you out, on this poor dead footman that everyone's been cryin' crocodile tears over. I'm guessin' you found out he was from Martina's Order, and so you made like the Russians, and had him dispatched with no further ado."

Acton was silent, and she prodded, "You discovered that he was an infi— inflit—"

"Infiltrator?"

"Yes, thank you. An infiltrator, and you're not one who tolerates infiltrators in any way, shape or form."

Her husband had apparently decided to make a clean breast, and he replied, "A strong message had to be sent, Kathleen. I will not be spied-upon."

"Too little, too late," she pointed out. "The Order had already done their spyin', and they'd already discovered a sackful."

"All the more reason, then."

But she shook her head in frustrated disagreement. "You could have just thrown the fellow out, bag and baggage, Michael; there was no need to kill him. I think you wanted your own revelation murder—you wanted the Order to know that you knew, and that you were not happy."

"A message had to be sent," he repeated. "And one they'll not soon forget."

Closing her eyes, she blew out a breath. "I know you like the back o' my hand, husband. It's not so much you wanted to send a message as you wanted leverage, and now you have it. They don't dare try to manipulate you, now, for fear you'll expose all their underhanded dealin's."

This was, after all, only to be expected; she knew from long experience that Acton was the grand master at turning the tables. She added, "I'll remind you that I saw this comin' from a mile away when we first found out about them, Michael, but I take no joy in it. Shame on you."

"I will not be an easy mark," he replied, completely unrepentant. "And I'll not allow a threat to you, nor to Edward. And so there must be repercussions."

Stubbornly, she insisted, "But you could have just warned them off, Michael; at heart, they're not evil people—they're just zealots."

This remark, interestingly enough, made him pause, and she could see that he was choosing what to say. "On the whole, I would agree with that assessment. But recall that their own ranks have also been infiltrated, in turn."

Puzzled, she frowned at him, trying to decide what he meant. "You're worried Martina's Order has been infiltrated? By who? Or whom, or whichever word is the right one?"

"Martina's husband."

"Oh. Oh—I suppose he *is* a wild card, just now."

As much as she hated to admit it, this seemed a fair point. Being as he was with the Order, Antonio D'Angelo was privy to the House of Acton's secrets, but Antonio D'Angelo seemed to have gone rogue, lately—involving himself in some questionable doings, with Tommy Dryden's murder serving as an excellent example. Not to mention he was playing least-in-sight with his poor cast-aside wife.

That's it, Doyle thought suddenly; that's who's wracked about marriage–poor Martina, who's got herself a renegade husband and loves him despite it all; I suppose we're birds of a feather, in that respect. But at least I have some control over my wayward husband; she seems to hold little influence, over hers.

And—speaking of control–this would also explain why Acton had visited the pawn shop, to gather-up the Antonio evidence. Martina had agreed to step down with respect to the Order's persecution of Acton, but Acton couldn't be certain Antonio-the-renegade was going to abide by her decision. Therefore, Acton's pawn-shop seizure was to gain the upper hand over Antonio by implicating him in Tommy Dryden's murder; Tommy's pawn tickets were Acton's trump card, so to speak, to hold Antonio in check in the event he wasn't going to honor Martina's agreement to let Acton's sleeping dogs lie.

Her husband's machinations suddenly began to make more sense—not that the footman's murder was justified, of course, but she could see the man's point. It was not necessarily Martina and her Holy Order he was concerned about, it was the people who might be privy to what the Order knew about him, with Martina's rogue husband serving as a very real example.

Recalled to their discussion, she continued, "The real lesson, here, is that you shouldn't have any horrifyin' secrets that need to be guarded in the first place, Michael, so that evil people aren't diggin' about to see what they can hold over you."

He didn't reply, and so she continued with some emphasis, "And the second lesson is that there are better ways to deal with your enemies than goin' to straight into battle, hammer and tongs, so as to annihilate each other. Faith, it's like everyone thinks they're still livin' in the Middle Ages; you, Martina's Order—even the Colonel's group and the Russians. For the love o' Mike; what was the point of tryin' to come up with a civilized system, if no one pays the least attention to it?"

"The stakes are too high," he replied in a steady tone. "When you are dealing with ruthless people, better to let them know you can be just as ruthless, in return."

But she stubbornly shook her head. "Everyone here seems to be forgettin' that all of this doesn't matter two pins, and that the highest stakes of all are what's goin' to happen to you after your brief life, here on earth. I suppose that's why religious beliefs are so hard to practice—I mean *truly* practice, in the day-to-day. If everyone else around you is practicin' every-man-for-himself, you're at a distinct disadvantage."

Much struck, she added, "I think that's one of the reasons poor Martina is so fashed; she's supposed to be the bigger man—the bigger Christian, I mean—and forgive her husband's many sins, but meanwhile, he doesn't care two pins about it."

"I think that is a very good insight," he agreed. "Even the strongest principles do not always hold up in practice when it comes to the personal—especially when one is personally at risk."

She made a wry mouth, because he seemed to be implying the exact same thing that Blakney-the-ghost had implied. "Next, you'll be remindin' me that I killed someone once, under just those circumstances."

"I wouldn't be so rude," he said mildly.

She had to chuckle. "You are so crackin' *annoyin'*, Michael."

He smiled. "Hoist by your own petard."

"Like I've have any idea what that means."

"It means your own actions have come back to haunt you."

"No more hauntin's, please," she said with a sigh. "Believe me, I've had more than my fill."

"Speaking of which, there is an apple, in the dashboard compartment—you didn't have a chance to sample the fruit plate."

"You are so crackin' *annoyin'*, Michael," she repeated crossly.

CHAPTER 33

*A*s could be expected, Acton dropped her home before he set out for the St. Margaret's crime scene. Doyle secured his promise that he'd wear a Kevlar vest—there was no cover, in the field, and the shooter could still be lurking about—and then he drove off, speaking on his phone even as the door closed behind her.

Since she anticipated that he'd be spending the remainder of the evening soothing any and all ruffled feathers over in Marsham Street, Doyle decided she may as well go straight to bed after she put Edward down; she'd had an eventful weekend, and besides, she was starting to feel tired, most of the time.

She was not to have an undisturbed sleep, however, because yet again, she was facing Bill Blakney in the quiet, stone-walled room.

With a knit brow, she complained, "Everyone's gettin' themselves killed, Mr. Blakney; it's like the Middle Ages, out there, and I'm half-inclined to hide under my bed."

"Good," he said. "Leave well enough alone."

Interestingly enough, his tone wasn't as belligerent as it had been previously–he didn't seem half as anxious, and he didn't seem to be listening for the door, anymore. A welcome change, it was, and one of those paradocks, or whatever the word was; all the living people around her were running around in a massive fret, but the two ghosts she'd seen this day seemed uncharacteristically pleased.

With some frustration she countered, "I don't even know what's the 'well enough' I'm supposed to be leavin' alone, though; between the sniper, and the footman-spy, and the dead doctors, it doesn't feel 'well enough' at all—instead, it feels as though we're fast-approachin' the crack o' doom. Mayhap Martina has the right of it, with all of her doom-sayin'."

"You should stay out of it," he repeated. "It would be for the best."

Frowning, she tried to catch his meaning. "Best for who? And besides, it's not as though I can make a ha'penny's worth of difference, when all is said and done. I'm shoutin' into the wind, with Acton–faith, he'd the footman killed, just like in the old days, and he'd do it all over again in a heartbeat, no matter how much I beg and plead. Between him and the Holy Order, I'm at my wit's end."

"You'll be needing your wits," the ghost warned, cocking a brow at her. "Stay sharp."

Annoyed, she replied, "I thought I was supposed to stay out of it?"

In a mild tone, he explained, "You'll be needing your wits to stay out of it."

Doyle held on to her temper only with a mighty effort.

"Stay out of what, though? I feel as though I'm in the dark, and wanderin' about like a hooded chicken."

As he made no reply, she calmed herself, and added fairly, "Except for the pawn-shop angle, of course. I should thank you for sendin' me over, since I did manage to twig-out that Acton's usin' Tommy Dryden's tickets to get the goods on Antonio D'Angelo." Brightening a bit, she asked, "Can you tell Tommy, if you happen to see him? Tell him I'm clearin' his name just like I said I would, and that Acton's usin' him as the assist."

But the ghost only shook his head in sad disappointment. "For fook's sake; look at that. You've already forgot."

Surprised, Doyle asked, "Forgot what?"

The ghost leaned forward to say with emphasis, "The biggest ticket-item that shop's ever seen, that's what."

She lifted her brows. "Oh—oh, are you speakin' of the necklace? I did forget." Mulling this over, she mused, "Strange, that he'd want Antonio's prints on it—he's already got the man dead to rights with the CCTV tape, and the pawn tickets."

"It's a trap," the ghost explained with heavy patience, and ran a finger along his starched collar, as though it was uncomfortable.

She nodded. "Of course, it's a trap. There's nothin' Acton likes better than springin' a good trap."

The ghost tilted his head at her and said with a great deal of meaning, "It's your trap, too. Don't forget about it, again."

She stared at him in surprise. "No—no, Mr. Blakney; I've nothin' to do with it, truly. And besides, I'm not clever enough to set a trap."

But the ghost only repeated, "It's your trap, too. Try not to forget."

With a sudden feeling of grave unease, Doyle ventured, "Am I settin' a trap for Acton?"

But the ghost seemed to find this idea preposterous, and crossed his arms as he made a rude sound. "As though you'd need one—he'd let you kick him down the stairs, and thank you for it."

Slowly shaking her head, she could only disagree. "Now, there you're wrong, my friend. I try to get him to stop goin' all scorched-earth, left and right, but he won't listen, no matter what I say."

"You're the one who's wrong," he replied. "And you should leave well-enough alone."

Thoroughly frustrated, she reasoned, "You're not makin' much sense, Mr. Blakney. If you think Acton's schemes shouldn't be my concern, then what is it that we're doin', here?"

"You should stay out of it, but you won't," he explained with some disapproval. "Don't forget about the trap." He then glanced over his shoulder toward the door.

Doyle decided she was tired of covering the same tired ground, and rather than talk 'round and 'round, she asked, "Is she comin' soon, the bride?"

"Yes. Yes, she is," he replied, and–to her amazement—his voice broke, and he quickly pressed his lips together, so as to bring his emotional lapse under control.

"I'm that happy for you," she ventured, but she received no response, because she was suddenly awake, and aware that her husband was sliding into the bed beside her, trying not to wake her up.

"I'm awake," she whispered. "What have you, anythin'?"

He drew her into his arms and pulled her back against his chest. "The scene was clean; the rain didn't help forensics, of course. Looks to be a professional hit; it was a single shot from a distance."

"Those pesky Russians," she pronounced, and drew her fingers lightly along his forearms, where they were wound around her. "CCTV? You'd think a fancy school like that would be awash in cameras."

"We tried to triangulate the shooter's site, but we couldn't be precise, so we'll have to review everything in the area—all feeds within a mile."

"Which was why it was done from a distance," she noted. "A professional."

He continued, "And even if we catch him on tape, I am not hopeful that we'll have any identifiers."

"No; not if the shooter knows his trade." She shifted slightly, to glance up at him in the dim light. "The Home Office can't be very happy that we've Russian snipers, lurkin' about London primary schools."

"True. And they are made all the more unhappy because they have not been covered in glory, with respect to Gemma's situation. Diplomatic mediations are ongoing, but I imagine the matter will be resolved with Gemma receiving a stipend from Moscow on the understanding that she'll remain in England, and stay well-away from Russian politics."

Surprised, Doyle's hand paused, as she considered this for a moment. "Faith, Michael; that's almost too good to be true."

"It makes the most sense, given the circumstances. She'd be constantly at risk, otherwise."

Soberly, Doyle agreed. "Yes. Next time the sniper could be after her."

"I imagine there will be no further objection to her adoption by the Howards. More likely such an action would be encouraged."

"Mother a' Mercy; better and better," she said in wonder. "And meanwhile, the dastardly Colonel is no doubt tryin' to explain himself, somewhere where it's very hot, and good luck to him."

But Acton's view was more philosophical. "I imagine his motives were not as dastardly as they might appear; he probably counted himself fortunate to be of service, in Gemma's return to glory. As I mentioned, such a marriage is not unheard of, in his tradition."

But Doyle wasn't having it. "There's no excuse for exploitin' a child in such a way, Michael. He's only one step up from the soul-eaters, forcin' the poor girl to hand her life over, with no choices to be had."

In a soothing gesture, he squeezed her slightly. "We are fortunate, then, that he did not succeed with his marriage-plans."

The squeeze inspired a new train of thought—her hormones were on a hair-trigger, after all—and so she turned over in his arms to nuzzle at this throat. "D'you know who *did* succeed in his marriage-plans?" she teased softly.

"Shouldn't you rest?"

Running a hand down his chest, she sighed. "You are so sweet, when you are tryin' to be noble, Michael, but if there was ever a time to go scorched-earth, it's now."

With a chuckle, he pulled her to him, and made no further protest.

CHAPTER 34

*M*onday morning saw Doyle back at work, and making her report to Habib with respect to Dr. James' homicide. "Office Shandera is reportin' that the clinic's been quiet, sir, and surveillance hasn't seen anythin' to spark an interest. The patients are spooked, of course, but hopefully with the staffin' changes, they'll start comin' back. The Health Professions Council is tryin' to keep a lid on the evil doin's, hopin' to avoid any more bad press—they've had their fill, in the past few years. They're pullin' in some volunteers from the other organizations around town, and makin' a push to do some door-to-door solicitin'; I know my doctor-friend is lendin' a hand."

Habib nodded. "The nurse is being held without bail?"

"Indeed, he is, sir. For his own protection, mainly—he's got to worry about retribution from both this evil group of perps, as well as the public. I imagine everyone on all sides wants his head."

Ducking his chin, the Pakistani man asked, "Is it possible the nurse is the killer, DS Doyle?"

Doyle shook her head. "Unlikely, sir. He was takin' a cut from the black-market operation, but he seems to know little about the particulars. Besides, if he was the killer, he wouldn't want to draw attention by leavin' the victim on-site. That's the topper; at first glance, we thought mayhap it was the villains, killin' one of their own, but because of the body's bein' left on-site, I think instead it may be a vengeful parent, doin' a revelation murder. Someone who wanted revenge, and who wanted to expose what was goin' on."

Habib heaved a small sigh. "It is a shame we cannot discover more about the chain of distribution for this operation. There must be a laboratory component, and payments which are being laundered, somewhere."

"Yes, sir," Doyle agreed. Habib had already directed personnel to make discreet inquiries of private medical labs in the area, but so far, there was little to show for it—it would be far better to find a witness who knew how to find that needle in the haystack. "I've had Officer Shandera tryin' to interview patients, but its tough sleddin', with that particular crowd."

Habib nodded. "I will ask DCI Acton for permission to withdraw surveillance at the clinic, then. It does not appear any more will be gained from that end."

Another homicide case that's going nowhere, thought Doyle, as she walked back to her cubicle. Because the working-theory was a vengeance-minded parent, the powers-that-be wouldn't be very motivated to solve the case–it was always a tricky proposition to drag such a righteous person into the dock, being as the public would be firmly on their side. The Met would then have the thankless task of trying to explain to that self-same public that—even though the Met hadn't managed to get justice done, itself—vigilantism was very much frowned-upon, since it only tended to get out of hand. Not that the getting-out-of-hand part was a drawback, for scorched-earth people like Acton and Martina Betancourt.

Abruptly, she decided to change the direction of her thoughts. *I've got to stop drawing parallels between Acton and Martina,* she told herself firmly; *they truly aren't very much alike, at all.*

Her phone buzzed, and the Desk Sergeant informed her that a Dr. Okafor was in the lobby, hoping to have a word. She'd brought flowers.

With a small grimace, Doyle replied that she'd be right down. It happened, sometimes; a relative or other member of the public wanted to thank them personally for saving the day, and it always made her feel a bit uncomfortable. It was her job, after all, and she was not someone who liked to be thanked for just doing her job. On the other hand, what was all in a day's work for a copper might be a life-changing event for a member of the general public, and so she should make the effort to pin on a smile, and try to be gracious.

Dr. Okafor was standing at the security desk, and smiled a brilliant smile upon sighting Doyle. "Officer Doyle," she exclaimed. "I must thank you many, many times."

Doyle dutifully accepted the small bouquet, and replied, "Thank yourself, then; you were brave enough to step forward, and to start the ball rollin'."

With an air of quiet conviction, the woman replied, "It was not me; instead, it was *signs and wonders, performed through the name of your holy servant.*"

"Absolutely," Doyle agreed. Recalled to her conversation with Habib, she asked, "Were you able to give Officer

Shandera any information about who else might be involved? There must have been other medicos involved in this scheme —a laboratory, at the very least."

With regret, the doctor shook her head. "The evildoers knew I would not approve, and so I was kept away from their evil doings."

"And you'd a black-eye to show for it," Doyle agreed, and then—suddenly struck with the idea—she asked, "Did they ever ID the perp who assaulted you? He must know somethin', or someone, so as to give us a lead."

But the doctor only shook her head. "I do not believe so, Officer Doyle—I have not been asked to identify anyone. Officer Shandera took his description, but he said it didn't sound like anyone who was involved with the clinic." She paused, and then added with a small smile, "He was a 'six'."

The number was police-code for a person of Middle Eastern ethnicity, and Doyle hastened to assure her, "It's just a shorthand-code used for descriptions, is all."

The doctor laughed. "Yes—yes; I took no offense, Officer Doyle. Officer Shandera and I thought it very amusing–he and I would both be a 'three', even though we do not share the same origins, at all."

Officer Shandera needs to be a bit more circumspect, Doyle thought, and was relieved that the witness didn't seem to feel insulted—often the police descriptors were a touchy subject. On the other hand, the woman's attitude might be directly related to the fact that Officer Shandera was a handsome man, which tended to smooth away any and all ill-feelings. It was a powerful tool, and none knew this better than Acton, who was himself a handsome man, and wielded it ruthlessly. McGonigal's poor office manager was probably still sitting up at nights, waiting by her phone.

Reminded, Doyle said, "We should thank Dr. McGonigal, too. He's the one who gave me the tip about your troubles."

The woman agreed, "Yes; he has been very kind—he often gives me a lift home, now, when my shift has ended. He says we cannot be too safe."

Ah--this was of interest, and Doyle had to hide a smile; McGonigal definitely had a 'type', it seemed, but he'd best get crackin', else Officer Shandera was going to steal a march. A shame, that Acton's take-no-prisoners method of courtship hadn't rubbed off on his shy friend.

Thinking to conclude the conversation, Doyle said, "Well, thank you for the flowers, and I'm glad everythin' worked out."

But the encounter was not at an end, it seemed, because her companion lowered her voice in a self-conscious way. "I must ask that you be certain to read the note. The note is not from me, but it is from my pastor."

Doyle blinked. "Your pastor?"

The woman nodded. "I visited with him, because now the clinic will be short on funding. His ministry controls a charitable fund, and he said he will do what he can."

The penny dropped, and Doyle remembered that the woman followed the former DCS's popular prison ministry. Ironic, it was, that the former head of Scotland Yard—now serving a sentence for corruption—would turn into someone who could be trusted with even the widow's mite. Signs and wonders, indeed.

Her companion continued, "He asked me to give you his regards, and asked if I would pass you a note. He said I couldn't tell anyone, because he is not allowed to pass notes." She indicated the small envelope that was attached to the beribboned bouquet.

Doyle touched the envelope and smiled. "Thank you, I appreciate it. And I'll be happy when we've rolled-up whoever is behind all this."

But the woman only shook her head slightly in disagreement. "The devil's minions are on the run, Officer Doyle—do not doubt it. *Don't put your trust in mere humans. They are as frail as breath.*"

Well, that's all very well and good, thought Doyle, as she returned to her desk; but some of us frail humans have to come up with a suspect, and try to bring about some manner of earthly justice, as imperfect as it is.

Settling in at her desk, she set the bouquet down and opened the note, curious as to what the imprisoned evangelist would have to say. The note was short, and rather ominous in that it did not identify the sender nor the recipient. It only said: *Code 2. Attempts to gain information about charitable contributions to my ministry, along with any other information I might disclose.*

Doyle blew out a dismayed breath. It referred to Acton, of course, and a "Code 2" was a warning to be wary. She ran a thumb absently over the card, and decided this wasn't much of a mystery at all; the Order of Santiago had been gathering-up information about Acton and his doings, and they'd no doubt attempted to delve into his connections to the prison ministry. In fact, this would actually be a point in his favor, since Acton donated generously; they needn't know it wasn't necessarily charity that motivated the man, as much as it was grateful appreciation for the DCS's efforts to protect the fair Doyle, on a best-be-forgotten occasion.

Unfortunately, the note didn't indicate when these attempts had been made, and that gave her pause. The DCS wouldn't know that Acton had already twigged-out the

Santiago people—and had put a period to their footman-spy, for good measure—and therefore the note may be old news. On the other hand, if such attempts were more recent, it might indicate a new wrinkle in the ongoing battle, which was just *grand*—nothing like giving DCI Acton yet another excuse to go all scorched-earth and medieval.

Fortunately, she had a way to sound out the situation short of hiding Acton's battle-axe under the bed, and so she rang up Martina Betancourt, and asked if they could meet again for tea.

CHAPTER 35

Three down; one to go.

After gathering-up some work, Doyle had gone home for the afternoon, since this was one of the usual days she did so, and a good thing; she'd reports piling up, and best make some headway before she forgot the details. With this in mind, she'd settled in at her desk in the guest suite at home, and had managed to put in a good two hours' work.

When they'd first married, Acton had sat down with his bride to teach her how to write a decent report—she tended to wander, and to use far too many words where just a few would do. Not to mention she would often use the wrong word—the spell-checking device wasn't all that helpful, when you were using the wrong word to begin with, and you'd think they'd fix this troubling deficiency.

She'd definitely benefited from Acton's instruction, but in the end, it hadn't really mattered, because she'd been awarded her two commendations for bravery and now she was bullet-proof, so to speak; a young female officer who'd twice managed to save the day, despite her questionable reporting skills. The brass couldn't push her forward enough, nor heap enough public praise. A shame, it was, that she was a "one", and so white as to be practically translucent; they'd have been over the moon if she'd been a bit more diverse. On the other hand, if that were the case she'd be thrown on the front line of recruiting efforts without a second's hesitation, and thus be given no time to nick the villains.

Indeed, she suspicioned that the only reason she *wasn't* recruited for more community out-reach, and PR assignments was because she was married to Acton, who was famous in his own right, and famously reclusive, to boot. Otherwise, she'd probably be paraded about like poor Mary at the political dinners, with a pinned-on smile and trying to be social even though the fair Doyle hated social gatherings, mainly because no one was ever telling the truth.

Acton protects me, from all that, she thought, as she checked the time, and closed out her computer. He knows what I'd like best—sometimes even more than I do–and then he quietly makes it come true; bless the man. He's my champion, and even if it chafes at me, from time to time, I have to remember that it's a fine thing, to have a champion, and that the same power he wields—the power that allows him to mete out justice as he sees fit, and get away with it–is also focused on protecting me, and making my life easier. It's a two-edged sword—although a sword is perhaps not the best comparison; better to say that you have to take the bitters with the beer, like my mother used to.

She stretched her arms over her head, and then rose to review her appearance in the mirror. I honestly think he's better than he used to be, she thought, as she brushed out her hair, and decided against lip-gloss—Martina wasn't a lip-gloss sort of person. Back when they'd first met, Acton had seemed firmly set on "self-destruct," and now—now he'd a busy household to run, and so he was too distracted to self-destruct, even if he were so inclined. He hardly drank anymore–or at least, not to excess–and he truly loved little Edward, despite the fact it was like setting off a bomb in the midst of one's quiet and orderly life–another reminder that God had a mighty fine sense of humor.

Thinking on this, she smiled at her own reflection. Dr. Okafor was right–there were signs and wonders everywhere; you need only open your eyes, to see them.

She tiptoed out to inform Reynolds that she'd another tea-date with Martina, and told him not to bother seeing her out the door—the servant was on a cleaning tear, and was elbow-deep in yellow gloves and scouring powder. "I should be back before Edward wakes, fingers crossed."

"Very good, madam," the butler replied in a low voice. "Have we any news, from Lord Acton?"

He was referring to Gemma's situation, and with a guilty start, Doyle realized she hadn't bothered to check-in about it. "The Home Office is involved," she whispered. And then, because she could sense his anxiety, she added, "Acton seems optimistic that everythin' will work out for the best, once everyone calms down. And he doesn't seem to think Gemma's in any real danger, herself—they're just bein' extra cautious."

The butler said with great relief, "I am very happy to hear it, madam. I will call down, and inform Trenton of your plans."

Doyle quietly closed the door behind her, and then

traveled down the lift to the lobby, trying to decide how best to raise the Acton-topic with Martina. She may as well be honest with the woman—after all, Martina had been honest with Doyle, when she'd warned her about Acton, and it had turned out to be a good thing, overall. In an odd way, they trusted each other–she and Martina–and so she would just straight-out ask the woman if the DCS's note was a fresh cause for alarm.

As Doyle crossed the lobby downstairs, she smiled at the concierge clerk. "Have you gone fishin', then?"

The young man laughed, as he hurried over to get the door for her. "Not as yet, ma'am. There's no place for it, close by."

"Ah," she said, and thought to herself; trust Savoie to break the rules, and fish wherever he pleases. "And where's our doorman? Never say he's on holiday—I'll not believe it. He's always here, sure as the cock crows."

Tilting his head in chagrin, the clerk admitted, "I'm trying to raise him; we may have had a mix-up, with the scheduling."

"Don't tell Edward," she cautioned, and the man laughed again, and then bade her have a good day, as he closed the door behind her.

It *is* a good day, Doyle thought staunchly, as she walked along the pavement and shoved her hands into her coat pockets—she'd forgot her gloves. First off, it wasn't raining, and second off, it was a shrine-worthy miracle that Gemma's situation was working out to the best that it possibly could— despite the sad fact it had taken a man's murder, to sort it all out. And thirdly, she was still feeling hale, and thank God fastin'; by this time with Edward she'd been as sick as a cat. Dr. Okafor hadn't managed to get herself killed, and the wretched *Curing League* had been thwarted from going forward with its evil deeds. It was indeed a good day, so why did she feel as though there was an ominous storm, hovering just over the horizon?

Thinking about this, she decided that it must have to do with Blakney's ghost, and his talk about traps being set, willy-nilly. There's more to come, she decided with a sense of resignation, and Blakney wants me to stay sharp, even though I'm to stay out of it, which is a mixed-message if I've ever heard one. Hopefully, I can glean a bit more from Martina, and thus head-off any and all looming disasters. I've got to keep in mind all those nice thoughts I was just thinking about Acton, and remember that it's all well-worth it.

CHAPTER 36

*S*he arrived at the café to discover that Martina had once again arrived first, and as the young woman rose, Doyle had to hide her dismay; in the short time since she'd seen her, Martina had lost weight, and didn't look as though she'd been sleeping well. She's that fashed, Doyle thought with a stab of sympathy; there's nothing like having a wayward husband to set your nerves a'fret, and no one knows this better than me—although mine doesn't want to stir a step from my side, which is much better, overall, than having one who'd rather pretend to be dead.

"Hallo, Martina," Doyle began. "I hope you didn't mind comin'; we had to cut it short, last time."

"No, I am so glad you called," the woman replied in a quiet tone. "I was hoping we could come to terms."

"That would be excellent," Doyle readily replied, rather relieved her companion had broached the subject so easily. "You truly shouldn't be fishin' about in Acton's doin's—you know he doesn't handle that type of thing very well." This said as obliquely as possible, because she couldn't very well admit that Acton had Martina's footman-spy murdered, although her companion must surely be aware of this unfortunate fact.

"Yes," Martina replied. "It has become difficult to move forward in our mission, which is why I am hoping you can exert some influence over your husband." She met Doyle's eyes with her own, hollowed gaze. "Our work is important, Kathleen—he might not respect it, but surely, you do. You wouldn't want evil to triumph."

"Which evil is that?" Doyle asked, at sea.

Surprised in turn, Martina ventured, "Surely, you know? *The Curing League* was suffering the innocent."

Doyle blinked as the light dawned. "Oh—oh; it was your Order, then, that killed Dr. James?" Faith, she was such a knocker; of *course* it was. Martina had been volunteering for the *League,* and the next thing you knew, the evildoers were falling-out dead. The fair Doyle wasn't much of a detective, not to have put two and two together—although they'd all been distracted by the vengeful-parent theory. Let this serve as a reminder that you mustn't focus on the suspect's motivation more than you focus on the evidence that's laid out before you, or you might wind up with no court case at all.

This thought reminded Doyle that she'd yet another dilemma in what seemed like an unending list; Doyle was a police officer, after all, and therefore should be arresting Martina forthwith, but she couldn't very well rock that boat for fear that Martina might rock the murdered-footman boat. We're at a stand-off, on all these revelation murders, Doyle realized a bit crossly, and I'm definitely not paid enough to thread this particular needle.

Observing Doyle's dismayed response, Martina hastened to assure her, "But not before she repented; I'll not send an unshriven soul to purgatory."

Doyle stared yet again, as the pieces fell into place—here was why the decedent had been tortured; she'd been tortured until she'd repented. It was all rather distasteful, when you thought about it, and Doyle had the sense that Martina took more pleasure than she ought to, in bringing it all about.

Taking up her thankless mantle yet again, Doyle replied a bit tartly, "You shouldn't go about killin' people, whether they're shriven or unshriven."

Martina smiled slightly, and explained as though to a child, "Hers was a righteous death, to protect innocent lives. Surely, you can understand this."

This was in reference to a church doctrine, which allowed the taking of life if it was to protect innocent life—someone who performed such a killing would be absolved from mortal sin.

But Doyle wasn't having it, and countered, "If you'd sent her to prison, those lives would have been saved all the same, and you wouldn't have blood on your hands, my friend."

Her companion only shook her head, certain of her convictions. "Earthly justice is imperfect, as I'm sure you've seen many a time, Kathleen. Evil is well-funded, and knows how to discern who is greedy or weak, so as to manipulate the outcome."

Stubbornly, Doyle insisted, "You can't be the one who's decidin', though; that's why we're supposed to leave it to God, to sort it all out. I'm the first to admit that it's not always straightforward—to understand what's expected of us, but we can't go about pretendin' that we know best. We're handicapped—because we can only see through a glass darkly—and so we shouldn't pretend that we know the perfect solution; that's not our job. Faith, most of the time it feels as though we're only tryin' to choose the least-worst of all possible outcomes."

Almost to her surprise, the young woman reached to clasp her hand, and say almost fervently, "Yes; yes—*exactly*. That is exactly the dilemma, Kathleen. How can we know what God expects of us? How do we choose between competing interests? *Wives, be subject to your own husbands, so that even if some do not obey the word, they may be won without a word, by the conduct of their wives.*"

The referenced dilemma seemed a bit pointed, and Doyle ventured delicately, "D'you think Antonio was involved in *The Curin' League*, then?" This, all in all, would not be much of a surprise; the man had already flown too close to the flame with respect to the money-laundering scheme, and it had cost Tommy Dryden his life. Not a pillar of virtue, was our Antonio.

Rather than answer directly, Martina withdrew her hand, and said with profound sadness, "I am trying to reconcile with him—trying to draw him back into his covenant with me. He hasn't been faithful, I'm afraid." A spasm of pain crossed her face. "He was tempted, like King David; tempted by the wicked harlots."

Not to mention that he killed poor Tommy, Doyle thought, but I'll not add to her burdens; I've the sense she suspects as much, anyway.

Martina drew a breath, and then continued in a steadier tone, "The wicked harlot repented, though; she repented of her sins, and I will pray for her soul."

Doyle blinked, as it appeared that Martina referred to Dr. James—another wrinkle, atop the mountain of wrinkles that already existed in this case. And if they were indeed lovers, it would explain why D'Angelo had led the coppers to the woman's moldering body.

Trying to hide her distaste, Doyle ventured, "I don't know as her's was a true repentance, Martina; not under duress, like that."

"It was the best that could be hoped for," her companion replied, certain of herself. "Only God can truly judge."

Tentatively, Doyle asked, "And Antonio? Has he repented, too? Her death must have come as a shock to him, and he does have a good wife, tryin' to steer him aright."

"I am working on it," the young woman replied, and pressed her lips together for a moment. "I am working on it more than he is, to tell the truth, but marriage–the same as any sacrament–requires sacrifices." She raised her gaze to Doyle's. "We are sanctified by our sacrifices."

The woman's abject misery was palpable, and Doyle offered gently, "You'll be with him through eternity. There's that, to hope for."

"It is my only comfort," Martina replied quietly, and Doyle could sense that her companion's profound sadness was tinged with a healthy dose of anger and frustration, that the wretched man wasn't paying attention in the here-and-now.

They sat in silence for a few moments, and then Martina said, "It is a shame you are not one of us, Kathleen. Few people understand."

But Doyle had to shake her head in gentle disagreement. "Not me, Martina; I'm one who thinks retribution should be left to God, who's the only one who's *not* lookin' through a glass darkly. Which brings me back to my original request; I'm hopin' we can call a truce, and that you'll promise that

ANNE CLEELAND

you won't be fishin' about in Acton's doin's anymore—it
won't work out well, believe me." Fairly, she added, "And
you mustn't put the DCS in a cleft stick, either—he's on the
side of the angels, too, even if he goes about it a bit
differently."

With a knit brow, Martina regarded Doyle for a moment.
"I'm afraid I am not certain what you are talking about."

Doyle blinked. "Oh; oh—the pastor at Wexton Prison says
that someone's tryin' to winkle-out information from him—
information about Acton's contributions to his ministry. I just
assumed that it must be you."

Slowly, Martina shook her head. "No. But if someone at
the prison is making such an attempt, it may be connected to
Mr. Javid, through his brother. I imagine they are a bit
desperate, with the criminal case pending."

Her tone was somber, and Doyle raised her brows at what
this seemed to imply. "Mr. Javid is involved in *The Curin'
League,* too? He's not a doctor, is he?"

It was Martina's turn to raise her brows. "Oh–I thought
you knew. He owns the laboratory facility that processes the
—the extracts taken from the children. He is an evil man. "
Her features hardened for a moment. *"Their portion will be in
the lake that burns with fire and sulfur."*

"Amen," said Doyle readily. It was interesting that
Javid's awful husband was involved in these matters,
which–while not completely predictable–wasn't exactly
unexpected, either. And—since the man was already in
criminal jeopardy for his involvement in the money-
laundering rig–it would be a simple thing for the CID to
expand that investigation into this one. After all, Mr. Javid
probably had been running the funds on both—the villains
needed a business-front, so as to launder the money. And if

this all came to light, little chance Sir Vikili would have of getting his brother off the hook; with these grisly charges added atop the heap, Mr. Javid was looking at a long stint in prison—small wonder they were looking for leverage, to hold over Acton.

And—come to think of it–Acton may already know about Mr. Javid's connection to *The Curing League*, but he hadn't mentioned it to the wife of his bosom because he didn't want said wife to hear about this ugly operation—he didn't know that Williams had already filled her in. She'd have to warn him anyway, just to make sure he was aware. Faith, Mr. Javid may be the very link they needed to bring the entire operation down in ashes and ruin–a fine bit of fire and sulphur, so to speak, courtesy of the CID.

Doyle was recalled to the conversation when Martina grasped her hand again, to plead with a fixed intensity, "You must allow us to finish our mission, Kathleen. You have influence over your husband, and it is no simple thing, to replace our members." She paused. "And Antonio is my husband, despite his sins—my husband throughout eternity, as you have said yourself."

Mother a' Mercy, thought Doyle in surprise; I don't much like the implication she's making—that Antonio's next on Acton's list of spies to be dealt with. Can it be true? Carefully, she said to the other, "I'll speak to him, but you have to remember that we are police officers, Martina, and we're not allowed to grant any favors. We are sworn to uphold justice, and we have to leave the redemption of souls to the church."

Martina watched her silently, and Doyle had the impression that she was greatly disappointed in Doyle's answer. "I understand, Kathleen."

With all sincerity, Doyle offered, "I'm truly sorry for your troubles, Martina. We can't stop lovin' them, no matter their sins."

"Yes," the other woman replied. "But we can't be made weak. *For neither their silver nor their gold shall be able to deliver them on the day of the wrath of the Lord.*"

"Definitely not," Doyle agreed, and then decided she didn't much like the turn the conversation had taken, what with all this talk about husbands and hellfire. "I suppose we just have to keep prayin' for them."

"And me," Martina said quietly. "Please, pray for me, Kathleen."

CHAPTER 37

"*N*eed 2 talk," Doyle texted her husband, and then thrust her hands in her coat pockets as she hurried home—the rain was picking up again.

And wasn't it just her luck, she thought a bit crossly, that she'd gone to warn-off Martina from mucking about in Acton's doings—being as such muckings tended to be hazardous to one's health—and instead she'd discovered a cascade of dismaying news that seemed to indicate she was well-late off the mark, when it came to preempting those aforesaid dark doings. Which only meant it was business as usual, but it was a bit dismaying, nevertheless.

Blakney-the-ghost had said it was the same old song, and now she knew what he was talking about. Martina's Order was on a crusade to take down *The Curing League*, but they'd been hindered in this aim because they'd made the fatal mistake of going after the illustrious Chief Inspector, on their previous crusade. Said Chief Inspector had immediately set about turning the tables, and had gone all medieval on them by taking out their personnel—Martina had definitely made it sound as though there were more than just the footman at Trestles.

Suddenly struck, she halted mid-step, as raindrops began to patter on the pavement. The limo driver from the concierge service—the Nigerian driver was a religious fellow, they'd said, and he'd up and disappeared. He'd up and disappeared, and the next thing you knew, a loyal Trestles man had been put in his place. It was as clear as glass, now that she realized what to look for.

Blowing out a breath, she started walking again. So; Acton was taking out the people from the Order who'd been spying on him, and meanwhile, Martina was in turn trying to take out *The Curing League*. There was an epic battle, going on behind the scenes, with Acton exacting his revenge and the other side still trying to get their objectives done for their cause. Although—although to be more correct, it wasn't necessarily revenge that Acton was after, but leverage, too. He was making certain the Order didn't dare come forward with what they'd learned about him; they were ruthless people, and he'd said himself that you had to show that you could be just as ruthless, in return.

So; he was serving-up a cold dish of vengeance, but he was also amassing leverage over them—only see how he'd arranged for leverage over Antonio, with the pawn tickets. Although it did seem—it did seem as though Martina was worried that Antonio was slated to be the next Acton-victim who was due to mysteriously disappear. What was the point of leverage, if you were going to kill the man, anyway?

The answer presented itself immediately. Acton would have the pawn tickets, so that Martina didn't dare come after him for Antonio's murder. If she did, he'd expose Antonio's own misdeeds, and in the process shine a bright and unwelcome light on her Order.

Everybody's got leverage, all around, Doyle realized a bit grimly, and so it's a stand-off—a stand-off of revelation murders, so that no one dares come forward to make accusations.

Her mobile pinged. "B home in 10. Meet out front?"

It wants only this; I'm slated for yet another wretched walk, she thought in acute dismay. That miserable man is taking care of me again–mayhap he'll forget to bring an umbrella, and so we'll have to cancel.

She texted her agreement, and then sheathed her mobile, trying to calm down, and pick up the threads of her thoughts. At least some good had come from this meeting-for-tea—an unsolved case was now solved. It was Martina's Order who'd killed Dr. James–Dr. James, who'd apparently been having an affair with Martina's husband, in the time that she could spare from serving-up children for soul-eating. She'd been killed, but not before she'd repented—which explained the burn marks; they'd applied a bit of torture to help her confess the error of her ways, and if *that* wasn't medieval to the core, nothing was.

Blowing out a breath, she hunched her shoulders against the light rain. A thoroughly miserable cast of characters; every single one, and on all sides. Yet despite all this, Martina was truly worried about her husband's fate—she loved him still; so much that she was willing to plead with Doyle to intervene with Acton, and save the wretched man's life.

Mentally, Doyle flinched; I don't much like the parallels, here, she admitted to herself. It's a little too close to home, with a husband who seemed bent on wholesale sinning, and a wife who loves him, regardless. I suppose that's me, she thought a bit bleakly; I'm an aider and abettor, and ever shall be, amen.

Which only reminded her that she mustn't forget to warn Acton about what she'd learned; Martina thought it was Sir Vikili or his loathsome brother, attempting to obtain counter-leverage against him—they must be feeling a bit desperate, to be trying to strong-arm the former DCS.

Again, she halted mid-stride, castigating herself for missing yet another connection that obviously should have been made. Dr. Okafor had described her assailant as a Middle Eastern man, and Doyle had been so busy being worried about hurt feelings with respect to the police codes that she hadn't asked herself a basic-detective question: Did she know of any Middle Eastern men who were ruthless enough to assault a nice person like Dr. Okafor? The answer, of course, was yes; yes, indeed she did, in the form of Mr. Javid. Not to mention that Martina kept bringing-up Mr. Javid in conversation—she'd been doing a bit of probing, herself, and Doyle had been too thick to realize it.

I'll lay the whole before Acton, she decided, even though he probably already knows the whole, which would explain his wariness, lately. After all, he's methodically taking all of them out, with Antonio D'Angelo serving as the final coup of grass, or whatever the phrase was. And in the meantime, he was being extra-cautious, since no one knew better than Acton that a cornered crook was a dangerous crook.

She continued walking briskly, as her building's entrance came into view. It was truly not a surprise, all in all, that the black-hearted Mr. Javid was smack in the midst of this scheme. And—in keeping with the theme of these events—he was yet another husband who served as his wife's cross-to-bear, although that metaphor was perhaps not the most appropriate one, with respect to the Javids.

The concierge clerk saw her coming, and hurried forward to open the door, but she explained that she'd just wait under the canopy, since Acton was due at any moment.

"Yes, ma'am," the fellow said, bringing a respectful hand to his cap's brim, and Doyle was suddenly reminded that their old doorman had mysteriously disappeared, just this morning.

Another one, she realized, in acute dismay. Another one, who'd been well-placed to report on all of our comings and goings. It was disturbing—to think that they'd been surrounded by spies, all this time—but it didn't excuse the scorched-earth manner with which they'd been eliminated. With a long sigh, she turned to face the street, and await her own cross-to-bear.

CHAPTER 38

*A*cton pulled up, and nodded a greeting to the valet as he exited the Range Rover. He'd brought along an umbrella, because of course he had; he was Acton, and he knew she'd forget. He lived to take care of her, even if his version of what that entailed might differ from her own version. It was the one thing she could count on, through thick and thin; her husband lived to serve her, and—ever since the day he'd caught sight of her from his office window —everything he did was to further this aim.

She surprised herself by blinking back tears, as she watched his approach. And—come to think of it—this was where all parallels with Martina's situation were put paid; Acton was devoted to his wife—sometimes over-devoted, truth to tell. It was his saving grace, in a strange way.

He hoisted the umbrella, and she placed her hand in the crook of his arm as they began their walk. "I love you," she said sincerely, looking up to him. "Sometimes I forget to say."

He leaned to kiss her damp head. "You don't have to say; not to me."

"No; and you don't have to say, either, because it's a crackin' wonder that you're willin' to risk water spots on your silk tie, just to take a walk-about with me."

"I am happy to do it," he said, and it was the truth.

She could sense that he was wary, though—he hadn't yet asked what it was she wanted to meet with him about—and so she began, "I had tea with Martina, as I imagine you already know, and I wanted to make certain you were aware that Sir Vikili has been fishin' about for leverage over you, and contactin' the DCS at Wexton Prison."

"I am aware," he acknowledged. "But thank you, all the same."

Trust Acton to have a finger on the pulse of all counter-plots. Thinking she may as well cut to the nub, Doyle continued, "Martina's hopin' you'll refrain from killin' her husband, Michael."

He walked a few steps in silence. As was his usual, he was not going to openly admit to his transgressions—after all, the man's wife tended to be a gabbler. Instead, he said, "D'Angelo is particularly dangerous, because he is unpredictable."

She sighed. "Aye–there's nothin' worse than a Pharisee, unless mayhap it's a Pharisee who's deservin' of a millstone 'round his neck. But the poor woman is that wracked about it, and I do feel sorry for her. She loves the man."

Acton made no response, and so she continued, "It's a sad thing to witness, Michael; she's gone from serene and certain in her faith, to all Book of Revelation, all the time. And it's mostly due to the fact she's a husband who's a prime candidate to be cast into the lake of fire, once we hit the end-times."

"That is indeed regrettable," he agreed. "But he's made his own choices, surely? *The wages of sin is death.*"

"Good one," she said. "Will you look at that; the devil's citin' scripture."

He chuckled, and leaned to kiss her head again. She wasn't fooled, though; he hadn't answered the let's-not-kill-the-wretched-husband question, because he was weighing his options.

Reminded, she said, "Martina's Order was behind the murder of Dr. James, but I imagine you know this also, which is why you were so careful to keep Williams away from the case."

"Yes," he admitted. "He'd already been assigned to the Benardi case before I understood what was at play, and I couldn't allow him to act as CSM on the James case, also, and come to realize that Martina's Order was the prime suspect for both."

"They killed Dr. Benardi too?" Doyle asked in surprise. "So, he was another doctor-gone-wrong?"

"Yes. McGonigal's office manager mentioned that he'd sold her a black-market youth serum."

"Mother a' *Mercy*—these horrid, horrid people," Doyle pronounced in disgust. "I half-hope he was tortured, too."

"Two of his fingers had been broken, ante-mortem."

Doyle nodded in confirmation. "Well, they had to do something different than burns, so that the CID wouldn't make the connection between the cases. You did, of course, and my hat's off to you."

"No doubt they used torture to obtain information about other potential targets."

But Doyle shook her head, and was actually a bit pleased that she knew something that he didn't know. "No, Michael; their aim was redemption, instead. A touch of torture was applied, until the victims repented of their sins, and then they were promptly dispatched, on the hope that this small window of opportunity into a decent afterlife didn't have a chance to close."

Lifting his head, he considered this in mild surprise. "Is this what she told you? It seems a primitive view, for such a sophisticated enterprise."

But Doyle, who'd been steeped in such a view all her life, only replied, "And who's to say they're wrong, my friend? Last Rites are based on a similar theory, after all. It may seem primitive to you, but that's because it's the same way they've been handlin' things ever since it all got started, which was a long time ago. And it only supports my argument that we should try to be the ones to set an example, here, and call a truce from all this scorched-earth-and-molten-seas."

"Very soon," he equivocated.

But Doyle wasn't having it, and shook her head slightly. "Let's lay off, Michael, and try to pretend we understand what is expected of us. Offer an olive branch, and resist sendin' Antonio to his unshriven fate."

He was silent, and she looked up at him to add, "Besides, we don't want to trigger another round of bloodshed just now, what with Sir Vikili's gettin' nervous about his brother's trial—who knows how it would end? You've leverage aplenty over all of them, so let's just stand down for a bit, and give everyone a chance to calm themselves down. This wretched *League* is full of desperate people who are all tryin' to arrange for the least-worst outcome, instead of just takin' their lumps. Mayhap a bit of reflection wouldn't come amiss."

In a mild tone, he suggested, "Perhaps there are times when the least-worst outcome is, in reality, the best outcome."

She sighed. "I suppose that's all a matter of perspective, my friend, and I'm not goin' to get into it with you, yet again. Let's wind-up the conversation with a promise that you'll stand down, husband."

With palpable reluctance, he agreed. "Right, then. For the time being, only–I'll not allow an active threat to you."

"Thank you." She squeezed his arm in appreciation, relieved that she wouldn't be an aider and abettor, this time around, and never let it be said that she didn't use her influence over him for good. "Despite my bein' such an archwife, I truly appreciate you, Michael. Don't ever let me browbeat you into abandonin' ship."

He smiled. "I promise."

They walked for a few minutes in silence, the rain pattering lightly on Acton's umbrella, and Doyle feeling as though she'd scored a major victory, all in all.

"May I ask how you are feeling?"

"You may, mainly because I am feelin' well—fingers crossed. A far sight from last time."

"Perhaps it is because you are eating more fruit, and exercising regularly."

"Good one," she laughed. "Although I tend to think it's because Tommy's not a trouble-causer. Edward's the chief trouble-causer." She considered this. "Tommy will be the loyal supporter to Edward's slashin' buccaneer."

Acton lifted his face to review the tree tops. "The world needs both," he observed.

CHAPTER 39

A shame, that all plans were regrettably on hold. None of them could be trusted.

ary, of course, wanted to attend Colonel Kolchak's funeral; the Home Office had kept a tight lid on what had been revealed about the man's plans for Gemma, and so—as far as anyone knew—he was the victim of the sort of random crime that happened in large cities, from time to time. However, due to the man's connection to a questionable Russian faction, Howard was reluctant to attend the funeral, for fear that it might be grist for the mill with respect to his stance on foreign relations.

Poor Mary, Doyle thought. She loves the man, but this is not easy for her; she's a simple soul, and not one who worries about whether one's actions can be turned to one's disadvantage by an opposing political party. The matter was resolved when Acton suggested Reynolds accompany them as his representative, which cast a mantle of acceptability over Howard's own attendance. As Gemma was deemed too young to go, Doyle had volunteered to watch her during their absence.

With Acton working downstairs in his office, Doyle sat with Gemma at the kitchen table whilst the rain blew against the windows and Edward napped in his nursery. Because they necessarily had to remain quiet, Doyle had hauled out the art supply box, thinking the eventual clean-up would be well-worth an hour of keeping the little girl occupied. As was her wont, Gemma eagerly launched on to a project, her little face a study in concentration.

Watching her idly, Doyle asked, "That's very interestin', Gemma. Can you tell me about it?" She'd already learned that you didn't ask a small child what it was they were drawing, as such a question implied that it wasn't at all clear.

"It's a ghost," Gemma explained.

"He's a lovely shade of purple," Doyle offered.

"It's a girl," she corrected.

"Of course," said Doyle. "My mistake."

"I saw a ghost, that time when I was at your house," the little girl offered, and reached to choose a different crayon.

Doyle stared at her bent head, and for a moment, had trouble finding her voice. "When—when you were stayin' at Trestles? What sort of a ghost, Gemma?"

Her little brow furrowed, Gemma began to scribble with the new color. "He was a knight, like in the fairy-tales my mum reads me. He said Mr. Reynolds should learn Russian."

Thoroughly astonished, Doyle decided to test it out, and ventured, "Was he like a knight in the picture-books? Did he have a shiny suit of armor, and a plume atop his head?"

Gemma paused, thinking about it. "No. I think he was a poor knight. His sword was broken."

"And he *spoke* to you?" The Trestles knight had never spoken to Doyle.

"Uh-huh," the little girl said, preoccupied with her creation.

Doyle could only sit in wonder—fancy that; the Trestles knight had taken an interest in Gemma, but mayhap he was all about helping-out his fellow aristocrats, and the little girl, after all, was as aristocratic as they came.

And Reynolds, of course, would immediately take such a suggestion to heart—especially if Gemma was the one who'd made the request; faith, nothing he'd like better, one would think, than to learn to speak Gemma-the-Romanov's native language—although it was the Colonel's language, too, which could only be seen as a massive strike against it.

Suddenly, Doyle stilled, struck with a thought so cataclysmic that she almost didn't know how to entertain it. With a mighty effort, she managed to gather her wits together, and asked, "Did the Colonel—did Colonel Kolchak know that Reynolds was learnin' to speak Russian, Gemma?"

The girl glanced up briefly, as she reached for the glitter. "I don't know. He didn't speak to Mr. Reynolds very much."

Of course not, thought Doyle, who was trying to think, over the roaring sound in her ears. Because to someone like the Colonel, a servant was the next thing to a non-entity. "*Holy* Mother," she breathed.

"May I have the green one, Lady Acton? It's under your arm."

"Yes—yes; excuse me, Gemma, but I've got to go speak to Lord Acton. Stay here, all right?"

"All right," the little girl said, and didn't look up, as she carefully drew the stem for the glitter-flower.

Doyle hurried down the stairway to Acton's office, and opened the door to slip within, leaning against it after she'd closed it again, and trying to decide what to say.

Understandably alarmed, Acton rose and approached to take her hands in his. "What is it, Kathleen? Everything all right?"

"Holy Mother of God, Michael; I think—Holy *Mother*—I think Reynolds arranged to have Savoie kill the Colonel."

Acton's brows drew sharply together, and he stared at her in profound surprise. "Why would you think this?"

"The fishin' pole. Remember, that we thought Reynolds was contactin' Savoie on the sly, to ask for money?" She swallowed. "What if instead, he was callin' in a favor? He must have found out that Gemma was in danger—remember, he was takin' Russian lessons? He must have overheard the Colonel say somethin' to her."

Quickly deciding that now may not be the best time to speak of ghostly-maneuverings, she explained instead, "Gemma referred to Savoie as the 'gun-man'; mayhap she saw them take one of your rifles from the safe, so as to smuggle it out in the fishin' case." Thinking this over, she knew she was on the right track, and slowly shook her head in astonishment. "*Holy* Mother of God."

Her husband bowed his head, as he held her hands between his. "I would be very much surprised, Kathleen. I don't think Savoie would take such a risk—not without informing me. And why wouldn't Reynolds simply come to me, if he'd heard anything untoward?"

She lifted her face to his. "Can't you see, Michael? It would be too risky. Reynolds couldn't be sure you'd be able to save the day—he'd no real proof, and besides, you haven't any authority, when it comes to Gemma. He couldn't risk failure, and risk that poor Gemma might be snatched away by the Colonel—it was too important. So, he had Savoie perform a revelation murder, and now all cats are thoroughly out of the bag. No one can whisk Gemma away without causin' international repercussions."

Thoughtfully, Acton lifted his head to stare out the window for a moment. "If this was the case, then why wouldn't Savoie tell me?"

This was actually a good point, since Savoie—unlike Reynolds—was much more likely to know that Acton would thoroughly approve of a spot of murder, so as to resolve all problems.

She frowned, trying to come up with a valid reason. "You'd think he'd tell you, but mayhap he didn't want to risk it, either. He's fond of Gemma, too—she's practically a sister to Emile, after all. And if Reynolds swore him to secrecy, about what the Colonel was planning—" She paused. "You've said yourself that Savoie has his own code of honor."

"It is possible," Acton admitted slowly.

In wonder, she shook her head. "Mother a' mercy, Michael; what will you do?"

"Nothing," he replied, and returned his gaze to hers. "I do not dare."

The penny dropped, and Doyle stared at him. "Which is why they used one of your guns in the first place—just in case you found them out."

He bowed his head in acknowledgement. "No doubt."

"Reynolds, of *all* people," she breathed. "Who would have believed it of him?"

But her husband replied, "I cannot fault him. He only did what had to be done."

Stubbornly, Doyle shook her head. "There's always another way, short of murder."

But this declaration fell on deaf ears, which was not much of a surprise. "He'd little choice, and I would suggest we say no more on the subject."

"Holy *Mother*," Doyle breathed, yet again.

CHAPTER 40

A clearing of the air was necessary, so that such a thing did not happen again. Or at least, not without his connivance.

The following day, Doyle eyed her husband sidelong, as he stood at the mirror, preparing to leave the flat. "You're not givin' Reynolds the sack, are you?"

"No," Acton replied with a small smile, as he deftly tied his tie. "I am not."

Doyle had figured-out that something was afoot, being as her husband claimed a need to go out on undisclosed business for a couple of hours, and Reynolds, coincidentally, had asked for the self-same few hours for personal time. This would not in itself be so unusual a coincidence, save for the fact that Reynolds was laboring under a strong and dismayed emotion, and taking great pains to avoid Acton.

Doyle ventured, "What's to-do, then? Can you tell me?"

Acton lifted his chin to smooth his collar down. "Nothing

startling. We will meet, and Savoie will join us for a private discussion."

"Best straighten up and fly right," Doyle guessed, with a grimace. "I'd hate to be in their shoes."

But Acton only disclaimed, "Not at all; we will enjoy a meal, and have a civil conversation. Perhaps there will be some suggestions made on how to go forward, in the future."

"You're knockin' a few heads together," she concluded. "Not that they don't deserve it, I suppose."

Glancing at her, he fastened-in a cuff-link. "Will you need help? I can call Mathis to assist." They were watching Gemma this afternoon, being as the Howards were meeting with diplomatic personnel so as to get everything buttoned-up with respect to the girl's future. Acton had already attended his own meeting, because the Russian stipend was to be placed in a trust, with Acton serving as one of the trustees.

"No—no need to call Mathis, Michael; if I can't take care of two small children by myself, I'm a sorry excuse. May as well get some practice in."

"Callie will start next week, if that is acceptable."

Doyle nodded agreeably. "Indeed, it is; poor Mary's got to be exhausted, after the wretched week she's had. Although everythin's turned out for the best, so I suppose she's got no cause to complain; Gemma will now have an ordinary life, lucky lass."

Amused, his eyes met hers in the mirror, as he shrugged into his suit jacket. "You are perhaps the only person in the world who would think such a thing."

Doyle smiled. "Me, and Mary, too—don't forget her, in your list of people who couldn't care less who's a nob, and who's not."

"You're a nob," he reminded her.

"That I am; and I've the tiara to prove it. Mayhap I'll haul it out, and let Gemma play dress-up."

In response to this teasing, he smiled slightly. "Don't let her paint it purple, is all."

Doyle laughed. "Only imagine Reynold's dilemma, if Gemma wanted to glitter it up a bit–he'd be caught 'twixt two competin' devotions."

"Gemma would win," her husband said. "As events have shown."

A bit sobered by this reminder, she asked, "Any chance they'll trace it back to him?"

"None," he assured her.

"Savoie knows his stuff," she agreed. "Which is a bit alarmin', all in all."

"I suppose in this case, it is more reassuring than alarming."

"Let's not wander back into the same old song, Michael," she warned, mainly because she was having a hard time justifying the idea that things shouldn't have been handled exactly as they had been. The Colonel's was a "just cause" murder, if there ever was one, and—as usual—she felt as though she was playing the part of the scolding schoolmarm in a Wild West tale. As she'd admitted to Blakney's ghost, it wasn't easy to sort it all out, sometimes, and—as Acton had pointed out–who was to say that the least-worst result wasn't the best result, on occasion.

As he slid his billfold into his inside jacket pocket, her husband cautioned, "Stay inside, please."

"The park's too wet for a visit anyway, Michael. Edward will have his nap, and I'll haul out the art supply box for Gemma—not to worry."

He leaned to kiss her. "Try to rest."

"Always," she teased. "Try not to turn Reynolds' hair white."

A short while later, Doyle had set-up Gemma with her art supplies, and was happily foraging in the fridge for an unhealthy snack—the cat was away, after all—when she thought she heard a card in the front door slot. She paused, to see if she was mistaken—unlikely that the meeting was over so quickly; Acton or Reynolds must have forgot something, and come back for it.

Carefully re-shelving the cheesecake, she grabbed the orange juice bottle, instead, and waited a beat or two before straightening up so as to not look as though she'd been caught in the act. She waited another few seconds, but heard nothing further. Curious, she stepped over to take a look toward the flat's entry door. There was nothing there, but her scalp prickled, and so she walked over to look at Edward's monitor, which sat upon the counter.

Ah—the wretched thing was off; surely, she'd turned it on, when she put him down? Now it would be no easy thing, to tiptoe into the nursery so as to turn it on without waking the boyo, but she should, since at any moment now Edward would figure out how to climb out of his crib—it was a wonder that he hadn't, already.

Gemma was preoccupied with her project, and so Doyle headed downstairs toward the nursery, walking softly, and then was brought up short to see that the nursery door was ajar. He's done it, she thought; the buccaneer was officially on the loose. "Edward?" she called out, as she surveyed the hallway. "Back to bed, you."

To her extreme surprise, though, the figure that appeared in the darkened nursery doorway was that of Martina Betancourt.

CHAPTER 41

$\mathcal{D}$oyle tried to hide her astonishment, as she and Martina regarded each other for a long moment. How had the young woman got past the security, downstairs? The answer presented itself almost immediately; the doorman—or former doorman, who must have been her cohort. The fellow must have concocted some sort of security bypass, and that's where she'd managed to lay hands on the flat's card-key, too.

"Explain yourself, please." Doyle was more annoyed than alarmed; she knew with a certainty that Martina was not a danger to her, and never would be. Nevertheless, this turn of events was unexpected, and the young woman was emanating a powerful emotion—anxiety mixed with a stoic fatalism, carefully hidden beneath her usual unruffled demeanor. Stay calm, and don't provoke her, Doyle thought; she's mighty unsettled, for some reason.

"I've come to bring a baby gift," Martina explained calmly. "I didn't want to wake Edward by ringing the doorbell, and I thought you'd be down here, in the nursery. I'm sorry I startled you."

This wasn't true, but Martina indeed held a small, elegant gift box.

"Let's go upstairs," Doyle said firmly. "And I will hear a better explanation from you, my friend."

"Yes—of course. I am sorry," Martina offered, and moved into the hallway.

A bit surprised that Edward hadn't been awakened by their voices, Doyle stepped inside the door to check on him, but was instead horrified to behold a sleepy Edward being held in the arms of Antonio D'Angelo.

Reacting on instinct, she advanced on him so as to seize her son, but D'Angelo swung him away, and warned, "Stay back; we've got a gun." He looked over to Martina, who dutifully pulled a revolver from the gift box, and leveled it on Doyle.

Doyle stood very still, her hands raised, and tried to think, over the panic that threatened to overwhelm her. Stay calm, she cautioned herself; there is something very strange going on, here—the emotions between these two are all crossed-up, and Martina doesn't mean me any harm, despite the weapon. Think, Doyle; what is your strategy?

Antonio said to Martina in an accusatory tone, ""You said they were all gone, and it would just be the nanny."

Martina replied, "I was mistaken; I thought she'd left."

This, interestedly enough, wasn't true—Martina knew Doyle would be here, and in a strange way it was reassuring; Martina must had led Antonio here for some reason, but what was she hoping Doyle would do? Despite brandishing the gun, the woman wasn't a danger—so, what was afoot? Mayhap Martina wanted Doyle to arrest her wretched husband, and thus put an end to his wholesale sinning spree. This, of course, was easier said than done, since she was out-numbered and out-gunned, being as her own stupid gun was sitting snug and sound in the stupid gun-safe, because the last thing you'd expect was armed blacklegs, roaming about in the nursery.

I wish I knew what my lines are, Doyle thought; but mainly, I've got to get Edward away from this man. Best start talking, and try to de-escalate the situation.

As calmly as she was able, she began, "What is it, that you're hopin' to accomplish, here? You're already on the hook for at least three major crimes, so far today, and if you're thinkin' of kidnappin' Edward, you'll have to shoot me first, which would count as a fourth and a fifth. And believe me, if that happens, there won't be a corner in hell for you to hide–but I imagine you already know that." Best remind them that her husband was not the forgive-and-forget type; after all, they'd already a body-count to show for it.

Edward, now having awakened sufficiently, was taking great exception to being held by a strange man, and began squirming as only a toddler can squirm when he didn't wish to be held. Wrestling with him, the exasperated man said to Martina, "Here, you take him; give me the gun."

"No," Martina said. "Just put him down—he's not going anywhere." To Doyle, she said, "Keep your hands where I can see them, please."

"Let's come to terms," Doyle said firmly, as Edward promptly attached to her legs, wanting to be lifted. "You want leverage over Acton; fine, let's go negotiate—" she caught herself before she said upstairs–faith, Gemma was up there, and she couldn't let them know there was another hostage to be had "—in Acton's office, down the hall. I'm sure we can come to terms."

Thinking furiously, she tried to decide what was best to do; ideally, she would whisk the children into the lift and initiate the alarm, but she was not certain how she could maneuver the situation so as to allow such a course of action —especially since they didn't know about Gemma, up on the main floor. I'll pull Edward into the lift with me, and sound the alarm, she decided; I can call security about Gemma once I have us both secure—it's my only option.

"No—we can't allow her near the lift," Martina calmly advised her husband. "It has a safe-room feature."

Thoroughly dismayed, Doyle wished she could catch a better idea of what Martina expected from her—the woman wasn't giving off any clues, and apparently she didn't want to see Doyle rescued. Yet, Doyle still had the sense that the woman was keyed-up, and grimly resolved–but resolved for what? Were they planning to ambush Acton, when he returned? Surely, they must know he'd be armed.

I've got to figure out a way to warn Acton, and to keep Edward out of the crossfire, she decided; they may think they'll use the boyo as a shield, but they can't appreciate how hard it is to catch him when he doesn't want to be caught. Hopefully I can distract them, so that he can dart away, and give Acton some firing-clearance.

But as it turned out, they were not awaiting Acton's return at all; instead, a third intruder appeared at the nursery door, and Doyle had to stifle her dismay at beholding Mr. Javid.

CHAPTER 42

The Middle Eastern man was all frustrated rage, and he addressed the other two after giving Doyle only a cursory glance. "His guns are locked down," he said. "He must have changed the security code."

No doubt thanks to Reynolds and Savoie, thought Doyle; thank heaven for small favors. It seemed that these people had planned to seize some of Acton's illegal arsenal, and to also take Edward, for good measure. Talk about leverage, that would be the topper; except—except that this plan did not seem to be Martina's plan; Martina who knew Doyle would be present, and who had lied to her husband about it.

"No matter," said Martina. "Go—keep watch, while we secure these two."

Faith, I hope Mr. Javid doesn't see Gemma, Doyle thought, trying to hide this concern as she watched the man slip through the door; mayhap he'll not venture into the kitchen, and mayhap she'll stay quiet, so that he isn't alerted.

"We're going to take them both?" Antonio asked Martina.

"It complicates things, that the wife's here. It's going to be harder to keep it quiet—she's very recognizable."

"Yes, we'll take them both. We've no real choice," Martina replied, and it wasn't true. To Doyle, she said, "Pick him up, please."

In the small silence, Doyle bent to gather-up Edward, carefully hiding her relief. Good–it seemed that Martina had some sort of plan, and anyways, Trenton would be at his post downstairs, so that Doyle would be able to signal to him. Since she held Edward, all would be well.

But matters took an unexpected turn, as Martina stepped before Doyle and moved her weapon's muzzle over to her own husband. "You must repent of your sins, Antonio," she said with a quiet calmness. *"Remember, therefore, from where you have fallen, and repent."*

Both Doyle and D'Angelo stood in astonished silence for a few seconds.

"Quickly," Martina urged, and lifted the weapon slightly.

She wants him to repent, Doyle realized, and then she'd going to kill him, hoping to squeeze him into heaven, by hook or by crook. And I imagine I'm here as witness, so as to raise a "just cause" defense—after all, the man's threatening my child.

Antonio found his voice, and blustered in outrage, "What nonsense is this?" Doyle was not fooled; he was in an urgent state of panic.

Martina intoned, *"In nómine Patris, et Fílii, et Spíritus Sancti, exstinguátur in te omnis virtus diáboli per impositiónem–"* and Doyle felt a chill; she didn't know the Latin, but she recognized the opening phrases from the Last Rites.

Antonio changed tactics, having apparently decided it

would be better to wheedle than to bluster, and offered in a gentler tone, "Come; don't be a fool, Marty. I love you."

Doyle duly noted that this was untrue, even as she tried to decide what was best to do in this strange situation—she was hampered by the fact she held Edward in her arms and was reluctant to let him go—Javid lurked somewhere, outside. I should wait, she decided; I should wait to see how this plays out, and try not to alert Javid that his cohorts were at odds, because he's the one who has the most to lose from this unexpected turn of events. And mainly, I need to get hold of that gun, because whoever winds up with the gun is going to win this.

"--*mánuum nostrárum, et per invocatiónem gloriósae et sanctae Dei Genitricis Virginis Mariea*," Martina intoned in an expressionless voice.

"Marty," D'Angelo said softly, pleading with her. "Marty, you can't mean it." With an outstretched arm, the man took a slow step in her direction, and without hesitation, Martina fired into his hand.

D'Angelo cried out and retreated, as he pressed his bleeding hand with the other and bent over forward, in acute pain. Edward, startled by the noise, immediately began to wail.

"Don't move," Martina cautioned in an even tone, and then repeated, "Repent of your sins, Antonio."

But D'Angelo seemed well-aware that his repentance would only seal his fate, and so instead, he began to bargain with his wife. "I'll change, Marty—I swear by St. James. We'll go back, and things will be as they used to be; remember? Remember Ciudad Rodrigo, and the river house?"

"*Ne reminiscáris, Domine, delicta fámuli tui , neque vindictam sumas de peccátis ejus.*" Martina intoned, unmoved.

This is not going to end well, Doyle thought in dismay, and tried to decide what was best to do—her priority was the children, but even if their odds were better with Antonio dead, she should at least make an attempt to prevent his murder—and above all, she needed to get hold of the gun.

"Martina," she interrupted quietly. "'Tis a grave sin, you're contemplatin'—the gravest sin of all, to take God's place. Who's to say he hasn't a purpose to be served here, despite all the sins he's committed? Only look at the DCS, and how his ashes were turned to beauty, within prison walls."

But Martina didn't waver, and only said to her husband, "*Salvum fac servum tuum–*"

With more urgency, Doyle pled, "Martina—please, please reconsider; it is not for us to decide such things. Let me call the Met, and we'll straighten it all out in Detention."

"Yes," Antonio agreed a bit desperately. "Look, I'm sorry—"

But since these words were probably the best she could hope for, Martina immediately took the opportunity to shoot her husband dead, with two more rapid shots into his chest. "*Amen,*" she said dispassionately, and watched as the man collapsed to the floor.

Doyle decided there was no time like the present, and hurled Edward at the distracted woman with all the force she could muster, causing Martina to stumble forward so that Doyle leapt upon her, landing hard atop the woman's back. Whilst Doyle pinned the arm that held the gun to the floor, Edward scrambled away, wailing in protest at such rough treatment.

"Let go of the gun," Doyle ordered in her best police-officer voice. "I don't want to choke you out, but I will."

"All right—all right," Martina gasped, but Doyle had glanced up, because suddenly Edward went silent, and was watching behind Doyle with wide eyes.

Instinctively, she rolled to the side as Mr. Javid's fist came down where her head used to be, the blow falling on Martina's head, instead. Immediately, Doyle lunged for Martina's gun but so did Javid, leaping atop Doyle with the full force of his weight so that she was sandwiched between the two, and the breath was knocked out of her body.

Whilst Doyle croaked and gasped for breath, the man wrested the gun from Martina's limp hand, and then brought the butt of the pistol down on the woman's head with a vicious blow, so that she went completely limp.

I've got to move, thought Doyle frantically, willing her gasping body to respond. I've got to move, and keep Edward safe; think, think—he's not going to kill either of us—he needs us for leverage—especially now, with all his plans in ruins.

This theory was borne out almost immediately, as Mr. Javid roughly scooped up Edward, and backed away toward the door, holding the gun on her. "You'll be hearing from me," he said. "Tell him I'll be in touch."

"You can't think you'll get away," Doyle rasped, her voice coming back as she gripped the crib's rails, and pulled herself to her feet. "Listen to me—you've better options."

Unhappy with this rough stranger, Edward reached out for her to take him, but his captor jerked him back, and slapped the boy's hand with the gun's barrel.

Tamping down her fear, Doyle managed to take a shuddering breath, and speak over her son's outraged wailing. "You should turn yourself in. You can blame everythin' on D'Angelo, now, and there's no one to say you nay; it will give your brother somethin' to work with. It's your only play—you know that Acton's not going to take kindly to any of this."

"No, but I will have his son," Mr. Javid pointed out, with an unpleasant, gloating twist to his mouth. "He doesn't dare move against me, not if he wants to ever see him again—or see what's left of him, anyway."

Rather than dissolve in horror, this threat only made Doyle feel an eerie calm. No one's going to eat Edward's soul, she thought; not on my watch. Stay steady, and do what you do best, Doyle—start talking. You stalled a man once, to gain an advantage; do it again. Think, think; what do you know about this blackheart? He treats his wife terribly, so no point in bringing her up. He's not afraid of Acton—more's the pity —and he couldn't care less about the redemption of souls. I've nothing I can offer—

"Say goodbye to your mother," Javid said into Edward's ear with an unpleasant sneer, and Doyle had the impression the man was very much enjoying her horror and helplessness.

"Wait," she said suddenly. "Wait; I have your family's necklace."

He paused in surprise, and she made a circular gesture with the hands. "I do; it's a collar of blue sapphires." She paused, trying to remember what Acton had told her. "It's from the Regentry era, or something—and the stones are from Burma. If you let Edward go, I will hand it over, and I'll not say another blessed word about any of this; my hand on my heart."

A calculating look had come into the other's eyes. "Show me."

"Not until you promise you won't take Edward, and you

will leave us alone," Doyle warned. "Upon your sacred honor."

He bent his head, as though considering. "I promise," he agreed, and it was a lie. With a show of compliance, he lowered Edward to the floor, and Doyle resisted the urge to snatch-up her son; she needed her hands free, and she'd only get one, brief chance.

"The necklace is in a safe-box, in the bedroom." With a firm stride, she walked past him toward the master suite.

CHAPTER 43

*D*oyle headed straight for the gun-safe in her bedroom, and decided she should pretend she truly believed that a blackheart like Mr. Javid would willingly relinquish his valuable little hostage, even though such a thing was patently untrue. Her main fear was that the boyo would follow her into the bedroom, and come within arm's reach of the man again, but it couldn't be helped, which was why she moved swiftly—she didn't dare look back, and thankfully Edward had gone quiet.

"I knew you were a sensible man," she offered in a placating tone. "And besides, the last thing you'd want to do is to try to manage a car, with Edward sittin' on your lap." She turned to throw a nervous, conciliatory smile over her shoulder.

"Very true," he replied, and Doyle knew he was very much enjoying her craven behavior, and the fact that she wouldn't be gaining anything by it.

She opened the armoire where the small, black gun-safe

sat, and pressed the entry code. Fortunately, he couldn't resist leaning over her shoulder to watch her actions, and so when she reached within to grasp her gun, she was able to swing around and fire, point blank, directly into him.

She'd hoped to hit the center of his chest, but didn't have the luxury of taking a moment to aim, and so she was slightly off-target, hitting him in the right side of his ribcage as he cried out in agony, and instinctively twisted away. She tried to follow up with a second shot, but it went wild, because he'd desperately lunged his doubled-up body into her, so as to pin her with a thump against the armoire. With a frantic gesture, he grabbed for her arm with his off-hand and then slammed her wrist repeatedly into the armoire's edge, causing her to drop the gun, and she immediately retaliated by bringing her knee up into to his groin with all the strength she could muster. She was off-balance, and therefore the blow wasn't a mighty one, but nevertheless, he grunted in pain and was staggered for a moment.

It was a brief respite, but it allowed for an opening to retrieve the gun from the floor. Unfortunately, her left hand was numb from its ill-treatment, and so she lost valuable time as she frantically switched to grope with the other hand.

Seeing her intent, her assailant fell atop her crouched figure, groaning as he impacted his injured ribs, and pinned her to the floor with the weight of his body as he groped for Martina's gun at his own waist, unable to move quickly because he, like her, was forced to use his off-hand.

She drove her elbow as hard as she could up into his right ribcage, and this brutal treatment made him pause and groan between clenched teeth, so that she had the opportunity to throw him off, and roll away. I've got to get to the lift, she thought—I don't know as I can handle the gun with my right hand, and above all, I've got to keep him from nabbing Edward. With this in mind, she scrambled out of the suite, and took off at a dead run down the hallway.

The hallway, however, was surprisingly empty, and she paused, panting in dismay. Where was Edward? She couldn't go into the lift without him, but he was nowhere to be seen— the wretched boyo must have taken the opportunity to clamber up the stairs. Frantic, she began to race up the stairway only to be grabbed by an ankle and dropped in place, hard.

She twisted to kick at her assailant, but he hung on to her ankle like grim death, and pulled her toward him on the stairs, the effort making him groan aloud. He has to use the same hand in order to shoot me, she thought; I'll knock him back when he lets go.

But—no doubt anticipating exactly this strategy—he released her ankle so as to stagger down a few stairs, gasping and nearly bent double, and pull Martina's gun from his waistband. "Where is the boy?" he rasped.

Merciful Mother, thought Doyle as she pressed her lips together and gauged the distance between them—please save my Edward—

Suddenly, a loud alarm sounded, and Mr. Javid looked up in surprise. Doyle took this opportunity to lunge at him as hard as she could, tackling him backward so that they landed in a heap at the foot of the stairs.

The gun, she thought, and managed to pull it from his hand as he writhed in agony. Holding it between both hands as best she could, she fired at his head, point blank, but heard only an empty chamber. Saints, she thought in acute dismay; no more ammo–Martina must have shorted it, just to be cautious.

Thoroughly frustrated, she backed away, trying to decide what to do—she could run and retrieve her own gun from the bedroom, but decided—since the alarm continued to sound—she'd need only another minute or two before help arrived. Her assailant made a groaning effort to prop himself up on an elbow, and so with both hands, she brought the butt of the gun down as hard as she could on the soft spot at his temple —the blow not as strong as she'd like, but it was sufficient, and her attacker immediately went limp.

The alarm continued to sound as Doyle raced up the stairs and toward the lift, cradling her numb hand in her good one. Martina must have taken Edward in there—she'd known about the security feature—and thank heaven for small favors, even though it probably meant that the fair Doyle would now have to refrain from strangling the woman with her bare hands.

Doyle quickly typed-in the security code, and the alarm abruptly ceased, as the lift ascended to the floor, the doors quietly sliding open.

But the sight that met Doyle's eyes was not Martina at all; instead, Gemma stood in the corner of the lift, her eyes wide as she held Edward's hand. A kitchen stool shared the small space with the two children.

"Gemma," Doyle breathed in wonder. There'd been no need to panic, and no need to sort out her allegiances to Martina, after all. No need, because it seemed that Gemma had quietly led Edward into the lift, and then had ascended to the upper floor so that she could drag-in a kitchen stool, and thereby reach the safety toggle. Because Gemma remembered that it was there; Gemma noticed everything.

The emotions of the past half-hour suddenly overwhelmed her, and Doyle sank to her knees, as she gathered-up the little girl in a heartfelt embrace. "Oh Gemma," she whispered. "*Go raibh maith agat; go raibh míle maith agat.*"

"Watch out, Lady Acton," Gemma warned, trying to wriggle-out from her arms. "Edward keeps trying to push the buttons."

CHAPTER 44

Suddenly, Doyle could hear urgent activity at the entry, and then she was treated to the blessed, blessed sound of her husband's voice. "Kathleen?" He was frantic, poor man.

"Da," proclaimed Edward, looking up with a happy smile.

"We're clear," Doyle called out. "We're in the lift."

"You're bleeding on my dress, Lady Acton," Gemma whispered, almost apologetically.

"Not my blood," Doyle assured her, and then mustered up a reassuring smile for her husband, who'd appeared in the lift's doorway.

"Do you need an ambulance?" he asked as he crouched before her, his worried gaze assessing.

"I'm fine," she said, pronouncing it "foine". "Although we've a DB downstairs, and two wounded—Javid's at the foot of the stairs, so best secure him first."

"Weapons?" he asked.

"There's one on the stairs, but it's out of ammo. And mine's on the bedroom floor, somewhere."

Over his shoulder, Acton glanced at Trenton, who immediately turned to head toward the stairway. Acton then rose to address the concierge clerk and the security guard who'd come in behind him, both men doing only a fair job of hiding their extreme alarm. "We'll need an ambulance and a field unit. Everyone wait outside, please, whilst I secure the scene. If you would take the children out in the hall? But no one leaves this floor until I give the all-clear."

He's that upset, poor man, Doyle thought with a stab of pity; his tone is clipped, the way it gets when he's teetering on the edge. Best let him know that everything's going to be all right.

Edward had already decided that his father should lift him up, and so the boy voiced his extreme displeasure at being transferred to the concierge clerk, but immediately became more cooperative when he was offered the man's patent leather hat, as they made their way over to the entry door.

Acton helped Doyle over to the kitchen table, and saw her seated. "May I leave you for a moment? You are all right?"

With a small smile, she assured him, "I am. I've hurt my wrist, but I don't think it's broken. And Martina's the one who killed her husband, just so you know it wasn't me."

She watched him disappear down the stairs as he spoke on his mobile, issuing orders to Williams. "We'll need a team," he said. "It may need special handling."

Naturally, thought Doyle; the last thing Acton would want is a gigantic scandal—especially one that might raise some alarming questions about the D'Angelos and what their mission was. Although with this latest disaster, they may have no mission left, at all. Tentatively, she tried to bend the fingers on her left hand and then jumped, when she heard the sound of a gunshot.

With some alarm, she half-rose but then stilled when she saw Acton emerge from the stairway, carrying her gun in his handkerchief.

"We'll need your prints," he said, as he handed the weapon to her. "Your right hand, please."

So; Acton had apparently decided he'd rather not entertain a loose-end in the form of Mr. Javid, and so had shot the man with no further ado. "Shouldn't I have had a vote, husband?" she asked a bit crossly, as she duly took the weapon and held it in her hand.

"No," he replied shortly.

He is indeed ruthless, she thought; and I can't say that I fault him, in this particular instance. "D'you want a report?"

"If you wouldn't mind. What happened in the nursery?"

"Well, they were tryin' to take Edward, but I think it was a false-flag by Martina; I think she just wanted to kill Antonio, with me as witness." Doyle paused, thinking about it. "She wanted him to repent, so that she could kill him whilst he was clean-of-soul, but she also wanted to be able to confess a justified murder, and thus not jeopardize her own soul. So she set it up so that he'd be shot, whilst trying to steal Edward."

Acton's brows rose as he considered this. "Extraordinary."

She nodded. "I think if she was honest with herself, it wasn't as much a 'just cause' murder as it was a 'revelation' murder. Antonio's sins will be exposed for all the world to see–there's a big element of revenge here, even though she'd never admit to it."

Tentatively making a fist with her fingers, she considered this. "Faith, when you think about it, Martina brought about her own private apocalypse—an end to her career, redemption for Antonio, and all of it mixed-in with bloody vengeance. It was a 'Revelation' murder, in more ways than one." She looked up at him. "Best put some flex cuffs on her, Michael before she decides to open the Seventh Seal, and burn the flippin' buildin' down."

"She's been secured," he said.

There was a nuance in his tone that gave her pause. "You didn't kill her too, Michael?"

He admitted, "I would like to, but I fear you'd object."

Doyle made a face. "She'd probably welcome it, truth be told—she's that world-weary. The only reason she hasn't killed herself already is because it's a grievous sin." Reaching over lay a hand on his arm, she said, "I know you're that angry, my friend, but let's call a truce, and cry peace. No more bloody scalps–we've won this round, in spades."

Any response was interrupted when his phone pinged, as the field team announced its arrival. He spoke to them briefly, and then rose to his feet. "If you would wait in the guest suite with the children, Kathleen? I'm reluctant to allow them downstairs as yet, and so I've called-in Mathis to assist you."

She nodded her agreement. "D'you mind if I shower, or do I have to be processed?"

"Bag your clothes, is all. And we should also see to your hand—I will call McGonigal."

She teased, "Tell him no one's pokin a needle in me for love or money."

"Right," he said, and scrolled for the number.

He's simmering—almost a'boil, she thought, watching him. And utterly frustrated, since there's no one left standing, to lay waste to.

CHAPTER 45

*L*ate that night, Doyle awoke, mainly because she was having trouble finding a comfortable sleeping position. She couldn't take a pain pill due to her pregnancy, and her poor body was protesting its rough usage from the afternoon. To the good, McGonigal had determined she need only strap a brace on her abused wrist for a few days, since no bones had been broken.

Acton wasn't in bed beside her, which was a shame, since he was that tired, poor man. After he'd helped Williams process the scene—even though he wasn't supposed to, according to protocol—she'd overheard more than a few phone conversations where he'd been adamant about keeping the tale under wraps as much as possible, being as he didn't want anyone else to get the bright idea that Edward was a valuable target. Thus far, it seemed to have worked; Doyle had been asked to sign a statement containing a much-abbreviated version of events, but there'd been no inquiries from the press.

Quietly, she slid out of bed and exited into the hallway—grimacing a bit, as she walked past the stairway with its memories—and saw that Acton's office door was closed. Mentally, she girded her loins; yet again, it was time to talk her volatile husband down from the ledge, and so she pushed the door open, and went inside.

He was drinking, of course, and sat at his desk cradling a glass, a half-empty bottle of scotch at his elbow. He did not look up at her entry.

"Ho," she said softy, and sat down on a chair across from him, pulling up her legs beneath her. "I miss you."

"I am not good company, Kathleen."

"Neither am I. I'd give a week's pay for a long pull o' that."

This turned the trick—directing his attention to her hurts—and he lifted his face in concern. "Tim said you may take an over-the-counter acetaminophen, as long as you are careful about the dose."

She shrugged, and ran a finger across her wrist-brace. "I'd rather not; poor Tommy's had enough to deal with, this day."

He regarded her for a long moment, and then said exactly what she'd expected he'd say. "It was my fault. I should have known they would be desperate." He paused, and then put down the glass so that he could lean back in the chair, and press the heels of his hands against his eyes. "I'd asked them to change all security protocols in the building, after the doorman was replaced, but they hadn't completed the task, as yet."

"Well, the only reason they got past the desk was because Martina had visited us before," she pointed out. "And so I imagine they weren't too worried. And who was to know, that Martina was hell-bent on settin'-up a righteous shootin' for her miserable husband; that type of thing is hard to game-plan against—even for someone as long-headed as you are."

But he was adrift in remorse, and would not be dissuaded. "You had the sense that she was on the verge. I should have listened to you."

Doyle tilted her head in acknowledgement. "That I did—only because she was that wracked about her awful husband, poor thing. Promise me, Michael–your hand on your heart–that you won't go off on a rampage, like he did. Oh—oh, wait—it's too late; that horse is already well-out of the barn."

This teasing—which was rather daring, all things considered—had the desired effect, and a ghost of a smile played around his lips. Apropos of nothing in particular, he said, "I believe it will be Mr. Javid, who will now bear the blame for both Rizzo's and Tommy Dryden's deaths."

She raised her brows. "Thank you kindly, Michael; I appreciate it, and I imagine Tommy Dryden does too, wherever he is. I wonder what Sir Vikili will have to say about it?"

"He has no standing to object," Acton replied evenly.

The implication contained in his words made her lift her brows in surprise. "Faith, Michael—d'you truly think Sir Vikili was aware of his brother's dark doin's? I suppose its possible–he's mighty long-headed, himself. But if he did, he had the same dilemma that Martina had; you're bound to the villain, and so you dither about whether you should take action to stop him, even as you resent the fact he's put you in this position to begin with."

Leaning forward, he absently fingered his glass. "One might say that is your dilemma, also."

"One might," she agreed. "But don't think I haven't noticed that you've refrained from sayin' 'I told you so', and remindin' me that I should have just let you take care of stupid Antonio in your own inminnatible—intimimable—"

"Inimitable."

"Thank you; in your own inimitable way."

He could not disagree, and lifted his gaze to meet hers. "I should not have been persuaded by you, perhaps. You are often very naïve, Kathleen."

But she reminded him, "Not so naïve that I don't find you out, every single time, my friend—which is the only reason I'm even given a chance to make a pitch to your better angel. That can't be a coincidence—that I always find you out. There's not a soul alive who'd say I was long-headed."

The dark gaze held hers. "No. It does give one pause."

She nodded. "I may be naïve, but I do know there's evil in the world—faith, we see it every day, in our business. I suppose I just don't see it the same way that Martina does—a fallen world, all hellfire and brimstone. There's too much beauty—too many people, doin' the right thing."

He tilted his head. "A strange thing for you to say, just now."

"Well, I'm not such a saint that I'm goin' to muster up a shred of remorse that these two are dead—a good riddance, in fact."

"A very good riddance," he agreed, and ironically lifted his glass in a toast.

She quirked her mouth. "I'm sorry that I've interrupted your well-deserved tipple with a philosophy-speech; shame on me."

With a deliberate motion, he set the glass down. "I must apologize, Kathleen; I should be stronger."

"Nonsense, husband; you've had a rough go, and deserve every blessed ounce."

His gaze on the glass, he quietly replied, "Don't say it; not after your ordeal."

They were wandering back into black-mood Acton territory, and so she decided she'd best keep him talking. "I was that happy to see the cavalry at the door, I must say. How did you get here quicker than the coppers?"

His chest rose and fell. "I check-in with the nursery monitor's feed on my phone from time to time, and I noticed it went dark. I couldn't raise your mobile, and so I called the concierge to have him check-in with you. He assured me that all was well, and that you'd called down not five minutes before, so as to admit your visitors."

Poor man, she thought in dismayed silence; lucky he didn't crash his fine car in his race to get home. Lightly, she offered, "It's gettin' to be old hat, these life-or-death struggles. At least no one will be givin' me another commendation, thank God fastin'."

"Don't say," he said abruptly; "I can't bear to think about it."

She leaned forward, and gently put her hand on his forearm. "Of course, I'm goin' to 'say', husband. You get to drink your scotch, and I get to do gallows humor. It's a trick o' the Irish, so as to cope with all the beat-downs we've had to take at the hands of the British nobility."

But he would not be teased, and replied rather abruptly, "I've been thinking that we should move from here. A gated estate, on the outskirts."

Lifting her brows, she stared at him in astonishment. "What's this? For heaven's sake, Michael, what's another couple o' ghosts? If you'd any idea how many murderous ghosts are lurkin' about at Trestles, your eyes would start clear out of your head." With mock-annoyance, she leaned back and crossed her arms. "Mother a' mercy, but you're a fearful *gombeen*, and I'm ready to wash my hands o' ye."

There was a small pause. "You are extraordinary," he said.

"Fah—don't be mawkish, husband; else I'll have to start hidin' the scotch. When I'm having a weak spell, you take care of me, and I do the same for you—that's how this marriage business works. Although it didn't work out so well for the D'Angelos, so I suppose the exception proves the rule." Reminded, she told him, "Martina hinted that her husband was havin' an affair with Dr. James—I wonder if that's what turned him into a black-hat?"

"Often a motivator," he agreed.

Doyle sighed in sad acknowledgement. "So; it comes down to sex—as it always does. That, and money; you'd think someone would come up with somethin' else, once in a while."

"Love," he offered.

She eyed him. "Doesn't that count as 'sex'?"

But he shook his head, slightly. "Not always. Reynolds killed the Colonel out of love for Gemma." He paused. "Martina killed her husband out of love."

Doyle made a derisive sound. "More out of an 'unsound mind', I think—it wasn't love. A very wise teacher once reminded me that *love bears all things, believes all things, hopes all things, and endures all things.*"

Her husband tilted his head in mild disagreement. "I would think that the nature of love is in the eye of the beholder. And I will point out that you tend to see things in black and white, with no shades of grey."

With a wry smile, she countered, "I think that's because it's very easy to get bogged down in those shades of grey, my friend, and wind up so paralyzed that you're unable to move.

But I will give you your point; love is the greatest motivator of all."

"As I know well," he said.

Touched, she took his hand. "Me, too. Come along; off to bed, now."

CHAPTER 46

*D*oyle's restless night was to be interrupted yet again, when she entertained another ghost-visit from Bill Blakney, who stood before her once more in his incongruous formal clothes.

His chin raised, he regarded her with a distinct air of vindication, and so she acknowledged, "Aye; one of your dreaded Russians has been neatly dispatched, and I managed to stay out of it, just as you wanted. But it wasn't because I figured-out what the two of them were up to; instead, I thought the fishin' case was to pass-along some money, and I didn't want to embarrass Reynolds."

"Doesn't matter why," he pronounced, with an air of satisfaction. "All's well that ends well."

"Well, it didn't end well for the Colonel," Doyle countered. "A man's dead, and the two of them are goin' to get clean away with plottin' a murder. It rankles me."

"It shouldn't," he countered with just a touch of

belligerence. "Cripes; you should have stayed out of the other fuss, too—it would have saved you a bad moment or two."

Slowly, she shook her head. "No—I can't be sorry that I asked Acton to stand down. I can't stay out of it–I can't just let Acton run amok. That's my cross-to-bear, even though you might think me naïve, too."

The ghost made a derisive noise. "There's some that deserve killing."

Doyle realized that perhaps this was an indelicate topic, considering her companion had been unjustly murdered, himself, and so she only offered, "You should have belonged to Martina's Order; you'd have fit right in."

But the ghost shook his head with a decisive movement. "Not me; I'm not one to hold a grudge."

Doyle frowned at this characterization. "It wasn't a *grudge* exactly; she's more a zealot, and thinks she's doin' holy work."

He snorted at her ignorance. "You're being naïve, again. It's a grudge. And once you've done one, the next is easier, and the next one easier still."

There was a small pause. "Acton can hold a mighty grudge," she mused. "He can hold a grudge like nobody's business."

"Ha," the ghost exclaimed, with a great deal of satisfaction. "And good on him. I'm only happy my shop could help him out."

Thus reminded, she offered with all sincerity, "Thank you, for remindin' me about the necklace, Mr. Blakney. Acton may have been usin' it to set a trap for Mr. Javid, but I'm the one who caught him in it, and it worked like a charm, I must say—winged him pretty bad, so we were more evenly matched."

Her companion nodded. "You can go claim it, now—the idiots running the place don't even know that it's real."

She made a face. "I don't know—I'm a bit superstitious about it. Mayhap I'll just give it back to Sir Vikili, and wash my hands of it."

The ghost cocked a knowing brow. "Your husband likes it. He'll not want to give it up."

With some dismay, Doyle asked, "He won't?"

"He likes his trophies."

With a sigh, she acknowledged, "Yes, I suppose he does—it's all very medieval. You'd think everyone would have got over all that, by now."

He shrugged. "The same old song."

She glanced up at him. "It's a bit discouragin', actually. I keep tryin', but I don't know as I've done much good, all in all."

The ghost chided, "Now, now; chin up, and none of that talk. You can't see what might have been."

She conceded "I suppose that's true. Small comfort, sometimes."

At these words, her companion glanced over his shoulder, and this time, the door behind him opened to reveal a bride, floating toward them in the profound stillness. She was serenely beautiful, in her ethereal white dress, her face obscured by a gossamer veil.

As she passed by, Doyle suddenly recognized the silent figure. Why—why it's *Gemma*, she thought in wonder; its little Gemma, and only see how beautiful she's grown-up to be.

As the bride glided through an open set of double-doors, Doyle managed to catch the barest glimpse of what lay beyond; a crowded church, with a very familiar figure, standing in readiness at the altar. A young man she'd seen in a dream once before, with chestnut hair, and oh-so-familiar green eyes. Her favorite buccaneer, awaiting his bride.

Doyle's throat closed with emotion, as the doors soundlessly closed shut. It's just as well that I can't tell Acton, she thought; he puts altogether too much faith in bloodlines, and he'd only be unsufferable, if that's the right word.

Finding her voice, she whispered to her companion, "She's so lovely."

"That she is," Blakney agreed gruffly, and she could sense the bittersweet emotions he was trying to conceal, beneath his tough-guy persona. "She'll not remember me, of course." He paused, and then continued in a stoic manner, "It's for the best."

Gently, Doyle offered, "We'll all try to love her as much as you do."

EPILOGUE

$\mathcal{D}$oyle sat at her desk, looking at the booking photo that was displayed on her computer screen. It was of Bill Blakney, taken back when he'd been arrested for fencing stolen goods, whilst running his pawn shop. It was not a very flattering image—not that booking photos tended to be flattering, of course—but she was having trouble finding anything else.

With a sigh, she rose and headed out to the main room, where Mary was sitting on the sofa with her feet up, mustering-up her strength for when the two children awoke from their naps.

Struggling with how to broach such a strange subject, Doyle sank down on the sofa beside her, and began, "I was wonderin', Mary; d'you have a—well, a little snap of Bill Blakney? I was thinkin' mayhap we'd give Gemma one. He stood-in as her da, after all, even if it wasn't for very long."

Mary, of course, didn't find the topic strange at all, and smiled warmly. "That is a wonderful thought, Lady Acton, but I do already have one of the two of them together, and we display it in Gemma's

293

bedroom, on top of her chest of drawers. Bill may have had his faults, but he loved her, and that's what's important."

"Aye," Doyle agreed, gazing out the windows at the endless sky. "That's what's important."

CPSIA information can be obtained
at www.ICGtesting.com
Printed in the USA
LVHW020309190422
716602LV00004B/34